THE BOX

Also by Mandy-Suzanne Wong

Drafts of a Suicide Note
Artificial Wilderness
Listen, we all bleed
Awabi

THE BOX

A Novel

Mandy-Suzanne Wong

Graywolf Press

This publication is made possible, in part, by the voters of Minnesota through a Minnesota State Arts Board Operating Support grant, thanks to a legislative appropriation from the arts and cultural heritage fund. Significant support has also been provided by the McKnight Foundation, the Amazon Literary Partnership, and other generous contributions from foundations, corporations, and individuals. To these organizations and individuals we offer our heartfelt thanks.

This is a work of fiction. Names, characters, businesses, places, events, locales, and incidents are either the products of the author's imagination or used in a fictitious manner. Any resemblance to actual persons, living or dead, or actual events is purely coincidental.

Published by Graywolf Press
212 Third Avenue North, Suite 485
Minneapolis, Minnesota 55401

www.graywolfpress.org

Published in the United States of America

ISBN 978-1-64445-249-3 (paperback)
ISBN 978-1-64445-250-9 (ebook)

2 4 6 8 9 7 5 3 1
First Graywolf Printing, 2023

Library of Congress Control Number: 2022952330

Cover design: Kapo Ng

Cover art: Shutterstock

THE BOX

Secondhand

At the beginning of the week before last, people in general began to understand that this snow we're having is strange enough to be disturbing not in the sense that all snow is uncanny as anything falling from the sky is uncanny, showing that the seams of the world between Earth and sky, sky and space, solid and liquid, between the present and unimaginable past are riddled with imperceptible holes, but disturbing in its perfect regularity, which you must admit is perfectly irregular: there was the blizzard, yes and very well, to whatever extent that there are facts of life the occasional blizzard is one; but after the wind died the snow lived on, and even after the biggest snowdrifts, the really unmanageable hillocks, were cleared away or melted by the hot breath of the city so it was obvious to everyone that the blizzard was over, snow continued falling straight down as it is doing now, continuing at a pace that seems for all practical purposes to be nearly proportional to the rate at which, with sporadic assistance from the occasional overworked municipal snowplow, the warm fumes from cars and buses, the hot and befouling eructations of the underground-train system, and all the lights and all the people going in and out of buildings relieve the streets of prior snow, which has discolored and been squashed, with the result that we are all of us to this day shuffling about in nigh a foot of powder, which being ever new is always white and clean; and just as in a costume unnoticeable seams bind the odd-shaped fabric cutouts which together make the garment, so too it seems that some precarious tension holds together in suspense the city's ingrained filth and the unremitting freshness apparent in this strange snow blown to us from god knows where on a wind that has forgotten it and disappeared.

I've never enjoyed snow, and unlike most people I take no pleasure in watching snowflakes fall to sidewalks even from behind a window at my home, although I like watching the rain and do enjoy the sound of rain blending with the river and pizzicatoing on empty streets, which may be why the snow, any snow but especially this haunting of a snowfall, this pale ghost of the blizzard that hangs around in neither determination nor indifference, makes me feel uneasy: snowflakes even when plummeting collide soundless with the ground, are subject to gravity but never to the noise which, with gracelessness of varying degrees, gravity summons upon impact from everything it touches excepting the ashes of combusted things and the heat our city belches from its countless pipes and chimneys to the farthest reaches of the world; and on insomniac occasions when I find myself looking through dawn's half-light at tumbling snow, should I drop a spoon for instance on the dead-tree surface of a table I must convince myself that their meeting produced a clatter as I must convince myself that besides the fire and refrigerator the rest of the house is mute and not about to produce any skittering noises no matter how I strain to listen in nervous apprehension; but you mustn't think I'm here because there's any comfort to be taken from the crunch of my own feet against snow-covered cement, I for one have had enough of ferrying snowdrifts on the brim of my hat, folds of my coat, crooks of my shoulders scrunched against the cold, and even on the day in question, last week or thereabouts, I was already fed up, for a blizzard followed by fourteen days of windless snow is quite enough, and now that three days more have piled on top of the fourteen, it is seventeen days of uninterrupted snowfall that we've had to endure, not counting the blizzard, seventeen days of nonstop snow, which you'll admit is quite beyond what anybody who is not a walrus or some sort

4

of yak should ever have to put up with; had I not had some obligation, which I no longer recall, I would just as soon have not quit my carpeted, blanketed house that day or anytime since the onset of the blizzard, and yet here you find me in this so-called café, here indeed you would've found me had you sought me yesterday or on any afternoon since the strange one of which I'm apparently about to give you an accounting even though I'm hardly the sort of person to give accountings except when they cannot be prevented as it seems this one cannot, just as it seems the events of that uncommon afternoon draw me back to this place day after day, despite myself and the serene, relentless snow, in a way that I can neither resist nor explain.

My house isn't even in this neighborhood, I came this way that afternoon because as I made for wherever I was going I was bent on keeping to unpopular streets that hold no attraction for the grimy buses which, once their wheels have masticated the fallen snow, never neglect to spray me with it, also because I've finally learned the only lesson that a lifetime in this city has to offer, to wit that if I am to survive a minute longer in this place I must become a proper misanthrope, there is nothing else for it; thus I turned onto the street where we are now, which the snow prevents you from seeing through the window, this dark and crooked lane wriggling between art galleries and so-called cafés as they devour one another in an attempt to make ends meet so that every establishment within five miles of here is a purveyor of questionable art and dubious coffee, the snow providing the advantage of obliging everyone to shut their windows, freeing the air of the canned music which would otherwise fly out of every hovel to do battle in the street and instead swaddling the sidewalk in an eerie sense of fragile solitude, a phantasmagorical impression enhanced by the silence of the cars parked along the curb, the dearth of moving vehicles, and the absence of pedestrians save myself and a man in a long coat and fedora: he was ahead of me on the same side of the street, moving in the same direction, some appointment bestirring him to hurry, when suddenly he stopped, looked at something in the distance, roused himself and rushed onward with purpose before stopping in his tracks as if the snow floating around us had become an impenetrable wall in front of him; he went on again and stopped again, his elbows bent perhaps so he could wring his hands, which he dropped when he went on, and then he stopped and seemed to listen, forming fists, and I thought he'd stamp his foot; his quivering posture gave the impression of an interior a-blizzard with what they call "snow" on television when the television cannot receive any signals and as such cannot communicate anything except a frightening suspension of communication on the part of those who presume to decide for everybody what things are worth, and it seemed to me that the swirling absence of meaning which from time to time envelops everything was suddenly obvious to him and too much for him and in consequence he didn't know what to do with himself, but his stop-and-starting made the lane uncomfortable to walk along, which further seemed to agitate him, so when he started up again it was with violence, "Bah!," and a throwing-up of hands; he plowed on as if so determined to end his misery that the noise of his progress drowned out the landing of a thing dislodged from his pocket when the throwing-up of hands disturbed his coat, and in retrospect sometimes it seems that this was his intention, that dislodging and drowning were theatrics he performed for the benefit of his conscience as the thing tumbled away from him, but at the time bemused by the irrational silence of the snow I was uncertain I'd heard anything at all, let alone the gentle landing of a small thing, and if I'd seen anything tumble from his pocket then it was as small and white as the multitude of small white tumblers all around us, and really I'd no wish to become involved with this unstable person and his renegade possessions if such there were, but I dreaded the possibility that my senses had deceived me, that my mind was as unsound as the preposterous atmosphere seemed to demand, that I was somehow infected with the absurdity of this taut symmetry between snow and city, and I hesitated while the man went zigzagging down the lane, the decision hemming me in like a hurtling mob, of whether to continue on and discover that he'd dropped a thing or that he hadn't, leading in either case to an encounter with his troubled mind or my own, or to turn back with no purpose except to leave this crooked lane and seek a different one.

Whether it was curiosity or dread that moved me I no longer know, but so that you will attempt to finagle from me not a word more than I shall offer, my concession in this respect being motivated by some begrudging consideration because if more people wondered as you do, asked themselves what a particular anthropogenic and to all appearances inanimate thing might get up to over and above what is conceivable to *Homo sapiens*, then this planet would not now seem a hostile alien one, you must understand three circumstances which told against my doing anything besides continuing on my way, circumstances which told loudly against my engaging some strange object that through the carelessness or otherwise of some human had littered this crooked lane: first is the circumstance that when last I went out of my way, thirteen or fifteen years ago in the dead of night, to investigate a fallen object in the street, my investigation revealed the object to be a young woman in such a condition that could never have resulted from a mere dispute with gravity, a state so pulverized and bloody it must have driven her out of her mind, closed her to anything outside her casket of pain and terror, and for her perfect ignorance of my existence whilst I summoned and waited for the ambulance and forever after I do not blame her in the least, in fact whoever she may be and whether or not she survived her injuries I do not know, since it was obvious she had been brutally set upon by some human or humans of the most rancorous rapacious kind, and the idea that it is possible for such people to exist disgusted me beyond recovery, lodged in me an incurable anthrophobia; second is the circumstance that I retired a month ago from the human resources department of the local branch of a multinational manufacturer of useful things' vital inner bits and in recent times of "global climate solutions" about which nobody knows anything except that they are COZY, CLEAN, AND COOL as they've plastered on the walls in all the train stations, the subject of cozy geoconstructivist cleansing and

7

computer-controlled cooling being the globe itself as though the very world were but a useful thing requiring only the proper bits to make it go the way the manufacturer wants it even as its human resources couldn't care less, their priorities being one-upmanship and various forms of insurance, as though the global ecosystem's basic survival, ·whence it's assumed *Homo sapiens'* immortality shall follow, could be manufactured as a commodity of determinable market value at which, in this epitome of blackmail, failing to buy in would constitute condoning the uncozy, filthy incineration of biological life; bringing me to the third circumstance which ought to have precluded the occurrence on the sidewalk outside this so-called café, specifically that in forty years' professional servitude, having sacrificed many a hankie to janitors in disastrous states of nervous collapse, I cannot abide littering, I cannot observe littering without wanting to burst into tears of rage, and because many litterers litter in paper or plastic, the presence of such items in states of abandonment and emptiness is categorically intolerable to me even though I am myself nothing but an empty animal who has resolutely abdicated from bothering about other duplicitous animals or this doomed Earth: I've retired from sympathy and community, I have done, and in consequence I've become an inveterate mumbler filling my blissful solitude with unwanted mumble, the bitter remnants of my vital forces dribbling from me in a slow leak, which astonished me on that singular afternoon by stopping itself up.

You'd think such a being as I, having witnessed what appeared to be a paper thing falling litterlike into the snow from the pocket of some human's coat, would in accordance with my character and circumstances have run away and left the thing where it had fallen; only that thing, a paper thing, white paper in the snow, exerted counterforces which I cannot define but which proved stronger than history and all my instincts: the little white box fit in the palm of my hand with perhaps a whisper of a rattle when it moved, was of a size that could've accommodated cigarettes or playing cards, a wallet or slim wad of cash, yet was absolutely self-contained lacking the door

or flap of the cigarette or playing-card carton, but then again it was
the opposite of self-contained being all-over seams, by which I mean
it was constructed of paper strips entangled as if haphazardly, shooting out as if dynamically between one another and diving under one
another in all directions; but so tight a weave it was that no strip
seemed to have an end, delicate as they were the strips held fast to
one another with a tension that resulted in an impenetrable rectangle, for neither fingernail nor toothpick nor so much as a breath
could've wriggled underneath those seams and not a one would yield
to pulling or prying, of that I was certain when I turned over the
curio in my mittens, a curiosity of kinetic rectangular perfection,
a hypnotizing snarl of gaps with all the vulnerability of paper in the
snow, and the devil of it was it belonged to someone else, the nervous
man who'd dropped it before my very eyes, which fact alone made
it a complicated, daunting thing: I might've kept it for myself, taken
it off somewhere although this notion did not appeal, for there was
something about the object which was as repellent to me as it was
attractive, I might've pretended I hadn't seen it and dropped it back
onto the sidewalk, let someone else chance upon it or crush it, or I
might've tossed it in a dumpster or beneath a car or done any number of things more characteristic of this city and myself than hurry-
ing after the stranger in the dated hat with the strange object in my
hand; but the infernal snow decided it, the snow kept on implacably
just as it's doing now, and although it's so far failed to smother the
city completely the small white paper box would have been devoured
and the fellow who had dropped it would've never found it again and
even if he did it would've been soaked through or squashed, no longer the closely woven secret that the man had carried with him but a
thing exposed, so yes I followed him on account of the weather and
the frangibility of paper, and he was easily overtaken for he made
no more than sporadic progress, stopping now and then to torment
himself; he was in the throes of just such an anguished hesitation
when I appeared at his elbow and as he looked at me I felt rather
like a ghost, so startled were the eyes between the brim of his gray

hat and his voluminous gray muffler, a reaction I understood whole-heartedly because, and I mean no personal offense, when a stranger appears at one's elbow in this city it is rarely a friendly thing, which is why I didn't speak a word but silently proffered the object that had fallen from his coat; and in his hesitation I saw him wish for the ability to pretend he'd never seen the little box in his life but, lacking the wherewithal for a feint of that sort, he made an effort to gather himself, thanked me earnestly, and with too much relief plucked the box from my mitten with careful fingers.

I meant to take my leave before the stranger could see my feelings stricken, yes, to my own horror, by his stricken look, the look of someone who is lost and unable to forget it, for I desired no resonance, no pity for this man to crowd my crowded thoughts, but when he said, "Were you able to look inside?" the forlornness of the castaway was in his voice wavering between dread and eagerness, and his question presuming to accuse me of presumption deserved no answer except the scowl I threw over my shoulder as I went on my way; yet he came after me, "Forgive me" falling from his lips in a voice which somehow penetrated even though it was more than two parts whispering, not conspiratorial but with a seemingly natural softness and sad smile as he said, "Most people would've tried to open it I think," and then he went on, this stranger whose dress bespoke a man accustomed to comfort without conflict: in conflicted tones he said, "Do you have a little time?" and in the pause born of the suspicious temperament which this city breeds in everyone, our wariness was as if embodied in the cold glittering curtain flickering between us on that cloud-shadowed day; "I need a moment out of the snow," he said, "to think a little, and I'm much obliged to you, you see, this," he said, "this"—and fell silent, holding aloft the box between his thumb and finger with a frown as if he contemplated giving me the thing even though or because we were strangers to each other and simultaneously as if he waited, waited intently for the box itself, woven closed, to express whether or not it should be given, and of course I knew I wouldn't accept it should it be offered, indeed I thought the man should put it back in his pocket, but it wasn't my place to say so and in any case the box wasn't what he offered, he offered himself, a delay of my errand, and an offering to which I knew I wouldn't agree and yet I did agree, so here we are: a moment, however drawn out, in this slouching lane, the pair of us huddling clumsily at this very table in this so-called café, and think of me what you will you would be right if you suspected I came with him to this place, the interior of which I'd never set eyes upon before, not because of my anomalous pity for him but because of his damnable box, that bit of self-enclosed and breakable white paper.

You'll observe that like the crooked lane in the crooked city which sprung it like a wart this café is all awkward angles and odd corners, you'll notice that the niche where our tottering table has been wedged, a triangular corner like a seam that is slowly being forced apart, is dark and uninviting and too narrow to accommodate the measliest repast at the stingiest degree of comfort, and yet that fellow made for precisely this murky recess and sat where I am now, calling for warm drinks, peeling away his coat to reveal a suit of the same gray, doffing the fedora to reveal a knit cap, also gray; he then proceeded by gentle brushing to remove errant snowflakes from the box, which seemed none the worse for it, he placed the box here in the apex of the corner as though it would function as a referee or chairperson, and if it was the box that had gathered us and stuffed us in this corner then it was also the box that imposed the straining silence between us, two jaded metropolitans with nothing else in common except the steam rising from the cups into which we glowered, each aware that the other had resolved, wretchedly it's true, straining almost to the point of breaking out in sweat, not to look at the box which was the reason for everything, each sensing that the other would rather swallow muddy snow masticated by the filthy wheels of grimy buses than be the first to mention white paper; and indeed it was the box that strained the silence to its breaking point, where at last with furrowed brow, a gaze turning inward and distant, and much pondering and prodding of words before daring to let them loose, the stranger began to speak.

"The other day, my cousin's first wife's stepbrother's eldest daughter decided to take a few days off from her job, which I'm told is very stressful," he began, "but on account of this weather, which makes even the journey to the next bus stop an uncertain prospect, for even the touted experts seem unable to guess when the snow will dwindle or suddenly whip itself into another storm, she and one of her girl-friends rather than trying to leave the city took it into their heads to make a holiday of staying in someone else's apartment, that is, some-one they did not know, had never even heard of, the idea being, I suppose, though one can really only guess, to immerse themselves in some alternate locale which was utterly unfamiliar yet entirely local: a place in a luxurious high-rise building with a view of the river and a private elevator landing that the two girls found on one of those websites via which people rent out their own homes for a few days here and there to whoever agrees to put down a deposit knowing nothing whatsoever about the owner of the place of whom the web-site displays nothing but a username, in this case 'Alex,' who in turn knew nothing whatsoever about the people to whom they gave the run of their apartment aside from whatever username the girlfriends used to make their reservation"; and as the fellow wet his lips he saw in a glance that I shared his horror of such a website, that even in my flimsy economic circumstances I could never do such a thing to my house or myself, and that he therefore had no need to ask my name or offer his, the pair of us having already come to understand something of each other's instincts, from which he knew without my utter-ing a word that he had nothing to fear from permitting his strange story as it bore down on him, heavy enough to stoop his shoulders, to slip into the air between us almost like this snow, which as if ac-cumulated and accumulated somewhere latent, beyond the threshold of being, until the accumulations overwhelmed the existential seam and caused it to develop fissures.

The attraction and adventure of this apartment were in its belonging not to a hospitality establishment but to a specific individual by and for whom it was idiosyncratically outfitted as a private nook or what is called a home, he went on; for every home, the hideout of a particular person who is by definition indecipherable, has its own indecipherable secrets: there are things in it that are precious, things that are haunted, things the existence of which would make no sense to anybody who hadn't chosen and arranged them, thus as a visitor to such a place you are at every turn confounded by puzzles, ciphers, enigmas which are dramatically or even painfully meaningful and yet the key to their decoding is hidden and sealed off from you forever by the contingency that you are who you are and not in this case Alex, who was in any case no more from the perspective of the holiday-makers than a name at the bottom of an email instructing them in how to make the elevator pause at the private landing and obtain the cooperation of the computerized front door; and so, as the daughter of the stepbrother of the former wife of my companion's cousin told her father, visiting this warren of possessions in the absence of their owner, that is, without the influence of the nostalgic or evasive looks which an owner cannot help bestowing on their trinkets when not ignoring them, offered endless distractions and opportunities to vivid imaginations "and in fact," said my companion, "from the young ladies' somewhat egotistical perspective it appeared that the owner of the place, who may or may not have been 'Alex,' understood how an owner's absence, boxed up inside the furniture and decorations, would prove diverting to guests and therefore purposely made the apartment"—something the word for which eluded my raconteur who searched for it in silence but eventually gave it up, saying instead that the apartment was small and square with four unequally proportioned rooms "if a minute bathroom and kitchenette may be called rooms," and then he hesitated, his frown betraying consternation as he blurted out: according to what he'd been told of the apartment "everything was boxes," and this was made apparent to the guests from the beginning in the photographs on the aforementioned website, which showed exactly what the girlfriends discovered on

arrival; every wall of the living room, including the walls surround-
ing the casement window which gave onto a snow-clogged balcony
overlooking the river, was itself walled in by multicolored brickwork
made of decorative boxes of every shape and size in wood, paper, felt,
tin, canvas, cardboard, and cotton; the living-room furniture was
built of square, rectangular, triangular, and elliptical ottomans, each
one hollow with a detachable cushion, and between the red sofa and
armchair thus constructed was a side table of ingenious engineer-
ing assembled from little boxes of mismatched hues and proportions,
crayon boxes, jewelry boxes, matchboxes, medicine boxes, boxes for
disposable cutlery and the like, which fit precisely together as in a
three-dimensional jigsaw to form a many-pointed star with a stable
and perfectly level top of convenient height; and besides the vertical
arrangement in the bedroom of sturdy trunks, each slightly smaller
than the one below forming a staircase between the higher bunk bed
and the floor whilst keeping hold of the spare linens, there was in
the kitchenette a fascinating structure, a recognizable rendition of
the city skyline in tea boxes, spaghetti boxes, plastic takeaway boxes,
breath-mint boxes becoming historic rooftops and skyscrapers, and
to the young ladies' delight this miniature city was as confounding
as the real thing, for anytime they wanted something, a napkin or
a cup, they had to discover the appropriate box, and in that recep-
tacular abstraction not only did no tea box contain tea, no toothpaste carton toothpaste, indeed no containers were what they'd once
been according to their superficial markings, but also boxes bearing
markings were outnumbered by boxes sporting whatsoever no outward indication of their contents; the towers, domes, and tenements
were so skillfully constructed that the guests could extract any box
from any edifice without toppling the whole, and such patient extri-
cations, which the friends undertook gently and one by one, replacing every box before removing another, proved to be the only way
in which to find a butter knife or a packet of biscuits living cheek
by jowl with staples, soap, and things in no apparent order, a box
of drinking straws in the spire of a tower under a tiny box of pine

needles, a cardboard box of sweetener packets the upper neighbor to a box of pen refills and a thumb-sized tin containing a dachshund figurine; and many of the articles were equally diminutive and strange, like the rose petal all alone in a jewel box, the single paper napkin in a flat container near the floor, the razor blade without a handle in a box meant for powdered laundry detergent, the scrap of tree bark in a canister for photographic film, the pewter pendant in the shape of a deer covered with rhinestones rattling inside a little wooden block wedged between a box of thyme and a box of pushpins, to such an extent that I for one upon discovering the pushpins would have found some difficulty in believing they were pushpins and not for example microchips or something even more unlikely, having by that point been thoroughly mired in and muddled by the city which was also not a city because it was boxes, the boxes which were also not boxes because they were rooms and quoins and windows in the city, the boxes which proclaimed themselves cereal boxes but failing to harbor cereal were also not cereal boxes, and the frightfully accentuated sense that things are not what they seem even as they are precisely so.

"I'd have gone mad in that place within an afternoon," said my companion, "but to that pair it was a lark, they went through every box in the kitchenette and bedroom as soon as they arrived, but I was told that being particularly taken with the side table they decided to 'save' the living room for the following day so as to prolong the moment of wondering, as though what amounts to nosiness or so to speak a kind of voyeurism by nonhuman proxy were a pleasure to be savored without consequence," and so once more my mysterious interlocutor brushed against my thoughts without my having to speak, for it occurred to me that this bizarre apartment must be the setting for a kind of game, and this along with the impression he evoked of the guests' cavalier enthusiasm for excavating every nook and cranny perturbed me as it did him, although I'm certain other people would've found it unremarkable or comical like a situation in a fairy tale; he wondered aloud what the game might be and what sort of person would enjoy creating such a thing or for that matter bumbling around in it, driven by fascination or the need for a toothpick to explore vertically and horizontally this compartmentalized maze; had he been the guest in that place, he went on, the question of who exactly was this "Alex" would've kept him up all night, but there I differ from him and the young ladies, for I wouldn't have touched a thing, which is hardly to say that I would not have wished to, indeed the problems which would've all but guaranteed my sleeplessness in that apartment would not have concerned the owner, who couldn't be of lesser interest to me, but the boxes and their potential: images of what might lie hidden, inert, entombed, or fit to burst with boxed-in energy would assail me from within although I'd never lift a finger to confirm their accuracy or falsehood; the possibility that there might be anything at all, such as a playing card, a lorgnette, a curl of hair, a swatch of paint, a bit of bone, a remnant of a candle, a map, an embroidered bookmark, the smallest piece of a nesting doll, a pen, a seed, an embalmed ant, or merely a lump of sugar, in whichever component of the side table I'd never touch would agitate my imagination to the point that it would foist magic on the place causing me to wonder if, should I open up a box, slip it back into its place, and after a moment open it again, I might find the contents miraculously altered, a battery where a minute before there'd been a spoon, and that ever-renewing possibility of amazement would make a prisoner of me there where I could neither bring myself to do a thing about it nor, as the two women did, put it out of mind for the night and following a takeaway dinner avail themselves of the small bathroom and settle with e-readers into the bunk beds, which entailed a great unsettling as ascending to the bunk beds required entering into relations with boxes as if they were otherwise than boxes, clambering up a staircase which being boxes was clearly not a staircase and so could not be scampered up without a thought but must be negotiated gingerly, bearing in mind, as the young ladies probably didn't, that whilst the boxes appeared to contain linens it is true of every thing that its appearance is only partly its reality.

The man stumbled into one of those unwieldy pauses that appeared to force themselves on him, heavy and thorny with some
meaning that eluded him or was all too blatant to him, as I thought
of a sudden, for although we were strangers to each other nonetheless it seemed to me that there was a quality to his latest dawdle,
something I cannot pinpoint but which caused to flash into my consciousness the question of whether this man's odd tale truly was the
tale of his cousin's ex-wife's stepbrother's daughter or of someone
closer to the tale-teller himself; for whilst I heard in his silence that
the crux of the matter had yet to be revealed and was dire indeed,
I sensed in the look he drove into his coffee as though nothing else
were safe to look upon that he'd press on with his tale-telling because he felt driven to do it in spite of himself, driven by something
external that had him in its power, spurring him to raise his eyes
to me and say in a thickening voice as though he'd stumbled into a
morass of confusion and straining to see beyond it only caused it to
congeal inside him: "Sometime after midnight, the guests were en-
sconced in their beds, not asleep, absorbed in their reading, when
there came a knock at the front door," and what knocking it was, this
truculent and vitriolic knock-knock-knocking, even though the possibility of visitors was unmentioned in the absent host's scanty correspondence, and only now, said my companion with vexation, did it
occur to the young ladies to wonder about this "Alex," now that they
found themselves tiptoeing to the door in the dead of night to meet
with a cheese cleaver they'd found in a miniature municipal admin-
istration building this person who refused to leave off knocking even
when the guests wrapped themselves in the cold silence of the not-
at-home, for how could anyone but Alex prevail upon the elevator,
which answered to a secret code typed on a keypad, to stop at the
private landing; how could anybody who was intimate with the elevator, Alex included, not have an equivalent relationship with the front
door; could it be that Alex knocked instead of barging in so as not
to alarm the guests, but if there was some emergency why had Alex
not emailed and if there was no emergency why insist on banging

without pause, why not leave off and wait knowing the guests were likely to be sleeping at this hour; and how were the guests to know whether the tormentor of doors was their host or not, having no idea of Alex's personal qualities nor any evidence that this Alex was a specimen of *Homo sapiens* and not, at the bidding of some corporate abstraction, some slavish algorithm or digital phantasm, a fantasy of that horrible website, that dissembling and calculating nonplace beyond which no such Alex existed?

The cleaver was not required, said my interlocutor, but neither was the person at the door expecting a puzzled and pajamaed holiday-making pair; she who had abused the door and defied the elevator, a tall woman of middling years, wild of hair, which the girls believed to have been blackened artificially, and bearing a prominent chip and twist in her front tooth, was profoundly horrified by the sight of the guests who in turn were horrified not to be expected, so they were all three of them thrown into such confusion that they froze there gaping and unable to speak for a ridiculous length of time during which the guests came gradually to understand that it was not their host who stood before them covered with snow, that the bewildered intruder must have reserved the apartment via the same website, which due to some glitch or oversight had allowed more than one party to claim the place at the same time, and so the girlfriends saw no choice but to invite her in, explaining with anxious laughter that they'd taken her for the owner of the place at first, to which she diffidently replied that she'd thought the same of them; and when the door was closed again, the three ladies standing awkwardly in the living room the tininess of which was no doubt palpable, the guests observed that the intruder carried no overnight bag and looked around her with a gaze like that of a captured animal, their babble about attempting to email Alex, who'd only given them an email address and now that they were all together in the apartment couldn't have done a thing about it, meeting with no reply from the wild-eyed woman who'd already uttered the last word she was to utter in the company of the guests and made no answer to their hesitant suggestion that although they'd established themselves in the bedroom they would never banish any living thing to the grim snow and gelid night and so the lady was welcome to use the living room until morning when the city must offer alternatives; and certainly I should feel a bit lost myself should I arrive under the warm roof I thought was mine for the night, having trudged across the city in the dark and this vile snow only to discover that there was no bed for me, that my refuge had been usurped by bewildered strangers who as the young ones later admitted wanted nothing more than to flee the discomfiting silence for the bedroom, but rooted to the parquet on which she stood the intruder looked not merely lost but overwhelmed unto despair as she gawped at the living room, shocked as though she'd never seen the website's photographs, appalled as though she'd no idea where to begin in an apartment besieged by boxes, how to exist in it even for a moment, and as no offer of a seat nor any amount of gentle banter could coax any more from her than this anguished goggling, the guests crept away, leaving her to the spot on the floor whence she hadn't budged a toe since crossing the threshold.

They shut the bedroom door behind them, but the memory of the intruder stricken mute with horror made that previously cozy barrack as uncomfortable as the living room, the presence just beyond the door of an unfamiliar human in a delicate psychological condition demolished every hope of merriment or relaxation, so after dithering awhile the guests discussed the situation in murmurs and although my companion was uncertain as to which of them raised the suggestion it was decided that they'd leave the apartment quietly in the morning, for neither wished to spend their holiday embroiled in argument with an intruder too distracted to control herself; and then, having resolved to take the matter up with "Alex," the young friends found themselves walled off from sleep by guilt and indignation, by the presence of the cleaver under someone's pillow, and by the intruder shuffling slowly through the living room causing the floor to emit small creaks, in response to which it was decided in anxious whispers that should drastic action become necessary the tenant of the top bunk would leap down on the older lady from above whilst the tenant on the bottom brandished the cleaver; and meanwhile the parquet floor confided in them from the living room, muttering when the intruder set herself on the sofa, went to the kitchenette, and returned after a moment, following which there was a silence of magnitude enough to suggest she'd gone to sleep, and the silence of snow falling steadily through the night enveloped them, that paradoxical sensation, too familiar by now to everybody in the city, of night holding its breath, daring not to tremble even in a breeze or flurry as if in thrall to its invasion from above by multitudinous cold slivers freefalling through the black sky.

And then a new sound slithered through the seams between door and wall and door and floor, a sound so attenuated that the guests, rigid in their beds with the strain of listening and not listening, thought at first that they had dreamed it, a sound they'd learned to recognize that very night, there in that strange apartment where the kitchen was only half a kitchen but was also an embracive if imperfect as if secondhand memory, a loving or ironic story without words of our overgrown ramble of a city: it was a noise like a whisper with no meaning but the meeting of things in motion, the sound of paper sliding over paper or brushing wood, the gasp of a small box emerging from its place in an intricate assemblage, and this swishing issued not from the kitchenette where the guests couldn't have heard it but from the living room outside the bedroom door where it could only have been the extraordinary star-table, the only small-box architecture in the living room whispering swish-swish as one by one the boxes slid from their places and back, emitting now and then the click or pop of a catch lifted or a lid removed, a box's secrets laid open to an ephemeral light; and the guests recalled their lingering in the kitchenette, their astonishment at the lonely peppercorn, the stories they'd concocted for the pewter deer, and weren't at all surprised to hear susurrations swish-pop-swishing in the living room for quite some time; the intruder must've opened every box in the table after which she spent a long while in the kitchenette, returning to the living room to lift cushions from ottomans and put them back again, rummage in larger boxes with haste and not a little noise, throw herself muttering on the sofa, and accost the side table again; and what, said my companion, are we to understand from this except that the woman was after something in particular and had come to the apartment for the purpose of searching every crevice for the thing she wanted, which implies, he continued in agitation, that the intruder knew something of this "Alex," that she'd expected "Alex" to answer her frantic knocking, but she evidently knew neither that the apartment might be rented nor even what it looked like on the inside; or, he demurred, she'd seen the website after all, invented a story to compel guests to let her in, and either feigned stupefaction at the sight of the interior or was authentically flabbergasted having failed to study the website's photographs; or, he proposed, rebutting himself again, she'd attempted to reserve the apartment through the website intending to gain access to the place whilst screening her identity from the owner, but as the guests supposed a problem with this damnable website allowed her to reserve the apartment even though it was reserved already; then again, he went on as alarm reduced his voice to whispering, the intruder herself couldn't have been Alex, for the owner of the place wouldn't have been surprised by it just as the owner's emissary wouldn't have been surprised and would've plainly told the guests that their host was in need of some object from the apartment; but what if that unstable woman had asked Alex for the thing she wanted and been refused and in a tempest of despair done something to Alex, "for," he added mournfully, "we prisoners of this city which doesn't understand its own desperation can no longer assume any of our fellow citizens to be beyond the reach of terrifying impulses."

No one is more confident than I that terrifying impulses are unexceptional in *Homo sapiens*, but the curious circumstances of that afternoon, the snow, the box, the probability that this man's story did not belong solely to the women who were its protagonists, and the story itself, most of all its mystifying setting, bestirred me to imagine monstrous impulses of other obscure origins; for I imagined myself in the mind of the intruder whose impossible task was to think not only as if from the mind of Alex but also as if through the apperceptions *of the apartment*, which place was also a thing that did not belong to the intruder but required as she sought the object of her quest that she ask both herself and the place-thing itself what it was that space, proprioception, appearance, and secrecy meant for a home-thing which was also a collector of boxes, and nor could she pose her questions as she'd put them to a human being: the apartment, the side table, the boxes, all the objects demanded she approach them as a fellow object, coaxing from them not with words but with hesitant gestures, postures, touches, some hint as to their inclinations, what they'd permit her to do, how far they'd permit her to dismember them in order to imagine that she'd caught a whiff of their secrets; and this sensitive and seeking attitude is what the apartment in the manner common to all things demanded of the guests as well, for whom such basic functions as sitting without falling through the furniture were of necessity inquiries subject to directives issued by the things themselves as they dictated for example that in order to make tea one must ransack a miniature city like a thief, the furniture and walls of boxes likewise demanding particular movements and refrainings, enabling particular operations and disallowing others, indicating that human sensations overall resemble nothing so much as visitorly responses to impulses of nonhuman hosts, with both parties ruled within by secrecy and strangeness.

The man fell silent bowing over his cup as if beneath an awful weight and inhaled deeply of the steam that was no longer there, his cappuccino or whatever it was having gone cold, and two considerations bade me signal the barista to refill his cup with something hot and contrary to principles do it at my expense, the first consideration being that he seemed to seek comfort from coffee-flavored steam as from caresses of hashish and the second consideration, the real energy behind my unaccountable behavior, being the irresistible pressure that hounded the story out of him, the very same force which, not from within but from beyond him, beyond both of us, and right there between our elbows, impelled him, *go on, go on*, as if with vengeful words and yet without a single muscle that could utter them; and being an unusual fellow with a heart easily moved, my companion resumed, submissive to that silent call, fearful for the guests and sorrowful for the intruder so distressed, and though he never spoke about these feelings they were evident in his reluctant tones as he said, "I'm not certain any of these possibilities occurred to the young ones and I'm not certain they didn't, the child," that is the grown-up stepniece of his cousin's former wife if this was her story as he claimed, "the child having reported that they were trapped in the pretense of sleep," especially when after another hour of listening to frustrated muttering, boxes fidgeting with increasing turbulence, and a spate of aimless pacing the guests were beside themselves with anticipation, unable to think of anything except the circumstance they dreaded, which to their horror came to pass: the light slipping through the seam below the bedroom door was walled off suddenly by the intruder's shadow.

There was no lock on the bedroom door, the apartment as a whole being so impenetrable, considering the chary elevator and intelligent front door, that apparently the owner felt interior locks to be unnecessary, and therefore it was the bedroom to which my interlocutor referred when he said with consternation, "She opened the door," pausing not in the bedroom but no longer outside it either with an almost inaudible clearing of her throat as though some desperate part of her hoped for the guests to wake that she might seek their help and confidence while some other part equally desperate dreaded having to explain herself and hoped for them to slumber on: I imagine her figure in the doorway, a silhouette against the light from the living room trembling like a windblown puddle in the dark, the silhouette not only her abstract representation but also her concrete totality at least from the perspective of the guests who from her appearance unannounced and mute derived nothing but that she was an opaque container of histories and intentions which, despite the plethora of seams through which we humans leak our stories in words and fluids and silent motions, remained so thoroughly hidden that they might have been lost in the darkness of a mind which had forgotten its own depths such that she was no longer any more than surface, an absolute silhouette, not a puddle but an empty box; "but what is even more disturbing," said my companion who was at pains to imply that he had the story not from the guests themselves but from the father of one of them, presumably the stepbrother of the lady who was no longer married to a cousin of the man before me if on this point the latter was to be believed, what he found truly alarming, unaccountably so, I thought at first, given the dubious quality of secondhand information in general, was that here the guests' accounts of their shared and simultaneous experiences began subtly to diverge.

The intruder tiptoed in and unpacked every receptacle in the bedroom from the portmanteau at the bottom of the box-built staircase to the sort of hatbox at the top, not sparing the overnight cases which the guests had brought with them, and replacing each and every article exactly as she found it; on this the guests agreed as they agreed they'd both spontaneously frozen in the feigned attitude of sleep permitting the intruder to believe that she ransacked the room without a sound, and one of the guests, said my companion, found a bit of a thrill in spying on the intruder as she spied on them, "for it was as if the tables had turned and kept on turning": just as the guests blithely believed themselves entitled to examine Alex's things, had even chosen Alex's mysterious apartment so that Alex's boxes might liberate their imaginations to set off frolicking on holiday, so now did this perplexing intruder examine the guests' things without so much as a by-your-leave, as though she'd every reason to expect the personal repositories of a pair of random strangers whose only prior connection to the apartment was that problematic website to contain something which would strike her meaningfully and personally as some kind of treasure; however, the other guest did not share the feelings of the first, finding no amusement in the vandalizing of her luggage, being of the firm opinion that while Alex had laid Alex open to scrutiny by lending the apartment to strangers in exchange for remuneration the guests had agreed to no such thing and their position was wholly different from the host's, who had promised them the private use of the apartment; as for the tale-teller himself, he seemed undecided as to which gloss of the situation accorded with his feelings and in his lowering silence I wondered whether the young ladies had ever existed, whether they were nothing more than figures of the man's irresolute mind, but this seemed unlikely given the almost fatherly way in which he spoke of his protagonists, seeming most of the time to disagree with both of them, baffled as he was by their perspective grounded in naught but youthful whimsy even as he was possessed by this story of three women that was not only the three women's story, indeed we were both of us in thrall to the magnetism of the recondite third party sitting tacitly between us, but whereas I was in the grip of it, bound to listen and if necessary lend my voice to its entreaty, *go on*, he was at the mercy of its commands, harnessed to its history, impelled to haul it forth into the open and thence into the future.

In any event, he said at last, in what seemed to him the most bizarre of all the bizarre moments of this adventure, the guests enjoyed or endured their invasion with silence and inertia too perfect and serene to pass for anything other than what it was: wide-awake lying in wait, listening with eyes wide open, frozen in fear and driven by pitiless curiosity, which the intruder could've seen right through had she glanced at the bunk beds; but she was absorbed in unpacking and repacking by the partial light leaking from the living room, and so just as the guests permitted her to believe that she proceeded undetected so she permitted herself to be taken in by their transparent pantomiming, and to my exasperated companion it seemed that this duplex charade went on with the conscious authorization of both sides, each shamming unconsciousness of their exposure by the other; he said, "That moment must've been, for the intruder foraging in half-light and the guests when they remembered to watch through half-closed eyelids, like peeking sideways into a box the lid of which is raised only a little because the person peeking knows very well what lies within but cannot bring themselves to look at it and so they close the lid again having admitted just enough light to send shadows swarming over everything"; and as he spoke, his voice subdued as if with every word and image, even the intruder's as she folded the guests' clothes, closed their cases, climbed the box-made staircase to dismantle it a second time, he interrogated himself from a distance which for him could never be distant enough, his hands squeezing the cup, his gaze drifting to the window that revealed nothing but snow in order to evade what lay directly and magnetically in his line of vision, deliberately to overshoot and overlook the thing that had drawn us together despite the snow which might have hidden it forever—the little white box on the table, unable to move itself and seeming to throb with the cry it could not utter, *go on, for god's sake, go on!*

"Beyond that moment the story begins breaking down like a ruined building which throughout its life has been so many things that nobody can agree on what it was at its inception," he said, and his speech became more hesitant than ever as though his words were rotting floorboards that at any moment could give way sending him crashing down through one dead room after another to plunge at last into a bottomless snowdrift; he said the moment of the intruder's departure was missing from the guests' account, he was told only that she rebuilt the staircase of boxes, was nowhere to be found when the guests peered into the living room in the morning, and left no trace of her presence, so the guests assumed that, feeling as discombobulated as they did in the apartment which they'd all three rented at the same time accidentally, a story to which the young ladies clung insisting the intruder had gotten carried away looking in boxes and mistaken their things for more of Alex's, she'd disappeared into the night like a phantom notwithstanding the snow and dangerous outdoor temperature, and when my companion pressed the point with whoever gave him the story he was rebuffed as if the lady hardly mattered, as if the visitation had no significance in comparison with what happened after, though on the contrary I've no doubt specula-

26

tions as to the visitant's inner qualities thronged my interlocutor's thoughts as they did mine: if intruder she was, to whom Alex was no friend at all, then what compelled her to appear at Alex's apartment with the intent of arguing or forcing her way in must have been some strong emotion, some need or hankering behind which lay turbulent histories; and if you imagine someone under such compulsions already near the end of her tether upon her arrival, which in the middle of the night cannot but have been an impulsive undertaking, tired, frustrated with Alex, angry with herself and the elusive object of her search, if you imagine her suddenly overwhelmed, face-to-face with hordes of boxes swarming wall to wall, imagine her invading box after box with supreme delicacy imposed and enforced by suffocating circumstances including the obligation to avoid detection by silly young ladies and not to smash the place to bits as she surely wished to do when the night wore on and she ran out of boxes and understood her prey had slipped through her fingers for perhaps the hundredth time, for the apartment of an enemy or stranger in the middle of the night cannot have been her first recourse, then her fury in the moment when she had no choice but to concede defeat, give up on even this audacious eleventh-hour excursion, must shudder your projective capacity, nevertheless you must go further and envision how in order to search the place entirely and extract herself from it that woman must in a terrible upheave of tremendous inner strength have crushed her own rebellion, stifled her frustration, swallowed down her rage, permitting herself not a peep or tear, you must bring before your mind's inconstant eye the thing that seemed to her to demand and justify such exhausting and devastating exertions—and then you will understand why my companion seemed not to know how to continue even though he knew he must, why his entire aspect hardened with determination not to look away from the window and with the horror of a storyteller thwarted by his story, which having lured us both out of probability's firelit salon conjured a fog and wrapped itself in it so that obeying the injunction, *go on, damn you*, meant entangling ourselves in mist where we were doomed never to say or discern all there was to be said or seen, doomed thereby never to know exactly what it was that we permitted to occur when my interlocutor set the story free, dismembered and darkened by its own protagonists, to slither out from that hermetic apartment to tunnel through this so-called café into me.

At last he said, faltering, that the conduct of his "sources" led him to suspect that they wished to "familiarize" him with events in order that he might "deal with the matter," and I don't know what he meant by "deal," you'll understand why I elected not to inquire, but simultaneously either the guests themselves or these "sources" sought to foment some subtle confusion so that precisely which individual was responsible would remain a mystery, to wit, said my companion, he'd been unable to find out which of them it was, but after the guests discovered by the flaccid light of the snowed-in sun that they were alone again in the apartment, one of them drew the other back to the bedroom and said she couldn't bear the secret burning in her any longer, claiming later on of course, said my companion, that her attack of conscience had nothing to do with the visitation but only with the fact that however trivial it was she'd dishonored a promise which the friends had made together: sometime during the night, she said, before the assault on the front door, whilst her fellow holidaymaker was in the bathroom preparing for bed, the guilty one tried her utmost not to think of the star-table which they had promised to "save," but the strength of her character and the weight of her promise were vanquished by curiosity which overpowered all resistance; as improbable as it is that she knew what she would find, my raconteur confessed that in moments of bleak confusion simply because the whole affair was so vagarious and twisted, he was unable to prevent himself from wondering whether by some freakish coincidence she did know something or had suspected in advance, but what she found serving as a brick in the star-table so disquieted her that instead of sliding it back into place as she had all the others she took the thing to her bed, whether the top bunk or the bottom my companion never could decide, and stuffed it underneath her pillow, confident that the box would not allow itself to be crushed, which inane assumption can have been spared ignominy only by some miracle of paper, papercraft, or neck musculature; she uttered not a word about it to her friend but pretended as agreed that everything in the living room was barred from nipping at her thoughts until sunrise, and as irrational as these maneuvers seemed she undertook them nevertheless, said the man across from me, "because she was certain that the thing should not have been in that apartment; whatever the actual identity of its owner, whatever this Alex meant by filling the place artfully with boxes, it was plain even to a visitor that at least one box did not belong there, as the errant guest believed she understood from the moment she laid hands on it; its presence there was unacceptable, that is the word I was given, it was unacceptable for the box to be sequestered there, and on this matter that was all I was given."

Not a drop of mumble escaped me during his narrative; he knew I was listening intently, sympathetically, analytically, as for forty years I listened to sweepers of floors, wipers of tables, answerers of telephones, and I was loath to interrupt him primarily because my curiosity was aflame but also at first because he seemed desperate to unburden himself, then because it became clear that he was laboring under an unwanted obligation which he didn't know how to satisfy, certain details having been kept from him which caused him unendurable frustration, and finally because even as my suspicions came to seem well founded concerning the small white box he'd let fall into the snow there arose in me a new and disappointing suspicion that the box itself was not as consequential to him as the questions of responsibility through which he couldn't see his way to solutions; for these weren't mere questions of fact, they far exceeded the matter of the box thief's identity, being instead, so I believed according to his words and manner, questions of morality: what made the larcenous guest, whoever it turned out to be, believe that she, unless of course it was *he*, and tale-bearer and protagonists were one, ought to take responsibility for the box only to encounter some obstacle or breaking point that seemed to deprive or excuse her of the responsibility and divert it with an incomplete accounting of events via some intermediary to the tormented man whose flailing gesture of despair in the crooked lane had fairly thrown the box away from him?

Human resources being predisposed to rumormongering, my quondam duties having included tedious scapegoating wherein accusers and accused were revealed almost invariably to be driven by pure malice and unmerited performance ratings, I must be forgiven for subsuming the gentleman's moral questions, which could only end in disillusionment, into ontological questions; because although questions of intent and motivation must lead to despair where humans are concerned, to ascribe moral responsibility to nonhuman beings is considered improper and in some cases insulting to *Homo sapiens*, and therefore as I do not wish to give offense, and also because the box thief's identity and excuses are of no interest to me, I shall wrap the question of responsibility in a question equally roundabout and relative, I mean the question of *what it is*: because only insofar as that insatiable, deceptive question may be posed at all do the directions, the demands that a thing such as a little box articulates by being exactly as it is, become meaningful to wandering beings such as ourselves; for despite that human agency has never been other than intricate dancing with nonhumanity such interfolding isn't often acknowledged although it must've been apparent to my interlocutor that the box had as if engineered an order of appearances which in the first instance averted the intruder's intentions, whatever they might have been, in the second instance rearranged the storyteller's impressions of his story's protagonists, and thirdly drew my gaze to the box itself with such consistency that the gentleman observed in me a powerlessness equal to his own, a mirror of his inability to resist the thingly magnetism weaving before our eyes in the inert form of a paper rectangle: holding fast to the indifferent expression appropriate to metropolitans, my poor eyes every time I dragged them to his face or to the window bounced back to the little white box on the table as if tethered by elastic bands, and even as he described the pilfering, the concealment beneath the pillow, he saw my weakness, saw my eyes, held them with his and with a little nod, almost undetectable, indicated that yes the box I had returned to him, the very thing which had arrested me in its self-supporting vulnerability, so finely woven that its complected gaps formed a delicate and authoritative impasse, had been stolen from a stranger's home, from inside an intricate piece of furniture, which one supposes now bears a rectangular wound.

I cannot account for my reaction to this news of his, this confirmation that I wasn't the first to fall under the subtle spell of the box and as a result conduct myself abnormally; but though it would've been ridiculous to hold responsible for the thing's magnetic aura the man who'd brought the box to my attention, my interlocutor smiled with so much sorrow as though wishing for my sake that I hadn't returned to him this object which was not his own, perhaps not even Alex's, that I had never been the receptive audience he'd craved; he said softly, "I tried to open it and couldn't" and with this question seemed to pounce, his smile falling away: "Could you open it, did you try?" and when I shook my head he sighed as if relieved that I'd been spared, and with that helpless sigh I understood so many things: that the man who told the story of the box was not its thief, that the thief had found a way in which to open the box without breaking its seams, and that what she found within, whatever it was that commandeered two disillusioned *Homo sapiens* to gaze upon the box and whisper as it lay in wait between us in this so-called café, was something beyond the thief's wildest imaginings, something that drove her to rashness at first sight, or at the very least something that convinced the man who told the story of the thing's terrible preciousness, leading him to suggest, by means of silences and stumbles and his little nod, that even he, obliged though he was to think in terms of moral culpability, couldn't help but suspect despite himself that a plain little box had compelled a young lady of his acquaintance to such behavior as seemed impossible to this naive gentleman whom life had clearly spared a career in human resources, to wit, that little box had induced a guest, a stranger, instantly, irresistibly, and with great shame to rid her host's apartment of itself, to claim it for her own, and then to inexplicably abandon it.

I need not tell you of the hours I've wasted since that afternoon returning daily to this table deep in contemplation of that box and its secrets; I need say nothing more than that there is no innocence anywhere, only insidiousness, but I think you know that already as I can see upon your face that in light of what I've said to you and what I haven't said, for example that I did not ask the man who chose me for his confidant what he'd heard from his "sources" about the innards of the box even though I sensed that he knew something and strove to keep it hidden, you think you wish to believe or wish you had it in you to refuse to believe that the stolen box, which I and my companion failed to open for want of effort, must contain the proof of some horrific crime, blood diamonds or an emerald with a curse on it, for you can think of nothing that would drive a rational person to such behavior as the intruder's, with such conspicuous urgency and rash untimeliness as she displayed, other than a desperate need to clear her name or that of someone close to her, to rid her reputation of some fetid stain which unjustly and erroneously makes her appear undeserving of the perquisites and protections that *Homo sapiens* confer on conformists; and if this speculation is as accurate as it is farfetched, then if she'd only had the chance, the intruder would have delivered the box and its secrets to someone supposedly in authority, some municipal or lawyerly human resources specialist to whom the presence of the box and the black pearl or crown jewel beneath its paper intersections would've proved the tall dark woman to be innocent of the corruption of which malicious rumor had accused her; thus you can imagine the alarm, the trepidation that gripped her when she discovered her rectangular savior had vanished, embarking on a journey somewhere beyond her reach and setting in motion who knows what obscure events which cannot help but be mysteriously charged, having unbeknownst to almost everyone derived this unusually energetic intensity from the desperateness with which the box and the woman who pursues it have infused each other precisely by each pursuing the other in their own way; but then again, when you consider what I've said to you, what evidence is there for the insidiousness of the box other than its strangeness, its secretiveness which we might call its privacy, its magnetism which may be nothing more than one's own curiosity making itself manifest, and the outlandish behavior of everyone who knew about the box or, as the intruder herself may have done, merely hoped for its existence?

No sooner had the thief made her confession than did the young ladies pack up and leave, one or the other taking the box from Alex's star-table, and whether she or the other confessed to her father or someone else, whether that which she'd discovered about the box, about her friend, or about herself left her so changed, altered forever, as I believe I am and the tale-bearer too, that those around her barely knew her anymore and subsequently wormed the adventure out of her, I do not know; it is obvious that my interlocutor censored himself, but his smile bade me not to ask too much of him, and in any case it does nobody any good to become too well acquainted with this city's intimate details; howbeit, when he allowed the box to conquer his resistance, in resignation and confusion lowering his eyes at last to its white weave of seams, I was writhing with the agony of curiosity and indecision, although I dared not let him see just how much I yearned to know and truly didn't want to know and miserably wished I'd been the one in the apartment and bitterly regretted setting foot outside my house; and after another of his silences he murmured to himself or to the box, "This ought not to have found its way to us, as the clouds ought not precipitate without reprieve," but this was no conclusion, it was no more than he'd made obvious already, and it achieved nothing but to cast the gray, indifferent light of winter on the doomed enigma that is "ought," and so he stopped, lifted his head, smiled his pitiful smile, and said with what I can only describe as sentimental uncertainty, "When we sat down together, I was at a loss for what to do with it, but you," he said, "you were never at a loss, from the very first, you had chosen your limits and accordingly you acted with an unquestioning attitude which I believe you've always understood to be dangerous, for you do not strike me as one to suffer fools, which means you've no patience for dogma nor the base stupidity that willfully or thoughtlessly emboldens dogma to become tyrannical, and yet despite the dangers, for my sake, you held your very self in suspension"; and for this the fellow thanked me and I assured him I'd done nothing to deserve his praise and had no use for his gratitude, whereupon he smiled once more and, rising to his feet with his trials and secondhand tribulations in this most comfortless of winters, he nodded like a man refreshed, the snow falling just as it had all the while, exactly as you see it now, and as I scowled, writhing and flummoxed, into this expensive muck that they call potable, he went out into the streets, taking the box with him.

Counterfate

JOHNVIAJOHN

To understand the catastrophe, you must look at all the artworks. There's no other way. The exhibition's name is *COUNTERFATE*. *COUNTERFATE* from *counterfeit* from *contra facere*, "to make in opposition." Also from *Konterfei*, meaning "portrait," which the artist interprets as "to make exactly like." Not "make exactly" or "make again." To make as if. As if the made thing were the real thing, which it isn't but which began it. The counterfeit thing exists to bear the burden of this secret, the secret of its nonidentity. The fake isn't what it appears to be, but in its own right it is nothing but a pretense of what it appears to be. It's as if counter fate, *contra* what actually occurs when the real thing occurs. Derivatives, paraphrases, rumors, secondhand stories are all counterfate. As if, to suit themselves, they decide what happened.

That's why *JOHNVIAJOHN* is like a door on the exhibition, a "front door" behind the actual front door. It dwarfs the door of the gallery, so enormous it consumes your field of vision when you step across the threshold out of the snow that blankets the whole city and into the separate corner that is the artist's tenuous world. As you must raise the lid to glimpse the contents of a box, you must deal with *JOHNVIAJOHN* before you can go any further. You must confront its afterness and consider that a warning: there's nothing original here. There are many originals. *JOHNVIAJOHN* foreshadows counterfeits that make much of their proximity to their originals, trying to hide behind them, almost. Also counterfeits that flaunt their fraudulence, trying to distinguish themselves. Reconcile yourself to this before seeking out *found secret*. Otherwise you won't have a hope.

The vast square of *JOHNVIAJOHN* makes minikins of us. White linen with delicate, perfect, horizontal lines, so painstaking they're painful, with uniform distances between, overcast-horizon blue with flecks of pink. The effect is almost of mass-produced notepaper blown up to apocalyptic proportions. Except the concentration in those lines, not meditative but backbreaking, the minuscule ripples indicating trembling, the occasional bleeding, the breaks here and there like broken stitches in a seam, show us that this was painted by a human hand. The lines' attenuated tension, this virtuosity of flatness, is undermined by towering black calligraphy, heavy brushstrokes heavily stylized as though the painting mistakes itself for a sacred scroll. You can't read it unless you're a specific kind of specialist.

After the vernissage, a cheeky review came out online. All these learned art-world minions, it said, bunged up the entryway as they stood in front of *JOHNVIAJOHN*, oblivious to those behind them stuck out in the snow. From specialists in action painting pretending to be certain they were looking at an action to literary enthusiasts pretending to recognize a foreign alphabet, all the contemplatively slanted heads, said the reviewer, looked like they knew what they were looking at, knew all along that they had no idea, and glanced around for the artist, meaning to corner her to say, "Of course that's an expressionist rendering of someone's ancient gobbledygook, am I right or am I right." Except nobody could find the artist.

What's painted here is our own language but not our way of writing. It's a shorthand system invented by a man named John over a century ago. The words rendered in it, in the artist's oblique way, are from a text about painting written by a different John. One John's system represents the other's words according to not what they mean but how they sound. Representation as a movement to sound. Like dancing. But the strokes are so big the edge of the canvas cuts them off. We have: *The despair of an artist is. Total it excepts.*

The quoted John never shredded sentences as if by accident and left them like that, in tatters. *JOHNVIAJOHN* misquotes. The text fragments are contradictory: a totality that admits exceptions isn't total. The artist magnifies the shorthand symbols till they no longer resemble writing of any kind. She mashes her sources' names together in the nonsense word that's the title of her effort. The work declines or fails to present all its own facts. It doubts itself. We doubt, faced with this picture, the ability of pictures, of writings, gestures, to transmit meaning. We doubt the artist. *JOHNVIAJOHN* is her first exhibition's outermost facade. It's the gate at the entrance to the maze of her imagination. But is there anything in this picture that's really hers?

Shorthand is speed-writing on factory-made steno paper. Making *JOHNVIAJOHN* took weeks. And so? Is there no more to it than irony? Another lamentation of metro-capitalist speed? Which, as if in revenge, the snow has slowed to a crawl. The gallerist here says *JOHNVIAJOHN* is about how things transmute with time. How time distorts transmissions. Time passing at different speeds simultaneously. Events spiraling in on themselves and outward.

□

If only *found secret* was capable of gestures, it too could be as if a vengeful anti-capitalist flourish. It could represent meditations on the nature of time if only it possessed some meditative quality. Even *JOHNVIAJOHN*—it's a picture of a scrap of notepaper. And it has yet to find a buyer.

Despite that reviewer's vision of enthusiastic hordes tripping over one another at the door, it's my understanding that the vernissage was poorly attended. This even though invitations flew out in superabundance. The snow, maybe. I'd rather we had one more great big

37

blizzard and let that be the end of it. Six and a half weeks of round-the-clock snowfall: who wouldn't stay home as much as possible? I've had to buy three new pairs of designer boots. I rotate them through the week so they have time to dry.

That said, it's unusual for an untested artist to exhibit at this gallery. They certainly didn't take me when I was painting, before I gave it up for conservation. So for this young artist (I can't pronounce her name; you can see it's unintelligible even when correctly spelled), missing her own exhibition's private preview is tragic. You heard about the bus. The only bus in service that evening when everyone who had to go somewhere was wishing for a sleigh. It skidded in the snow and struck a streetlight sideways. She was on that bus along with too many others. She was standing, fell over, and was crushed. Broke her shoulder, had to read about her debut vernissage from the hospital.

The gallerist didn't learn what had happened till the following day. He went ahead with the event, unfazed, assuming she'd forgotten it. This happens with artists. I didn't receive an invitation; my predecessor at the ZV Collection briefed me later. She noted ten or twelve attendees and the loud absence of a focal point. The event must've had a wrong-note undertone all night.

Right now it's daytime. It's only us. The gallerist is somewhere out of sight. The front door is closed but transparent. It invites this silver light. The light brushes the air and the quiet. As light would fall into an empty box after the shipment or relocation is over and done with. Normally, even at private views, this gallery has to keep the front door open. The heat needs an escape. The noise. Pontificating, private jokes, champagne, shameless self-promotion by and by means of established artists with connections in droves. Maybe that night the door was open out of habit. Maybe they put the velvet rope across it. The gallerist must've kept on peeking at it, hoping to see as usual the headlights from one car after another sweeping up and shining in as it dispensed some big shot before sweeping off again.

Instead he saw empty night. Not even breezes wandered in. The snowflakes kept to the outside along their perfect paths, perfectly perpendicular to the ground. Have you wondered why it falls like that? When I met the *COUNTERFATE* artist at last, she said she thinks we're being exposed to the stuff in a regulated manner. More and more of it but only little by little, like the city is a fish tank in a laboratory. She thinks the snow is a toxic infusion of calculated subtlety, and outside someone is watching. Someone who fears toxicity and approves of slowly killing fishes. This too happens with artists, susceptible people. Their paranoia tends toward a blend of the creative and clichéd.

This artist insists her pictures be freestanding or suspended rather than avail themselves of the walls. Having slipped behind *JOHNVIAJOHN*, we must slither between canvases. We must be like fugitives ducking in and out of strangers' shadowed doors. Imagine the vernissage. Barely as many viewers as there are artworks, so the next person to pop out from behind *secondhand world* could be the gallerist resolving not to wonder if he's made a mistake.

Permit me to clarify a distinction. A gallerist and a curator are both hangers of pictures: both coordinate an oeuvre's encounters with viewers. But our responsibilities are really very different. A gallerist exhibits the work of an artist with the aim of furthering her career by, for example, facilitating the sale of her best pieces. A curator's concern is the collection that grows under her auspices and subsists in her care. A curator of a culturally vital institution oversees its collection's presentation, conservation, and promotion under many layers of public, professional, and scholarly scrutiny. It's on her sole authority that new artworks are purchased. Her selections are contingent only on the approval of the collector or committee that finances the collection. I still don't understand why ZV, the collector who would become my boss, insisted on attending *COUNTERFATE*'s vernissage. Or why he dragged along my predecessor, the then-curator of the famous ZV Collection, oldest and finest collection of masterpieces in the city.

She said the ambience resembled that of a department store on its way to bankruptcy. People spoke in huddles about other people who weren't there, people who weren't this artist. My predecessor knew almost everybody. She saw nobody with use potential except ZV. She said everyone drank too much, and there were too many waiters. The artworks seemed irrelevant to their own party. Like interlopers. Skip those canvases. They're uneventful. Come see the box.

secondhand world

A copse, one critic called it. Four quadrate canvases of middling size face one another in a square, their backs to everything around them. Secured by wires to the floor and ceiling, they suggest to the uninitiated eye the walls of a shipping crate forsaken by gravity and coming apart at the seams. An art professional unlucky enough to be female, like me, will also see the tall, broad backs, squared at the shoulders, looking all alike and rigid, of the art world itself. The key is to slip between the walls, for there are gaps. Here we go.

And now we find ourselves boxed in. There's not much room. It's very awkward. The installation is called ". . . secondhand world . . . ," or From Ema's Husband, Memory. Punctuation and all. "Ema's husband" is a renowned artist whose relationship with painting is as if subversive. With the From and that comma, it's as if the maestro is a popular address in a famous city.

Maybe I should tell you to forget the title and just look. The installation is a tetraptych like the multipaneled altarpieces of the past. But unlike them, this has no terminus. As a city square has no terminus. None of the canvases has any visible priority. All four are flawless as far as technique goes. In the images she made by hand, the energy of her hand, the weight and warmth of her arm and shoulder are in the canvas, coming through it, not imposed on it. The images reach across the distance, sometimes overwhelming, sometimes unnoticeable, between life and death. I ought to say this to ZV. This gathering of images captures our inability to feel the motion of time.

Maybe I won't say it. It's a bit much. Anyway, you can't forget the title. If this work means to say anything, then the title is the cipher. Unfortunate.

What she's done is to *as if* recreate one of the maestro's paintings four times in four different ways. Not one of his masterpieces but a painting he rejected and destroyed. She could only have seen that painting in the rare photographs he took of an attic that served him briefly as an early-period atelier. These photos aren't online. They're not at all easy to come by. And the artist claims, unless I've misunderstood, to have painted from memory.

It's true the maestro won his reputation with deliberately inexact re-presentations. He painted photographs. Sometimes private snapshots, other people's family photographs. Sometimes advertisements, models, or criminals featured in the press. He painted them enlarged, the images perfectly to scale, but as if the photographs they came from were imperfect. Blurry, grainy, faded, disrupted by a chance, involuntary motion of an unsteady hand, even when the originals weren't like that at all.

In this painting, which we cannot call the first, our artist seems to discourage her memory from embellishing the maestro's second-hand image, a scrupulously blurry painting of an enlarged snapshot of a smiling man crouching beside a poodle. It appears she tried to paint them exactly as he did, a counterfeit of the maestro's counterfeit.

The next one, counterclockwise, is an attempt to reproduce the maestro's painting of the unidentified man and poodle's black-and-white analog photograph using digital technology, which neither photographs nor paints. Somehow our artist transmitted the photograph she never saw to a computer, which instructed a digital printer to spray the canvas with the image of the maestro's no-longer-extant painting. Note the lack of texture and movement in comparison to the windblown feel of the manual painting. There's less variety among the ambiguities of grays.

Turn again, counterclockwise, and we have, once more by hand, a reimagining of the same stranger and cloud-white poodle in brilliant acrylic colors without blurring. Not an attempt to paint them as they really were but to make the colors lead us through the image. The act of looking becomes adventuring instead of pausing to lock ourselves in a moment.

I should point this out to ZV. How the black under the man's chin, where his throat goes down into his maroon shirt, guides the gaze to the shadow under the dog's ear, behind which the man's hand and arm disappear, then to the shadow above the dog's crimson collar and the black, uncertain shape of his closed mouth, to the dog's unreadable black eyes and the man's pink, fatuous grin. Yes, I should probably point this out. Although it's not as if she pioneered the technique. It's not historically striking.

Maybe I won't mention it. It's more as if she's trying to insinuate herself into the maestro's history. She's pretending she had access to the atelier photographs and was allowed to study them without anyone knowing, which can't be possible. The photographs are in the maestro's archive. The archive has no record of anybody studying them. Beyond that, she's presuming to appropriate an image that disappointed the maestro enough for him to destroy it. Does she think she can somehow elevate the rejected image by reviving it like some kind of zombie? Does she think she can succeed with it where the maestro failed?

Ema's husband painted from snapshots because at the time he thought snapshots eschewed hidden meanings. They aren't secret drawers or puzzle boxes, which the maestro had no patience for. But *COUNTERFATE*'s instigator enjoys indirectness, say the critics. Photographs and videos have forsaken their credibility anyway. That goes for images everywhere, not only in what's called "art." Hardly anyone expects what is called "media" to represent the truth. What passes for directness nowadays is illusion and ideology.

And so turn once more, against the clock, to what for us is the final canvas. Black and white and gray again. Brushwork that is delicate without seeming so. An exactitude of blurriness that would've pleased the maestro. What he'd think of her misquotation I can't say.

This canvas undermines all the others. If you haven't seen the atelier photographs, and almost nobody has, you can no longer tell which of these four paintings represents the original image and which represents a misremembrance or a lie.

The white poodle is as usual, though he's blurrier, more ghostly. But in the dark, familiar clothes, the face above the shadowy seam between the throat and masculine collar, is the terrorist whose image became one of Ema's husband's most notorious paintings. The terrorist was a girl whom the maestro never knew. He painted her in prison garb but almost smiling, just as she was in the photograph he found in the newspaper. She smiles the same smile in our young artist's mash-up, though the position of her body is that of the man behind the poodle.

This girl is what society values most. Pretty, youthful, white fecundity. And she's what it fears the most. The misfit with an idea that's become a violent obsession. She's shown in a common pose, a featureless landscape, having fun with a pet. You couldn't tell what she was if you didn't already know her face. In another famous canvas, the maestro painted a newspaper photograph of her dead body. Presumably because, as he did in personal snapshots, he saw in photojournalistic images some denial of complexity, some straightforwardness that's no more than *as if.* This girl supposedly killed herself in prison. But his rendering of her corpse was so lovely, so vivid, seeming almost tender, that after people saw the painting they couldn't help but wonder if such a person really could've taken her own life. They wondered if the police had killed her, confected the suicide story and the images in the papers. But what does a spectral poodle have to do with this?

The gallerist dared to quote at me: *History is not just human. History is selective in favor of the human despite itself. It is causes and effects mediated by gaps, insinuations, and shadows.* Make sense of it if you can.

Secondhand images pile on one another and themselves. Like the snow outside, almost. And like the snow, sometimes pieces of the truth evaporate. It could be because of the terrorist that *secondhand world* hasn't sold. Or it's a deeper, conceptual problem. I've revisited this installation more often over the past few weeks than I care to remember. Because if any work of hers could be historic enough to deserve the Collection's consideration, it's this one. But secondhand retellings aren't historic. They might be history, but they are not historic.

They're helpless. Every counterfeit is a complex of helplessnesses. The elemental helplessness of the counterfeiter is the inability to create the real thing. If the counterfeiter could conjure real, minted currency, she'd feel no need to fake it. If she'd been the actual maestro who'd made the actual masterpiece, she'd have felt no urge to make-believe it. She names her things *COUNTERFATE* to pretend helplessness doesn't exist. But even if *fate* just means your present circumstances, pretending you have the power to remake them all in your own image is patriarchal, imperialistic trumpery.

For example, she thinks this weather is deliberate. She thinks someone's figured out how to regulate snowfall in the synthetic, mechanical image of the city where people live on preservatives and move according to the clockwork of trains and buses. That such industrial-grade arrogance will only ruin everything is the lesson of the past several hundred years. *found secret* is arrogant, too, but in another way.

I haven't said it to anyone because it wouldn't be kind, but I find this installation frustrating. Three men, one woman, four dogs boxing us in. And so? What do you feel? *Secondhand stories of a city in despair where hope is either hidden or counterfeit*, said the artist to *Art in Public* magazine. Meaning what exactly in regard to people with poodles? Ambivalence is rarely a selling point for a creature like billionaire-business-baron ZV. In the words of my predecessor, "Wishy-washiness will get you nowhere." Trying to be ambivalent, *secondhand world* has gotten stuck.

At the vernissage, there was a woman no one knew. Not even the ZVC curator, who wasn't yet its former curator, recognized this person. She'd made an effort at "evening casual" but couldn't pull it off.

She had lots of black hair that didn't suit the way she'd styled it. "She didn't fit well in herself" was how my predecessor put it.

She, that is, ZV's then-curator, and presumably everybody assumed the outsider was a friend of the artist, whose absence unaccounted for would've then explained the stranger's lost expression. She didn't presume to think she was anyone important. She didn't force her acquaintance on anybody. But it must've been unsettling to watch this person wandering the gallery wearing yellow, like she'd forgotten about winter, and a permanent grimace. My predecessor said she looked "like she never really understood where she was. Like she was doomed never to find anything that made sense, and she knew it or suspected it. All the time." She kept chewing her lips. So her front teeth often showed. "Capybarical," said my predecessor, referring to a rodent of some kind. "And one of the teeth was chipped and crooked. And she didn't even bother having it fixed before imposing herself on an *aesthetic* gathering."

The old curator remembered almost bumping into the stranger as she walked in her cheap shoes around *secondhand world*, looking at its unpainted outsides. She walked, said my predecessor, "like each step was an explosion. A leg exploding forward. An almost pause, a struggle to hold herself in, hold back, stop this. But no, there goes the other leg. Another small explosion." No contact was made, no words or looks exchanged. They kept near-missing and near-colliding all night long. I don't suppose there were many options for chance meetings drifting through this half-empty mausoleum of half-stolen things. But turning her back on the interloper, seeking distraction in a critic who'd already been permitted to pay court, only to glimpse a flash of yellow between dark suits or a slip of black hair slashing through *The Seven Presents* like a will-o'-the-wisp, the old curator found herself hunting the woman and hoping not to find her, longing for the relief that would wash through the whole gallery when the apparition disappeared into thin air.

I don't know my predecessor well. We've only spoken once in person. She's not a fan of photo-painting or mixed-media work. She said art for her means ground cinnabar and linseed oil. I'm trained in the conservation of traditional, digital, and mixed-media work. ZV chose me, he said, because I "come with the latest algorithms."

□

Stalking the woman who'd driven her to distraction by looking out of place, the old curator found herself in the armpit of the gallery. A poky corner at the back of the exhibit space, which everyone ignored because they thought they were supposed to. A case of the gallerist redoing his office and the junk-removal truck failing to get through the snow. No one, anymore, would've been offended or surprised by this. But when the ZVC's curator, still curator for the moment, peeked into that graceless corner, she almost dropped her champagne cocktail.

The talk in that corner was too subdued to hear. The old curator noted thoughtful listening poses. The stranger with the fake-black hair and tasteless color palette, not pretty, not young, a paradigm of the perfect nobody. And ZV himself. The man to whom everyone from CEOs to socialites yearns to toady up and almost never has the chance. Even I had never dared to dream of an interview, let alone employment, with the connoisseur they call ZV. Yet there she was. A nobody. Murmuring so nobody could hear but him. He allowed caesuras to pinprick his eternal monologue for her sake. And the gallerist confirmed what my predecessor saw. ZV and the interloper hushed and huddled before *found secret*.

Implausible as this cozy little conference was, the gallerist was unconcerned at first. Nobody'd have the guts to infiltrate a vernissage of his without an invite, he thought. He assumed his inability to recognize this person meant she was from out of town. A secretary or ghostwriter for one of the big bylines. Someone of the old school, the gallerist thought. Because while keeping an eye on the interloper and chatting up someone else, he dropped the name of a hotel. And at the sound of the hotel's name, the interloper turned and looked at him.

"A flicker of a glance," the gallerist told me. Which makes me doubt it ever happened. But it reassured him that, since she was from out of town, she must be staying at La Blue Boite, the hotel he'd invoked. In the old days, every visiting critic and collector stayed at the Boite if they were somebody who mattered. So, based on evidence gleaned by name-dropping and eavesdropping, the gallerist surmised that this woman had every right to be inside his gallery in conference with ZV.

Observant art professional that he is, the gallerist didn't recollect until later that while talking with ZV, the interloper seemed "frightened." In turn, my predecessor said, ZV looked at the interloper with "concern." He frowned and sometimes gestured at *found secret*. Both of them looked at *found secret*. And ZV listened.

His curator didn't dare interrupt. She sensed she'd be unable to even if she tried. She dreaded someone coming up to her and asking to be introduced to the nullity who appeared to know something ZV wanted to know about an artwork. She didn't trust herself not to brain the woman with her champagne flute. So she left them. Ran into the gallerist, didn't want to speak to him, found herself commiserating bitterly with him about the stranger who was everywhere and the artist who was nowhere.

Later I asked the artist about the visitant. At that point, she was in no fit state for conversation. She was in tears. She almost screamed: *Obviously* the woman no one knew was a *manifestation*, a spiritual emanation by an object. Or something. I stopped listening after "obviously."

More to the point, nobody's drafted a sales contract for *found secret*. No one's made an offer. No numbers waft in the ether. What happened was a remark tossed like a crumb. That remark was catastrophic.

After his furious curator left him to his own devices at the vernissage, ZV said something to the gallerist. When the artist was unearthed, the gallerist (everybody knows he's the opposite of reckless), spoke to her of reckless "promises." The artist burst into triumphant tears, witnessed by nurses who heard all about these promises. The nurses told the physiotherapists and god knows who else. The curator was informed eventually and as if offhand by the billionaire's assistant. My predecessor assumed the man was joking.

Then one day ZV asked her if the *COUNTERFATE* artist was still in the hospital and, "If so, have flowers been sent?" The curator, being a curator and not a personal assistant, had no idea. (I've remembered it wasn't just the artist's shoulder that was broken. It was her collarbone as well. Also one of her wrists.) But that's how she, the curator, came to realize ZV wasn't joking. When he realized his curator thought he was being whimsical, he was indignant. Like he doesn't know "solid art" when he sees it but must wait for her to tell him what to think, as she said he said.

Inanities come as cheaply to ZV as everything else. "Solid" art? The curator was fuming but had to appear conciliatory. She asked him reasonably what he saw in *found secret*. He called it "intimate." He called it "personal." He said it "couldn't be left out in the snow or some dingy studio where nobody and anybody could get at it." He said, "It gives you a deep-down shock. Then it refuses to console you. But it isn't indifferent either. Since it isn't indifferent, it's different. Its walls resist and its inertia condones."

My predecessor concluded that the man had no notion of the piece at all. As curator, she felt duty bound to speak her mind. If there's any sense of intimacy in *found secret*, it's the counterfeit intimacy of a burglar or voyeur, she said, and even that's grasping at straws. She warned me not to underestimate what I must do: she'd told ZV the "promise" he'd given the gallerist was catastrophic. For art as such. For the history of art. Like it or not, the ZVC plays a pivotal role in determining what such things are. And for ZV's reputation as a man of taste but also, more than that, for his curator's reputation, a pair of receptacles thrown together like a bankrupt department store's discards is no good.

She expected a countertantrum from the billionaire legatee and financier. ZV's unused to being contradicted, "however liberal he likes to appear," she told me. But no countertantrum came. He waited for her to go on. There was no going on. There was no more to say. ZV winked at her and said, "But you're just beginning to wonder!" He sauntered off, thinking he'd been most profound and set his curator on the path to revelation.

Actually, she was disgusted. Not only by our boss but, from the moment she set eyes on *found secret*, by the thing itself. She can be volatile. You've probably realized. Her tendency to shrill presumption, snap reaction, and exaggeration clinched her early successes. But her first impressions of *found secret* couldn't have been as gripping as they came to seem in hindsight. To be sure, it was intended to make gripping first impressions; otherwise it wouldn't have been on view. But from back there in the cobwebs? It's more likely that she didn't see *found secret* at all at first, only ZV and the woman with the crooked tooth. Because of that woman, *found secret* became the bane of the ZVC curator. And for what? One question alone arises from that piece. Why is it on view, at the vernissage, no less, flaunting an absence of skill that the artist clearly possesses?

The Seven Presents

In the handling of brushes, colors, proportions, our artist of the unpronounceable name is uncommonly dexterous. Witness *The Seven Presents*. This is a great painting.

It's without a buyer. If ZV's eye were as cultivated as he thinks, he wouldn't have passed it over for *found secret*. Here it is dead center in the space, directly in line with *JOHNVIAJOHN*. No undead furniture, no litter of canvases in some backward formation. *The Seven Presents* is an oil painting in a frame on an easel. The artist made the frame herself, carved and painted the gilded antique filigree. The easel is an easel. The gallerist wanted a square of velvet rope around it. The artist thought velvet rope would be too much.

I should've said it might've been a great painting. The disagreement over a corral of velvet rope shows how ambivalent the work is about its own ambitions.

The subject sits on a flat surface of dark wood. Some kind of side-board, I imagine, at right angles to an open door. All this I'm getting from the light. We can't see what kind of object the wood surface belongs to. Most of it is beyond the canvas or covered by the subject. What we see is this gentle light showering everything askance. Like daylight slipping in through a small opening and diffusing, gifting us the grain of the wood, the glisten of the plastic shopping bag. And all over the subject's body, this shopping bag in hunter green, the shadows writhing.

Here in the furrows of the slouching plastic bag is a remarkable black. The kind of black that crawls, that growls. Nightmare black. The shadows twist and groan with the struggle of a metamorphosis they can't complete. Like the secrets in the bag. Out of sight behind green plastic, the secrets bulge and strain the bag so it can't keep its shape. The sleekness proper to all things plastic is undone. Are puppies wriggling within? Are we looking at the excess energy of an unnecessary purchase that'll look ghastly when it comes out of the bag at home? The department store's gold lettering is crumpled. Smudged as though it's been out in the snow. My predecessor says this picture makes her think of indigestion.

The title refers to a flight of fancy by the John of *JOHNVIAJOHN*. He once eavesdropped on a guided tour because the docent looked to him like a strange creature. After the tour, he continued watching her. He saw her leaving the museum with a green plastic bag from a department store. And he imagined that in the bag were seven presents. What the presents might've been, celebrations or consolations, whether they even existed, were arcana known only to the docent, whom he shadowed but never approached.

My assistant forwarded me a quote he'd received from someone on our staff whose son or niece saw it on a blog (it's on my phone) that mentioned *The Seven Presents* in a tangent: . . . *so moving because it feels, as with grasping fingers that cannot grip what falls between, the unsolvable mysteries of things belonging to others. This painting beds down in the longing that is symptomatic of individuality: a fraught condition that bars each of us from dissolving into all others.*

But, as in *JOHNVIAJOHN*, nothing specifically *of the artist's* is discernible in this piece. Besides her skill with brushes, which makes a plastic bag such a pretty thing. But expecting people to see beauty in plastic bags: to anybody who's seen the river, the idea should be downright horrifying. *The Seven Presents*, wrote someone on social media (people keep sending me accolades for *COUNTERFATE* from all and sundry), is *the most profound portrait of contemporary humanity: plastic with all our logos corroding.*

Maybe we're learning the world-historical power of plastic. But plastic has never been profound, only convenient. And as I said, the secondhand is not historic. Look closely and you'll see nine bulges in the bag, not seven. Not necessarily another misquotation, this could still be a bag with seven objects in it, one or two of which bulges elaborately. The painting makes a show of addressing the problem of the historic but as if with a mute address. A look that doesn't see. Looking that, uncurious or skittish, doesn't seek seeing. And this sort of sideways as if squirming look is inquisitive only sometimes. Sometimes it's acquiescent. It shares a certain shallowness with *found secret.*

□

And so you see me here on my free evening. As the gallerist sees me again and again. Fishing, if you want the truth. Struggling to sound the depths of *COUNTERFATE*. He worms over. "If I may suggest . . ." as though I asked him for suggestions. He goes on about my being "thrown" into my position, the "unbalanced" influence of my predecessor, the artist's youth and situation, the billionaire—"such a powerful man," he says, as though chauvinists aren't all alike. "Given all this intimidation and extraordinary pressure," the gallerist tells me I must take especial care not to let prejudice cloud my eye as a responsible professional.

"Political consciousness must be ecological. Ecological consciousness requires deanthropocentrism," he proclaims, surely misquoting some theorist. "Thus," he continues, even those who find such ideas "intimidating" must recognize COUNTERFATE "as an historical act" because it challenges humanity's vision of itself as the only player in its power games.

"Intimidating," he says. Again! And dares to "thus" at me. The truth is he parted badly from my predecessor. But let's move on. Mustn't let him catch us with *The Seven Presents*. He'd start in on the shopping bag as a pawn in a mistreated-packaging conspiracy.

He's revised his opinion of the interloper, you see. Now he thinks she was a spy. This gallery's gallerist, an educated purveyor of fine art, thinks a box manufacturer found out about COUNTERFATE's "invocations of packaging" *before the vernissage* and regarded the exhibition as an affront. This mysterious corporate entity, which the gallerist couldn't name, sent a nobody in bright yellow as a covert infiltrator. After the vernissage, she informed her superiors of ZV's interest in *found secret*, and the box makers orchestrated the vandalism, driven by a baseless thirst for vengeance against the artist. And her gallerist, of course. Delusions of grandeur go together with persecution manias.

As for ZV, after he winked and spoke of flowers, his then-curator was determined that they should both forget about *found secret*. She refused to engage in any discussions of contemporary art. She knew the gallerist couldn't formalize an offer, which in any case hadn't been made, without the artist's evaluation. And the artist (she also had a concussion) was in no condition to evaluate. The gallerist didn't want to be accused of taking advantage of her debility in an eagerness to secure a commission.

But rumor outran everyone. ZV's interested. Suddenly everybody's interested.

News media. Rival galleries. Some museum wanting to be first in line when the ZVC sent *found secret* out on tour. One of the auction houses hinted they'd buy it off him if ZV bought it first. Mobs of hangers-on found sneaky ways of connecting with the curator. Many were too influential to hang up on. Unbelievable numbers popped out of their mouths, tangled up in specious questions about *found secret*'s aesthetics, intended to provoke some telltale pause or quiver that might measure the seriousness of ZV's promise. They let fall these absurd numbers, my predecessor said, as you'd drop a muffin wrapper to bring a swarm of pigeons. All of which goes to prove that the most interesting thing about *found secret* is the rumor that ZV might find it interesting.

Amused by what a whisper of a whim of his could do, ZV entertained himself by answering everyone equivocally. The artist lay in the hospital, where her wounds became infected. And the ZVC's then-curator floundered in an enfilade of calls and messages. She was the sole force of resistance against the fake enchantment that *found secret* cast over the art world by sleight of hand. Volleys of sidelong questions posing as how-are-yous drove her to self-medicate with absinthe. She spent a fortune on aromatherapy massage.

The worst, she said, was when the other phone calls started. Not a culture journalist digging for a tip. Not a critic angling to make sure he was sailing with the current. Not a nosy relative, ZV's or her own, hoping one of them had finally gone crazy, but a voice my predecessor had never heard before.

She described it as "presumptuously quiet." Like a single snow-flake expecting to be noticed. Like this voice and what it had to say were so important that the rest of us deserved to exhaust ourselves trying to hear it. As soon as she heard that voice for the first time, she knew. She knew it without recognizing anything about it.

It was the stranger from the vernissage. The interloper who'd as if possessed ZV.

He never admitted it. The woman with the hair too black to be true was "just an interesting person" whom he blessed with a few seconds in his company. That's the story he gave his old curator with a grin. A grin, she said, that said he knew she knew that he was being coy and that she should take it as a challenge. And like it.

How the interloper got around the ZVC's legion of docents, interns, and assistants is a mystery. The woman's name is a mystery. She ignored all demands that she identify herself. Needless to say, the then-curator hung up on her. But not immediately.

"Something about her voice stopped you." My predecessor rarely listens to anybody, but even she understood that what gave her pause was the opposite of power. "Like desperation from another world. But a world so near to ours it shares our language." She said her massage therapist talks often about fissures. Anthropogenic fissures, or was it atmospheric? Fissures causing other kinds of splitting in the seams of space-time.

"If you knotted all the fissures together, tangled them up so they'd no hope of unentangling or of being told apart, then they amounted to something impassable. Something as if sealed airtight." My predecessor analyzed the stranger's desperation as though it were a baffling work of art. Connoisseur of color on canvas, the old curator followed a sense of incompletion and stubborn closure, a "self-interference pattern" that she called "blank *blanc*," through the interloper's vocal timbres to images of her face.

That face almost haunted my predecessor's memory. The stranger was almost so nondescript as to be unrememberable. Which added to the then-curator's feeling that this person's defining aspects were sealed off or nonexistent. It was useless to try to ascertain where she'd come from or what fueled her. It was more "faithful" to the interloper, said the old curator as if unpacking some maestro's latest, "truer" to the "effects" and "affects" that this individual created, *not* to project aspirations or backstories onto her ambiguous facade. That would amount to "misinterpretation of inviolable desperation," said the former curator, who was drunker than she looked.

All she really saw at the vernissage and later heard over the phone was an out-of-place woman who thought nobody would understand her. The interloper resigned herself to that belief to the point that she was cowed by it. Her actual question was the same as the tabloids' and forgotten art-school cronies': Would the ZVC buy bad art by a nobody? It was the stranger's way of asking that was different.

She asked, "Will you hold on to it forever?"

When others asked, art-world parasites, they spoke of the rumored purchase as a secret that, wink wink, nudge nudge, they were already in on. The interloper asked, "Will you hold on," as though she knew everybody else only thought they knew the kind of secret that it was but didn't really. As though she knew they couldn't possibly appreciate its significance. Ever. Nor could they comprehend that the secret of *found secret* had to be protected or contained at all costs. Unluckily for her own agenda, the interloper failed to specify what kind of "holding" she thought *found secret* should submit to. Did she mean preservation, imprisonment, or burial? My predecessor said the interloper's regard for *found secret*, like a species of fear, was "in her timbre, not her words." The timbre of secrets.

This city. Work like *COUNTERFATE*. Living with things like this teaches us to be afraid of quiet. My predecessor, who never listens, couldn't get that nobody's quiet out of her mind. She, the ZVC's soon-to-be-erstwhile curator, came here after midnight. She looked at *found secret*. The gallerist stood with her in the dark, looking.

The calls came almost every night. *Unidentifiable*, said the then-curator's phone. How the interloper found the ZVC curator's personal number is a mystery. Dazed with alcohol, sex, disrupted sleep, she knew long silence was the interloper's first word. And lay there. Waiting. Waiting to strain to hear the question before hanging up.

"Will you hold on to *found secret*?"

Every night the same silence and the question. Knowing that the interloper might call anytime, the curator who'd soon be as if démodé carried around "a creepy feeling like the instant before a shiver." And what went on between them was very like a nervous vibration, movement without movement for weeks on end. The stranger knew she'd be dismissed, but she kept calling. The curator knew what she was in for but kept answering. Only to hang up again.

I wouldn't have hung up on her. She would've revealed herself in time. I've little doubt she was just another artsy type seeking fame's magical doorway. But I don't judge without firm grounds, unlike some people.

One night she asked a different question. First the usual. The old curator said nothing as usual. But before she could hang up, the interloper asked, "Has he opened the box? Have you?" I think that's beside the point. She must've realized she didn't need to know. As it hazily occurred to the then-curator to ask if the artist was a friend of hers, the stranger hung up.

But this interloper so solicitous of *found secret* was for my predecessor just another glare bouncing around the hall of mirrors where all the obstreperous reflections were *found secret*. ZV delighted in the frenzy and in teasing her about *found secret*. She regretted the torrid affair she'd begun with *found secret*'s gallerist while her "chakras were a jiggling mess." Some time elapsed before she realized she no longer heard her phone at night.

She flew to the conclusion that the snaggletoothed interloper had connected with ZV himself and so no longer needed her. She confronted him, demanded to know if he'd been in contact with the freak who'd crashed a vernissage in preworn shoes. The billionaire laughed, and she exploded. *"You will not* purchase that appalling thing. *You will not* undermine the Collection's history by soiling it with junk," and so on.

A billionaire's whims aren't to be trifled with. Spurious though his intentions may be, a mere curator cannot enlighten him to the fact. ZV said of course he was going to buy *found secret*. He said he'd do it as soon as the artist was well enough to be unable to make excuses when negotiations didn't go her way. The curator found it horrifying that he'd disregard her expert advice. ZV found it horrifying that she'd dare to argue with him. The curator, at the limit of her endurance, accused the billionaire of presuming to mistake her for an impotent tool. She said his sporting with *found secret* was despicable. She tendered her resignation with a shriek that the whole business was an affront to art itself.

Later, ZV laughed when the box slipped its restraints: another catastrophe. My first assignment as curator is to deal with the mess. While the art world watches with bated breath. They watch because imprudence is what art and billionaires have in common.

The Wardrobe Is Embarking on Its Escape

Out of solidarity as a former artist and former nobody myself, I'm trying to think the best of COUNTERFATE. Try as I might, I can't elude the sinking feeling that the only energy in this exhibition is a wish to be notorious for something. Skip those pieces. Look at this. *The Wardrobe Is Embarking on Its Escape.*

Look straight on to start. You seem to be looking through a pane of glass at a wall-mounted canvas. The glass hangs from the ceiling. It was once a sliding door. The image on the canvas, done in acrylic paint with almost uncanny realism, is a wardrobe. Slender, about the height of a person. The wood is cracked in places, the whitewash discolored as if from too much sun. One door is slightly open. The mirror on the door's inward side is partly visible. The artist has painted a green picture frame around the wardrobe. She's partly painted the open door over the picture frame.

Now step to the side. See the work in cross section. What appeared from the front to be two surfaces, one behind the other, is actually four. The found glass at the front. Behind it, the wardrobe is painted not on canvas but on the verso of a large mirror suspended from the ceiling. On the mirror's smooth posterior, the artist counterfeits the fluctuating crisscross texture of canvas. Behind it is the mirror itself, unadorned. We regard ourselves obliquely. There isn't enough space to squeeze between the mirror and the wall. But on the wall in line with the mirror is a canvas. A real one. A painting of the same wardrobe. An exact replica, it seems, of the wardrobe behind the mirror. Again the wardrobe's door is open. So when we look in the real mirror, we seem to see ourselves looking out of the painted mirror in the wardrobe's door.

The chances that people will peer askance at this work are slim to none. Even peering sidelong, it's impossible to really look at the painting on the wall because the mirror is too close. The painting is besieged by layers and layers of surface. But if you squinted, looked through a telephoto, or had the misfortune, as I did, to have the cockroach that you'd blissfully unnoticed leap out and catch your eye as for the ump-teenth time you sauntered innocently by; well, you'd notice two small differences between the painting on the fake canvas behind the mir-ror and the painting on the real canvas before the mirror.

The latter has two additional details. The sticky note, looking real enough to grab, in that corner of the wardrobe's built-in mirror. And the life-size cockroach peeking out of the wardrobe through the gap between the partway-open door and the rest of the ward-robe's body.

See whatever you want. Cite the artist's juxtaposition of inanimate and living things, including a live hexapedal oracle of death. It makes no difference: that cockroach, regardless of symbolism, disqualifies this piece from the ZVC's consideration. I refuse to spend my work-ing hours in any proximity to any cockroach. I refuse to get cozy with that cockroach for the sake of the sticky note. You'd need a magnifier to read it anyway. The gallerist is happy to provide the text: *The wardrobe seems penetrable because it has a door. But inside is a closed surface, the worst discovery taking form. The world is not human, we are not human. And the inhuman part is truest. The thing of us.*

A mash-up of misquotes masquerading as a coherent thought. That is, if you believe a certain clique of critics who substantiate their analyses by citing one another. But, barring the cockroach, there's no reason to let them pass unchallenged; neither the critics' delu-sions nor the artist's evasions. If I could do it without the cockroach (not an option; they'd say I missed it, call me careless, reject and ridi-cule, etcetera), I'd challenge this work in print. Why bother with a note that's too tiny to be legible in a negligible corner? Why diminish or deny the artist's responsibility for the vicious words she painted in her own hand? "The inhuman part is truest"? Any normal person would find that plain offensive.

My point, driven home by that disgusting cockroach, is that comb-ing *COUNTERFATE* for significance that will valorize the ZVC is a degrading first challenge for this curator. It makes one almost feel like taking revenge on something.

No matter. I'm equal to the challenge. When I know how to defend these works, then even if ZV goes on with *found secret* or I succeed in selling him a picture of a shopping bag, our decision will appear sound from the outside. Even if its soundness is counterfeit, if deep down even the artist knows we were duped, as the first curator of the ZVC in its new era I will convince everyone that we were right.

The old curator staked her career on an incontrovertible truth: for art and artists, for history, the ZVC and all its visitors, for paper-crafters and interior decorators everywhere, it'd be best if *found secret* had no connection with the name *ZV*. Here's the thing.

I know *found secret* is garbage. But I'm tempted, perhaps to an irresistible degree, to convince ZV to buy it.

□

Somebody from art school told me about the ZVC's sudden vacancy. My appointment was announced. Unkind rumors sprouted. They said my résumé was "scattered." The billionaire chose a failed painter to spite the old curator. The old curator chose an "unfocused" multimedia conservator to spite the billionaire. There are always unkind rumors. ZV and the staff welcomed me with enthusiasm and, I think, relief. My predecessor told me everything in a bar.

Then came a glorious week of settling in with monumental masterpieces. I've known them all since childhood. Suddenly they were mine to care for and arrange, exhibit and hide away as I saw fit. Their visibility, their existence, was in my hands. In spite of everything my predecessor said, her undoing by *COUNTERFATE* and a small box, I forgot about moldy cabinets and swollen notepaper. I took no calls in that first week except from staff.

The interloper never called. Mentioning her to my staff made them uncomfortable. To learn their former curator was bandying about the story of her downfall embarrassed them on her behalf. The head of docents thinks the unidentified caller and the interloper in yellow cannot be the same person. My predecessor thinks the opposite. A conviction based on fleeting apparitions, tipsy conspiracy theories, and not listening.

And I doubted her. I questioned that conviction. In answer, the former curator launched a rant with table-beating. But that isn't why I feel, though all I've done is listen to a nervous art professional throw her life away . . . maybe she could be right.

One of the artist's advance-publicity strategies was an interview for online broadcast. In the video, we see her holding the box. Turning it over, turning it over. Paraphrasing and misquoting, she goes on about the withdrawal of beings. "The unspeakable suchness of a thing." She said nothing's fully accessible to anything else because things are too intimate to know one another. "The box is its own secret, not mine," she says. Her gallerist informs me that the discrepancy between my ideas about the box and the box is irreducible, meaning I'll never "subjugate" the box, and neither will anything else.

For some reason, this "unspeakable such-and-such" makes me think of the interloper, who has yet to contact me. Rather, it makes me think of my predecessor's idea of the interloper. An idea that's half silence. As if resembling a rumor so rampant it's exhausting its own meaning.

Which brings me back to *found secret*. Nobody would notice it had it not been vandalized.

It happened in the second week of my new life. It must've happened while the gallery was open. There was no break-in. The gallerist could've been cowering in his office as he is today. Some think he was in on it. They say he and the artist conspired to devalue *found secret* temporarily. Or to boost its value with the myth of hooligans so affected by the piece that passion moved them to possess something of it. They say the artist and gallerist thought to use the crime as an excuse to appeal to the ZVC. Proof that *found secret* belongs there even as a sort of refugee.

My predecessor formed her own conspiracy theory. She decided the interloper was an actress hired by the gallerist to "disrupt" the vernissage and turn ZV against his curator. In which case the interloper was just pretending to be desperate and had even dressed the part. The gallerist rehired the actress to harass my predecessor with midnight calls. He vandalized his own gallery, she said, to create a scandal. Because in the eyes of the market, scandal would obviate even the ZVC's then-curator's assessment of COUNTERFATE.

Besides, it was she who was the gallerist's intended victim. Or so the old curator has convinced herself. "That vindictive little skunk" meant to undermine ZV's confidence in her, make ZV want a "trendier" curator receptive to the gallerist's "innovations." "That glorified pawnbroker" either had the box in his office all along or squirreled it away with "one of his shady associates whom he thinks nobody knows about." I make no comment except that I'm not sure it's possible for news of the vandalism to have leaked to the media without the gallerist's knowledge. He says that's what happened. I offer no opinion except that it's unlikely anyone would want the box for its aesthetic properties alone. I forbore to ask my predecessor what she meant by "shady associates." The actress, maybe, or a dealer in fugitive furniture. But let's not get carried away. This gallery's reputation is unstained.

I could no longer avoid the enfilade. Financial media, popular media, the art world, some kind of investigator offering his services, offering them to me although we haven't bought the thing. Someone from television said, "The contemporary masterpiece that ZV selected against his curator's wishes has been stolen." As if to drop a sordid hint. Then: "What happens now?" As though my permitting sacrilege to happen on my watch will deprive thousands of children of their last crust of bread.

ZV told some reporter, "We're still thinking about it. The work isn't what it was, so as an investment it'll have to be carefully reconsidered." You see how he strings people along. As if the artist couldn't fix it without lifting a finger. In all photographs and reports, the stolen component's crisscrossing seams are straighter and tighter than any hand could make them. Even the hand that painted JOHNVIAJOHN before it shattered under the weight of a dozen strangers. It's a machine's work, a mass-produced trinket.

The artist swears it's unique. She moans that *found secret* is forever ruined unless the box is returned. If an artist believes her work is ruined, it's ruined. So really it's in poor taste for her to continue hoping for something from ZV. If she won't fix the piece of interest, we have nothing to negotiate.

You think I'm unkind. I humored the gallerist. I came here to meet the artist. The distraught little thing was bandaged up and bolted together like a broken puppet. Weak as she was, she said she understood why my predecessor "didn't take to" *found secret*.

The box, said the artist, "gave off creepy energies." "Uncanny resonances," she said, that would discomfit anybody. Even though nobody would find the box (she said, grazing a contradiction) if it fell in the snow. That she'd opened this creepy box was a serious matter, she thought. Regarding what she found inside, she felt a compulsion "stronger than magnetism" to be silent. She said the box "almost had voices." With energies almost acoustic, barely beyond sensibility, the box compelled her to keep its interior secret. And keep its secret as *her* secret.

She was confused, obviously, given her concussion and what must be an interesting variety of painkillers. I think her overall gist was that nobody can understand the box unless they open it for themselves without breaking it; but nobody should dare to open it lest they miss the point or worse.

It's all theatrics, of course, meant to link this artist with disturbed-genius stereotypes. That said, she's really lost all sense of judgment. First she "understood" my predecessor's aversion. Then she implied my predecessor was the vandal.

Anybody in the city could've done it, I replied. Hoping she'd take my implication too, you understand. But no, she was emotional, begging me to persuade ZV not to "abandon" her but to buy a different piece. Otherwise the vernissage will have brought no sales, and for a long time her ailments will prevent her from working properly or at all.

I said that's most unfortunate, but the relevant question is: What appeals does *COUNTERFATE* spark, what conundrums? The works assert themselves, but they ask nothing. A ZVC masterpiece can't just make assertions. I need questions. I need more. Something to do with history. With time. She had nothing to add except an excess of detail concerning her physical ailments. Like a beggar in a train station.

I tried easier questions. How did she make the box? Was it woven wicker-like? Was it a block wrapped in crisscrossing paper sheets? One sheet artfully folded? Sheets wadded together by something like a garbage compacter and dipped in varnish? Was it like a snail? An octopus wrapped in its own tentacles? Could anyone peel or unravel it? Must it be split open like a peanut?

Well, she began to cry. She asked if she could please speak to ZV. Her one-track wheedling put me in mind of the interloper who'd driven my predecessor to the unthinkable. I started to ask about the stranger, but the gallerist interrupted: "If I may suggest . . ." I would've said that he may *not* suggest. But I was digging through my handbag for a tissue for the artist. His suggestion was "perspectives. Instead of history. Perspectives, as in differences," said that minty little man, "could be fountainheads in the ZVC's new era." I said next time I required suggestions, I'd have someone contact him. And then the artist: "But it isn't about perspectives. Or history. It's about just the things." "Things are political," said the gallerist. And I thought he'd start all over again with that nonsense. But the artist said no. She said things are "irreducible to relations." Every leaf and antimacassar is "a secret deviation and deflection." Thinking maybe of the snowflake that was one too many for the bus.

Then she said the snow has made everyone in the city form an unconscious obsession with history, time, and change. Possibly because (this could be a complete distortion; she was blowing her nose and babbling) we're experiencing what she calls a "matched precipitation rate" that neither eases nor intensifies. She thinks we're imprisoned in what should've been a passing moment. Seasons are supposed to pass. Our bodies know it. Our bodies fear or sense our abandonment by time and our imprisonment by something else. And maybe we understand this but don't believe we understand it or wish we didn't.

The gallerist checked his phone, nodding along. I let her ramble on. Even as artists go, she's the most pitiful I've ever seen. She said the idea is (whose idea I don't know) that we keep waiting for a blizzard, a glimpse of the sun, an explanation, some announcement, anything that isn't this. We're in suspense. We're stuck in it. And the anxiety building in us doesn't have the "matched melting rate," or whatever, that dispels just enough piled-up snow to confuse us. To make us think we can keep going. The anxiety just continues building on itself inside us. So all our other sensibilities are as if drowned out by it. Except our desire, growing too, for some hint that our sense of time, of progress, wasn't mythical to begin with. And somehow this brought her back to "just the things." She said, "Humanity's insignificant except where it converges with a thing."

The gallerist jumped in and said she didn't mean humanity's insignificant. She meant, he said, that the "absence" of whoever is "behind" the secondhand elements of her work is sometimes total absence manifesting as "the extra-thick presence of a gap, blackout, knot, or pileup of walls." In a sleight of hand intended to herd the artist's wild assertions back into his own corral, the gallerist linked *COUNTERFATE*'s surplus of "fissures" with the fissured history of the *found secret* box. As far as anybody knows, that history consists of the myth disseminated by the gallerist himself.

So, as the story goes, the artist found the box in a café. Abandoned on a table. Nobody could tell her where the box had come from, who'd left it on the table, how long it had been there. Why they left it alone, drinking, wiping, sweeping around it. Not throwing it away, not seeking its owner.

If this is true, I said, why couldn't the box's owner have been the so-called vandal? Stealing it back, perhaps, after searching half the city just to stumble on a picture of the thing in an art blog. What right did the artist have to take it in the first place? Putting it in the

cabinet, bringing it to a gallery, signing it with her name as her creative accomplishment, trying to sell it: by what right did she do all
this? Then someone takes the box from her, and she raises an uproar
but doesn't call the police?

"But that's different, you don't understand," and so on. "His" artist, the gallerist insisted, had every right to take the box and use it
because the café was a café and not an "abode." If she'd taken the box
from someone's abode without permission, that would've been "an
objectionable violation." Stealing. "Because the things abiding in my
abode" (he really said *abiding* and *abode*) "are my possessions, belonging to me and not to others."

In contrast: things on tables in cafés. Sugar packets. Paper napkins.
Such things are provided for customers' convenience. Thus they belong not to the café but to its customers, whoever they might be. And
this is the case even if the café has no customers except *in potentia*,
the gallerist added wildly in an argument full of holes.

Either way, put in the artist, the box was too distinctive to have
been "forgotten" in the café for so long. (How did she know just how
long the box sat in that café, if it ever did?) Nobody who'd had the
box in their possession could forget they'd ever had it and thereby
forget that it existed, the artist insisted. Even if they'd left it there
by accident to begin with, their forgetfulness had to become deliberate after a certain point. If we were talking about something "less
unique," the artist argued, any old generic box befitting paper clips
or raisins, then it would've made sense for the person who forgot it
to forget it till the day they died. But nobody who "abandoned" such
a complex object as the box "belonging to *found secret*" (note the cart
before the horse) would've failed to go back for it unwittingly. On
the basis of which she reasoned, bolstered by her gallerist's bobbing
head, that the "person previously in possession" had deliberately
decided not to reclaim the box. Unless of course they'd met in an accident, said the artist, loudly not mentioning buses. Either way, she
concluded, any "hypothetical owner" of the box had forfeited their
ownership via the café.

"Stealing from an art gallery is another matter. That might be worse than stealing from an abode." This is the gallerist again, of course. To rob an art gallery is to rob "the art-loving public," which suddenly meant everybody extant and unborn, of a chance at inspiration. And this meant depriving culture (still the gallerist) of an opportunity, maybe *the* critical opportunity, to reimagine society's potential. This deprivation, "dismembering the collective imagination," said the artist, is exactly the kind of violence the police don't want to stop. At which point the gallerist wised up and shut her up.

found secret

And so. We stand before it. Infamous. Insignificant.

Wood cabinet, provenance unknown, worthy of a dump. It has clawed feet. Its ankles sag. A little square of paper props up one of them, discouraging the chest of drawers from wobbling.

Toward the top of the cabinet, the drawers are progressively smaller. The top row has three little ones side by side, the next row down two longer ones. A single drawer runs the width of the cabinet at the bottom.

I learned nothing about this random furniture from the artist. She couldn't decide whether to follow her mind and try to steer me to another work or follow her gallerist and persuade me that I want ZV to keep his promise. The gallerist tried to wrap the cabinet in mystique. This "chiffonier," he said, could be hundreds of years old, but its history is a secret that the thing keeps to itself.

Note the cracks in the drawers. The unattractive syrup brown. The gallerist doesn't know I know that when things started to look desperate, my predecessor sent a furniture appraiser. She estimated a zero value for the cabinet. A mass-produced attempt at replicating old motifs, the appraiser said. She named a secluded, smelly, scary row of junk shops somewhere near the river as the only place for such a cabinet. She hinted that the artist could've dredged it up there in the first place. The gallerist wouldn't let the appraiser touch the cabinet. Note the velvet rope. Yet he expects ZV to give him money for it.

There appears to be a vertical panel of solid wood between the two drawers in the middle row. The horizontal panel between the top and middle rows also appears solid, as in any chest of drawers. But we can see even from here that the floor of the middle drawer in the top row is removable.

The artist left that drawer wide open. She lifted the false floor. She propped it up inside the drawer at an angle. She wants us to see how the secret is unconcealed.

From beneath the counterfeit floor of the top middle drawer, a fourth drawer rises perpendicular to the others, surfacing like the head of a river serpent from what seems to be the solid panel between the two drawers below. The artist propped up the secret drawer so it sits visibly in the hole where it is hiding.

The face of the secret drawer rotates away from a hollow the size of your palm. An empty hole dug out of the heart of a broken piece of discarded furniture. This is *found secret*.

Before the theft, a small white box balanced on top of the hole. In photographs it seems poised. Either to fall into the hole or fall out of the secret drawer into the "real" drawer.

I've only seen the photographs. Remember I'd heard of none of this business before the fall of the former curator. When I took over from her, there was no time. Then the theft.

The box disappeared, leaving the cabinet to gape. Like a comedian who's forgotten the punch line.

The relationship between the cabinet and the box was always counterfeit. The artist told the gallerist, as he muttered to my predecessor while they were intimate, that *pace* the furniture appraiser, she, the artist, had found the cabinet on the street beside a dumpster. If that's true and the café bit is true, then the "artistry" of *found secret* is its use of found objects to stage, as in a tableau, a story that never happened.

We're meant to think we're looking at the discovery or revelation of the little white box in the cabinet's secret place. Why wouldn't we think so, if we simply viewed the work and weren't subject to sales pitches? But that's precisely where the artist *didn't* find the box.

"Collage," said the gallerist. "An art of resistance against categories and the ideological sanctity of 'great' things." And why, I asked, should masterpieces not be cherished? And which categories does *found secret* resist? He went on as though I hadn't said a word: What matters is that this artist found the box and the cabinet and "orchestrated their provocative convergence." The man is an endless flow of sophistries.

The box made an unreasonable impression on my predecessor. "A sawed-off little mummy," she said. At the height of her squiffy derangement, she said she wouldn't be surprised if the box contained a human finger, nose, or tongue, bandaged white in open concealment in hope that someone mad with curiosity would attack this *found secret* not in order to "dismember" it but to expose it, causing a far greater sensation. Whoever took the box meant to unmask it as a conspirator in something scandalous, she thought. And she believed that the entire rigmarole, from truncated digit to dismembered artwork, had been choreographed in order to depose her as ZVC curator. Paranoia, I'm afraid, has gone gangrenous in her.

There's a simpler explanation. Without perfumes of blood and scandal hovering around it, how many people care about damaged art, assuming that's what this is? Wrap it in suggestions of shadows of villainy layer upon layer, and the hangers-on have a field day. And they did.

The chest of drawers represents the city in microcosm, someone published. *Crossing without meeting, the seams of the box represent individuality's self-sacrifice to geometry for the city's sake. To permit the death of individuality is to consent to mass extinction.* Vague and unoriginal but very serious.

I asked ZV for his impressions. His analogy was a gift wrapped in many layers of paper to keep the recipient guessing. He said the paper from which the box is made or in which it is covered waits to be decorated like a canvas. I suspect he doesn't believe it. He said another strange thing too. He laughed when he learned about the theft. But when he spoke to me about the box, he said it was "no good" that it was taken.

I sensed this wasn't just an aesthetic disappointment. It was something else. Something that stayed with him and worried him. But it wasn't only that. I asked if he knew what was in it. ZV said he didn't. He said it quickly. He said that even before the box was stolen, he'd been unable to see a way to open it without ripping it. Yet the artist claims to have done it.

Stranger still, when I asked about the interloper, who she was, what she wanted, do you know what that man said? He said he hadn't spoken to anybody at the vernissage except the usual people. He said he had no memory of a woman with phony-black hair, a chipped tooth, and a yellow dress. He'd stumbled on *found secret* and judged it for himself, he said.

Then he seemed to have shaken something off. He said lightly that he'd once bought a luxury apartment just so nobody else could. Then he laughed and said I should pay him no attention, said he was only reminiscing. I can't pretend to understand him. Such pretenses could be fatal.

The box was empty. That's what I think. The drama of this artist has everyone carried away. Not the drama of *found secret* but of the artist. Anything with the slightest connection to her personal tragedy seems to acquire grave significance, and she eggs on that impression. Her greatest talent is for smoke and mirrors. Past the smoke and in the mirrors there is emptiness.

That's my honest opinion. I meant to keep it secret, but I suppose I got carried away myself. Not out of pity. Pity isn't my job. Nothing in *COUNTERFATE* deserves the ZVC. It doesn't even deserve this gallery. I've known it from the start. ZV pretends not to believe it. But if he didn't believe it, he would've had his lawyers draft a sales contract. He would've voiced some suspicion or excuse when the artist refused to contact the police. He would've tasked somebody with solving the mystery of the box.

Even if he pities her, he's said nothing about any of her things except *found secret*. He shows no sign of ending the public game he's grown so fond of, keeping everybody hanging on his equivoques. It's almost like her other artworks don't quite exist for him.

And so. Why am I here? Why do I try so hard to speak for *COUNTERFATE*? Why waste my breath and precious hours poring over trash? Why plumb it for excuses to make notepaper or a poodle pretend to monumentality? Simply so I can sully the ZVC with it?

The answer's simple. I must see if I can.

Glutted is the vast art world today. It needn't tolerate failures. If an unpronounceable upstart should fail to sell something to the ZVC, that's only as it should be. But if I can convince ZV to bestow the name of *masterpiece* upon a shopping bag? To take a thrift-store dresser with a hole in it under the wings of the Collection, which preserves the very best that humanity has ever offered up to history? Then I'll know the extent of my power over him.

If I don't convince him, what of it? I'll still learn what I need to know. If I'm to succeed as curator, I must know the limits of my persuasion. I must know what I can make him do.

If I can make a financier expend hundreds of thousands on preserving an ugly cabinet from the ravages of the future, there is little I cannot do.

Changeling

I

... an odd number of sides, and there's always at least one side that can't be heard from any other. Here we have the box which, possessed of singular size, color, shape, and extraordinary obstinacy anent its patent withdrawal from intelligibility, has forever altered the neighborhood.

It isn't a time-share developer, birdie. It's a box. It sits in places and looks pretty.

Yes, but if you'd think the thing through, flower . . .

Done enough of that for both of us, you have. I'd just as soon use my nights for sleeping.

. . . you'd realize the human elements alone cannot account for the events.

Only because we don't know all that happened. And that's because we weren't invited to the meeting and most human elements are liars. Now, do try to refrain from scaring off our visitor.

Consider the Seeker and Keeper. The one dark and looming, the other light and lithe. Each in her own way helpless.

You just mean distraught. Or wanting to seem distraught. Both the sneaky old Seeker, so eager to find this box, and the poor little Keeper wanting to be rid of it.

She didn't want to be rid of it necessarily.

We call them Seeker and Keeper, not knowing their names. "Keeper" like a jail warden for tigers, says birdie here.

I think she was uncertain whether to cherish or resent it. Possibly frightened of it.

Who'd ever have thought my birdie would be frightened of a box!

I am not frightened. I'm cautious. For if there's anything to be gleaned from that horrible meeting or this horrid snow, it's that even things which appear to be inert catalyze far-reaching changes beyond all expectations.

Yes, birdie. Now, you promised not to go working yourself up. We mustn't aggravate your wheezing.

A thing that flaunts its secrecy is a thing of which anyone would do well to be careful. There are any number of reasons why even the Seeker would be wary of the thing she sought.

Such as?

Years ago, when that writer came in, you remember? He didn't want to see our first edition of the book he'd published when he was young. Not being young himself, he was frightened of its worn spine and of its saying something other than he'd wished. When the things we make slip through the seams of our control, when our own deeds escape us through gaps in our perspective, it is terrifying; for our doings are still ours.

You're thinking the Seeker made my box? We know she's wrong in the head. Now you're telling me she took a paper ribbon long as your leg and twisted it into this precision-rectangular pocket of solitude?

You don't know how it was made, flower. You can't even open it.

Told me not to, didn't you. As though a pretty thing like this could bite me. And you don't know it wasn't a paper ribbon once upon a time.

You don't know the Seeker was wrong in the head.

You don't know my box was ever hers. You're speculating.

We didn't pay much attention when she came in.

Maybe you didn't pay attention.

She didn't scrutinize our shop as it appears she did the others. She flickered between bookcases like a fish in reeds. Then she was gone.

Leaving her scowl to haunt our dreams forevermore.

It was rather unforgettable. The Seeker's scowl. Almost like a separate entity that had the Seeker in its grip. Or as if some invisible force had taken hold of her from within and shadowed forth to manifest as an eclipse of her face. A desperation so intense it obfuscated all her other qualities, everything else she might have been. It wrapped her in itself, leaving almost no seams at all, not a slit through which she might snatch a breath of air. Swaddled head to toe in the lack that's driving her pursuit, she'd nothing to gaze upon except her own interior, where that same lack was suffocating and metastasizing—until a frightful panic broke through to the outside as rage. The Seeker's rage glowed with her terror of herself, and the glowing quickened her every move, energized everything she touched, heated the very air she breathed. You felt frantic yourself, simply being in her presence.

We felt it, anyway.

And all the objects in the shop, from this stub of pencil to the most expensive book, trembled one by one before her laser gaze, the Seeker seeking in each thing the solid counterpart to her restless hollow. With but a glance at a box of staples, she revealed its insignificance and all at once bestirred in it the potential for new significance. Each thing withered in her disappointment and at the same time awoke to the suspect possibility of being the thing the Seeker sought. Each thing, oscillating between withered and awakening, shivered in suspense on its own wavelength, in the suspense of maybe being just the thing, just what she needed: the Seeker's just-right thing. Only nothing that she saw was what she wanted.

None of the things she looked at were this pretty box of mine. And the Seeker loathed them for not being it. Hurled her look at things, she did. "Mean old bookshelf. Selfish light bulb. Horrid inadequate antagonistic book!" Her going round the shop was like a one-woman knife fight, every which way that scowl of hers stabbing and jabbing. And after all the trouble she took to get here.

Your wet ankles are aware, no doubt: the snowplows don't come here.

Not important enough, are we. Lungs and stomachs in the fancy districts, those are worth something, aren't they.

Never mind. We're managing all right.

Yes, we're quite all right with our bent shovel and balding broom. And keeping track of whose turn it is to be the snowplow has done wonders for our relationship. But I was saying: the moldy-chair fanatic . . .

Antique-Furniture Specialist.

. . . popped round to tell us about the meeting they didn't invite us to, where it came out that the Seeker had gone round all the shops. She spent a long while two doors down in the fustian-footrest fanatic's venerable establishment. Which is how the latter came to know the Seeker's wrong in the head. "All that hair of hers, too long, too black for her age," she said. And isn't she a fine one to talk. But once the redyed-rug fanatic said her piece about the Seeker's hair, the man with the junk shop remembered the Seeker's scowl. And the man with the other junk shop piped up about the Seeker's odd front tooth that stuck out. And so it turned out she'd searched them all for this little box. And slammed the door on her way out.

We mustn't call them junk shops, flower. They don't call us that.

Pity for the Seeker she didn't turn up later; although my little box looks so nice among our hoary tomes that, while it's lovely for you to be interested as well, whoever you are, really I couldn't dream of selling it.

It was uncharitable of everyone to find the Seeker so alarming just because she declined to grin. Grinning is a sneaky late-capitalist entrapment strategy.

She didn't decline to poke through the sunken-storage-ottoman fanatic's inventory. When she thought she wasn't looking, she went so far as to rummage.

75

You don't find such futile furtiveness suggestive of a person who's more than anything ashamed to be seeking what she's seeking because she believes a thing shouldn't elude its creator?

The broken-escritoire fanatic said when the Seeker despaired of finding what she wanted, she didn't politely request assistance but went making accusations. "You there! You're harboring a little white box!"

Desperation.

Presumption! "You don't understand, it must be here!" An honest-to-dogs conniption, said our chipped-sideboard fanatic.

Which undeterred merchant endeavored to impress upon the customer that she really wanted something else. A stock item, naturally.

Well, the others agreed she's cracked.

No, it was avouched to us by the Antique-Furniture Specialist that all the shopkeepers claimed unanimously to have been "alarmed" by the Seeker, whom they subsequently assumed to be cracked. But it wasn't unanimous, was it. I wasn't alarmed, nor were you, and nor was Max. Max would never be alarmed by mere appearances. Besides, it's foolish of anyone running a shop round The Bend, a place of secondhand inclinations, to be alarmed by any protest that the wedding ring, old desk, first-edition thesaurus, pinking shears, compromising photograph, or whatever might go missing from the household of a gambler, drunkard, or artist simply *must* have found its way down here.

You're probably right in Max's case. Especially if the thing went missing at knifepoint.

Max only gave the Seeker a second thought because of the Keeper. And if anyone's of unsound mind, it is that young lady. Carrying that box all round the city not even knowing what it is or what it was doing to her.

You'd fancy the box was some wild animal, the way you go on.

Nobody professed alarm over the Keeper. As though anyone young and fair is above suspicion. Whereas anybody dark, unsmiling, particularly a woman who isn't pretty and even in middle age gives every appearance of being alone, should put everybody on their guard. Even Max, who couldn't care less about the Seeker, knew any accusation on behalf of the dainty Keeper would be believed. That upped the stakes for everyone.

Not jealous, are you, birdie?

My flower, don't be ridiculous.

II

And now. The scene of the Seeking and Keeping and august meeting. Behold The Bend. Where the mighty river makes a shifty little wiggle like a card shimmying up a sleeve before the sootiest, slinkiest, slimiest, squintiest bridge in the city. Huddling about this murky kink are five retail establishments of varying repute, and mind you know how to find them when you want them, for not a one bears any indication of its name or wares. Shutting up her shop and making certain of the door's abundant locks, slooshing thenceforth through the snow as it sprinkles us with obstinacy, is the Antique-Furniture Specialist.

Self-styled.

Passing our little shop, which is asleep, another shop with a roller shutter drawn over the display window, and another without a window but with contraptions on the order of bicycle locks securing the front door in triplicate, she slooshes westerly as far as she can sloosh without stumbling under the bridge.

Which you shouldn't if you like living.

Who's telling this story, you or me?

Well, it isn't your story just as much as it isn't mine.

Thereby came the Antique-Furniture Specialist, with little clumps of snow festooning her hat and shoulders, to the place where old things go when people decide they can do without them after all.

They go in the river if Max won't take them.

Thus Max's establishment, affectionately known as The Last Stop . . .

. . . is rather literally a dump.

Flower, I do hope you'd never say as much to Max. For our visitor's sake I ought to clarify that we of the shops around The Bend don't really know each other. We suspect each other. Neighbors in proximity we are, but not in spirit. We stay in our shop. We conduct our business. The others stay in their shops and conduct their business.

We're none of us wanting to crush each other, but for example if your roof was needing a bit of help, you wouldn't borrow a hammer from the likes of Max unless you were wanting to pay double what your house was worth. Not that it bothers Max herself, having a roof like a shoebox and a lean-to with a stink so strong it props the whole thing up.

Flower, let's not be unkind. It isn't as though our roof's ever so hearty. And it's been ages since our last peek into Max's.

I remember she had lots of rusty metal crates. And dirty wooden crates for sending fruits and things on ships. And useful tools like crowbars and brass knuckles. And do you remember we saw a knife with a handle like a little finger?

Max's is a place for desperate things and desperate people.

Call a fence a fence, birdie. They say there's people wanting to foist all sorts of things on Max. Dogs and children and all sorts of dreadful things.

Loathsome place at the best of times this city is. With even the best of people trying to pretend it isn't getting worse.

Now, don't start, birdie.

Construction projects, food deliveries, taxi drivers.

Here we go.

Delayed, delayed again, delayed till someone just gives up somewhere along the line. The taxi that never arrives never gets paid. Takeaway that comes in cold never gets another try. Traffic trying to come into the city comes to a stop as city-center traffic crawls because nobody can see out of their windshields. Lorry driver who was sacked because he couldn't deliver his lettuces before they went off.

Refreshments, anyone?

Construction workers who've not seen a paycheck in how long because the weather doesn't suit the safety regulations. The man and dog who slept on the bench beside the river . . .

Unless the junk-shop fellow ran them off with somebody's dead grandfather's umbrella.

. . . would normally wait out the snow under the bench. Now it's as if the snow is waiting us out instead.

Right, that's enough, birdie. Our visitor who's come to see my box doesn't want to hear you snivel about the bank not being built on time. You're as bad as the knackered-credenza fanatic two doors down. All this talk of snow not being snow or never stopping, it's rubbish.

It isn't rubbish.

But it's convinced her that her ceiling's sinking from too much snow on top. Mind, she knows it's got a matched melting rate as well. I think it's pretty. Always liked silvery skies. But she says each day that brings no change piles on her heart atop the other days that's all alike and piled up there already.

It sneaks into your mind, the snow. Like a noise that's too far off to hear but trembles the air for miles around. For even in the obstinate self-containment of each thing, things reverberate one another.

The woman's just impatient. And really, a bit of snow.

A bit of snow. Three months, is it? Nearer four?

And you and I are running the shop. And having our lovely discussions. And we like reheated takeaway just as much as usual. And if the weatherpeople on the telly can't explain the unusual persistence of silvery skies, I shouldn't think a pair of antiquarian booksellers any more equipped to do so.

Stuck under your silvery skies, which I call dreary gray and never amount to proper daylight, never proper evening either, I'm telling you this isn't a proper bit of snow. It isn't right for snow to never proliferate or cease. Especially here. It's not Antarctica. Not that Antarctica ever saw matched precipitation either. The absence of seasonal shifts where they ought to . . .

The problem isn't the snow, birdie. It's people. As the problem with the box isn't the box, it's just people. We'd be in back in our old shop right now if not for people wanting to buy rubbish off of websites instead of coming in person to meet beautiful old books. Safe, central, and snowplowed that location was. Its own car park and everything. And above all, it was *dry*. Whoever heard of antiquarian books happily bedding down in the damp beside the river with all the mold in? Lost the lease on that other place, we did. One of those courier services that's got its own airplanes and would even lick the envelope for you offered more than we could ever afford. And I shan't soil your eardrums with its name.

My one-and-only refers to CytyBox. But never mind. As I say, we're managing.

What's a bit of snow after being turned out of your own shop, I'd like to know! All those people in other places with bombs going off all round . . .

What have I told you about pseudoquantifying? As if it's possible to ration sympathy according to whose catastrophe is bigger. It's an impossible calculation. Starving in a war zone versus starving in endless snow: you cannot say the one is more horrible than the other therefore people suffering the other ought to man up and not breathe a word.

Like what you're doing now? It's only all that wheezing like a geriatric steamboat sounds a good deal like not-breathing, and don't say I didn't warn you. There's people who aren't good at weathering, that's all. People in our own city can imagine the world exploding but can't imagine a dearth of imported coffee. But we were talking about Max.

You never listen.

Yet here we are after all these years. Now, I can't imagine The Last Stop to have undergone radical renovation since last we found some clothespins for our sniffers and took a peek. Can you? No sulking, birdie.

Well, I suppose. The shadows can't have gotten any thinner. The corners can't have gone uncreepy. More dagger marks in the counter, maybe. Fresh dimples in the bulletproof bit.

Which they say Max got installed for free.

I should think the taxidermied salmon is still there. Likewise the recliner with the bloodstain.

Still having to go sideways for getting to the register so's not to touch the questionable box that's on the floor. Thus spake the slantwise-cupboard fanatic.

Well, you never know with boxes. Then again, she also said the Antique-Secondhand-Memory Distributor was given the questionable box to sit on.

He wasn't going to sit in the recliner. The cracked-curtain-rod fanatic . . .

Antique-Furniture Specialist.

. . . said she got a wobbly two-drawer filing box, her being a connoisseur of seating. And the other junk-shop man . . .

Antique-Useful-Goods Broker.

. . . made do with a suspicious portmanteau with a bent lid. Max pre-
sided from her corner on a sort of throne which I believe is from a
church.

We don't resent not being invited. The Antique-Furniture Specialist
said what Max called an invitation was rather an unsubtle hint.

Hinted she knew something, Max did. Something the teetering-
tallboy fanatic should know was being spread about.

Only Max wouldn't tell her what it was. Not on the telephone.

Bait-and-reeling. Worked on the junk-shop fellows too.

And so, sometime during the night, a decent while after anyone
could hope for after-hours custom . . .

Indecent, you mean. Max wanted the suspense to stir up panic in
all three. At least she wasn't such a fool as to sprinkle any hints
round here.

It's only that we're irrelevant. Make us stink as horribly as she does,
would our Max, given a half-credible reason. Still, I think we were a
bit incredulous, weren't we, when the Antique-Furniture Specialist
brought round the story of the meeting. What could Max have known?
What ignominious secret could've lured them all, three insignificant
shopkeepers with nothing in common besides a crimp in the river, to
trudge through snow and darkness to The Last Stop?

For all her hinting, Max didn't know which one had done the dreadful deed. She wanted them all where she could see them. And the guilt
on the guilty face.

To get them where she wanted them, trapped in her dark domain, she led each person to believe that she and half the city, as if anyone would care, suspected them of using a changeling to defraud a customer.

III

You opened it, didn't you! You told me not to try, but you tried and you found something frightful in it, didn't you!

I've done nothing of the kind.

My little paper box, which if it fell in the snow would be drowned and lost forever: you're calling that a changeling!

Max summoned the meeting because she believed that pursuant to a sales transaction one of our neighbors surreptitiously swapped your box for the purchased item.

Which not even Max knew what it was.

Until the meeting's grand finale, when it was alleged that someone swapped the box for a very small, expensive picture. Whilst this "picture," if such it was, remained in the shop, the customer, none the wiser, went off with the box. The word for a thing in that position, even a little box, is *changeling*.

Birdie. A changeling is a monster that's dropped off in exchange for somebody's fat baby, which the monster's mum has gone and eaten.

Similarly, for a merchant not to give you what you paid for but to saddle you instead with something that is worthless to you is a kind of violence. A dirty trick like that undermines the basic trust on which depends every relationship between merchants and customers. What is that basic trust but the fundamental premise grounding the exchange economy?

All right, if you say so. Just remember to breathe.

Of course, that such an economy would undermine itself was only to be expected. A systemic totality consisting of individuals each of whom is driven by private notions of possession and profit which, in competition with others, undercut and double-cross . . .

What did I say about working yourself up?

But as a specific act of violence, how egregious a changeling is depends upon the things themselves: changeling and kidnapped thing. The thing that's left behind, the thing that's never seen again. Max must've known that, being an antiquarian bookshop, our shop doesn't carry little boxes, therefore the changeling wouldn't frighten us, therefore she didn't bother asking us to her little gathering, which in my opinion she arranged for a lark as much as anything. It tickles Max to have people in awe of her in all her squalor. Hardened criminals, police detectives, media people. As though there weren't plenty of those owing their crooked necks to old Max. I expect they're never enough. The true collector has no concept of *enough*.

Got information too, Max does. For sale and barter. And the freedom to sell what's in her bulletproof cases and legendary back room. Shaky seam she skates and no mistake. She survives because the blackmail market ever waxes.

All of us round The Bend trade in secondhand stories, things that people are willing to forget for a few bob. But Max's stories ruin people. No matter who you are, she'd ruin you in a heartbeat with a whisper and a grin.

Rumor says it's rumor that's Max's secret weapon.

Frightening trivial shopkeepers with rumors of accusations that the Keeper never made, that's simply what Max does.

I expect she'd another motive too. More tangible, let's say.

The Keeper didn't like to accuse anyone. She gave us her story when, after visiting the others, she stopped here in exhaustion. To look at something irrelevant after she'd given up hope.

The story concerns the Keeper and her young man.

He's no longer her young man. The changeling put paid to that.

IV

The Keeper popped in some days before Max's meeting. Sometime before that, she and the attorney who at the time was her young man had a little anniversary. They slooshed to a romantic venue that hadn't got fed up and put the CLOSED sign out.

Out of sorts he was. She'd quite a time persuading him to explain.

He said he'd foraged the whole city for the just-right little present to commemorate their anniversary. He'd discovered it at last in the most unlikely place. The shopkeeper wrapped it in paper. The young man put it away. He took it out again when the anniversary came round. And only then, that night, did he notice as he let fly dismayed expletives that the paper box which he now stuffed into his pocket was not the paper-wrapped parcel he had purchased. But, running late, he'd no time to decide what to do with a thing he hadn't bought. He explained to his young lady that the purchase and the changeling were of roughly the same size and shape but, on reflection, the papers which encased the one and seemed to constitute the other were not the same shade of white.

Ever so upset, he was, the Keeper told us.

She received the news without surprise. For although this young man prided himself on never overlooking things, the young lady was secretly relieved to find he hadn't forgotten the anniversary, blaming his oversight, as he was wont, on some hijacker or bank robber. The mere fact that he'd turned up gave her hope, she said, that she wasn't just a cheap accessory which made itself available or invisible at his convenience. Laughing, she proposed that he'd swept up the wrong thing in his excitement.

Not paying attention. As usual.

The young lady joyfully swore to love whatever he had brought simply because he had brought it. The young man refused to hear of it.

Thought the shopkeeper had done a switch on him.

For if there's one thing he knows about himself, he said, it's that he knows a hoodwink when he sees it. Not a criminal in the city could outsmart him, and he would prove it to his young lady. He would prove to her, he said, that he would not be made a fool, he would have his revenge, that dastardly shopkeeper didn't know whom they were dealing with. The young lady asked to see what was after all her present and decide about it for herself. He thought all she wanted was to laugh at his misfortune, but he delved into his pocket. He slammed the little white box down on the table with the candle and the rose. And lo, the changeling came unto the Keeper.

My box.

She didn't laugh. Something about the box precluded laughing. The way it coiled around itself, perhaps. The paradox of the self-contained container self-sufficient as a brick and fragile as a poem. The "air of pandemonium" about it as like a poisonous plant its mere existence "filtered an intrusive, disruptive element into the atmosphere."

Birdie's being silly. Misquoting something or other. The Keeper never said a word of poisoned airs.

She wondered if there might be something inside it, what with its being a box and boxing boxes' calling.

Got that sort of sound as well.

But she couldn't see how to open it. Each of these uncountable seams, where if my flower is correct the original white paper ribbon criss-crosses itself, stratifying upon itself: each of these looks like a possible way in. So it appears the box must open along one of these diagonals. But which? There are so many, the thing is all diagonals, their crisscrossings have got no visible order, and when you follow them with your eye, not a single one makes sense as an ingress after all. If, say, this diagonal were an opening along which, provided you could get your fingernail in, you could pry open the box, then somewhere at least two other diagonals must be hinges.

Which you've not even tried to locate, have you, stubborn as you are that other people mustn't.

Only none of them look like hinges. And if you did pry this bit up, it appears the most you could achieve is loosening this strip. But the strip can't be loosened, so resolutely does it burrow under these two strips at either end, perhaps continuing out of sight to wrap around the whole. It doesn't make sense, you see. The one way in is with a knife.

Except apparently your way. I'll find how you got in, birdie. Just you wait.

As I was saying, the remnants left to the Keeper of her little anniversary numbered but two. She had a memory of her young man thinking he'd been made a fool on her account. And she had the changeling, a stranger's unuttered secret. She hoped he'd forget them both and allow his mad wish for vengeance to drift away. And what a thing to have to wish for. That a celebration of their love should drift from the mind of her beloved. Days elapsed. Time enough for her sad wish to become reality. When next she met her young man, she expected to find his equanimity restored. It wasn't.

First thing he says is he's hot on the huckster's trail.

You'd think revisiting the scene of the culmination of one's shopping would be a straightforward matter. Not so for this young man. He'd lost his sales receipt with the shop's address on, and he couldn't bring to mind a single detail of the place. The knavish shopkeeper whom he was keen to persecute might've been an extraterrestrial or an elephant. The attorney-at-law simply had no recollection. Why should he remember one shop out of a hundred? Just because he'd spent a bit of money in it? Seems incredible to the likes of us, but for this young man it mightn't be so farfetched.

Flighty as a fly in a fruit basket, he is. Goes about with two eyes on his telephone, the Keeper said.

It was the phone that brought him here. A place of last resort in his quest for the just-right thing. He'd used the phone to find The Bend, and the phone remembered.

Sort of. It showed a map of the river and how it wiggles. But it couldn't say where on the wiggle was the place he'd forgot to notice while he was in it. Lucky for him, he told the Keeper, a wiggle can't hold many shops.

He was in a frame of mind, the Keeper told us, to either convict somebody or perish in the effort. She saw the ease with which a frame might close around a mind, the imprisoned intellect becoming a danger to itself and others. And she told him to drop the matter. He got angry, but she stood her ground: *she* would confront the shopkeeper, she said. She'd learn the history of her little present and rescue her beloved from embarrassing them both and however many others with serious accusations which she knew he couldn't prove. The young man made a fuss, but he relented, leaving the "investigation," as he called it, in the Keeper's hands.

Poor child.

So she went and made the same mistake as before. She trusted too much to time. Given time, she thought, and love, he'd let it go. She put the box where he'd never find it, and she got on with her life.

An attorney herself, the Keeper is. For the electric company.

She used her work as an excuse to put him off. For not a day went by without a message from him. Not the cartoon hearts and tender abbreviations she was used to but two words. Words she never would've believed a man would fire at his beloved. The only place for such pitiless words was the lair of the uniformed men whose hearts had frozen blue. His "hounds," the young man called them.

Confession yet? What nonsense.

She knew it was lots of questions loaded into one. Had she found the shop? Had its owner recognized the box? Had they admitted to deploying it as a changeling? But popping up out of context again and again, those sharp words began to feel like inflamed lesions. As if *she* stood accused by her beloved.

And she's telling us all this. A pair of strangers.

When suddenly they stopped. Quickly as they'd morphed into the bleating of a tyrant, his messages reverted almost to what they'd been before. Let's meet at such and such a time, that sort of thing. If swooping hearts were rare, the Keeper supposed to her own relief that he was busy with work as usual. Perhaps he was a bit snappish, but the sulks had never been unusual with him. She began to think she might allow herself to hope that time and his mercurial character had finally succeeded in washing away vengeance and sweeping some impersonal, lawyerly disturbance onto his changeful inner shores. Maybe something in her knew that she hoped foolishly. Love would not permit her to do otherwise.

How was she to know he was the sort to lie in wait? She thinks they're having a little rendezvous when suddenly it's: "By the by, what've you found out?"

She said her heart sank like a stone in the river. She told him she'd found nothing and was weary of the whole affair. Just because he'd made a mistake didn't mean life should stick in the moment of his blunder and never again move on. The young man didn't like that at all.

"I knew you hadn't done a bloody thing about it. You don't care about my being made a fool, you don't take my reputation seriously. You don't even take my present seriously."

Simply put, the root cause of his picking up the wrong parcel was his young lady's refusal to worship and obey him *ex post facto*.

He knew the truth deep down, just took it out on other people without a thought of being responsible for his own self. Even though he makes his living making people own up. She fought back, the Keeper did. She'd had enough of his nonsense.

She was also hurt.

Haven't spoken to each other since. Instead she picks her lonely way down to the sick heart of the city. She stands right where you're standing, poking through her little handbag for her hankie, saying she just can't understand their disintegrating over this.

Which is why she's unstable, flower. She did understand. She only wished she didn't. A person reveals his true colors when the lowliest of things destroys his best-laid plans by doing nothing except existing. A paper box, let's say, reveals to an attorney that he's never had control over much of anything and any illusions to the contrary are side effects of thinking too much of himself. A sniff of those hard facts awakened a vindictiveness which not even his beloved, who thought she knew him, could've imagined. Confronted with his obliviousness to things other than himself, he set his sights on an enemy whom he couldn't so much as identify. His obsession with convicting another of his own carelessness was in reality determination not to risk a glance at his own limitations. When the Keeper saw this hidden side of him alight with the blaze of his own savagery, she was repulsed.

And loved him still. Plain as the nose on your face it was.

V

How much time between the Keeper's breaking with her young man and coming to The Bend? Couldn't say. According to the squashed-cushion fanatic . . .

Antique-Furniture Specialist.

. . . the mournful little thing drooped in with her little box, asked the shopkeeper whether she remembered a distrait young man as might've picked it up after buying something else, didn't spare a sniff for the rolltop that was offered her instead, and drooped out without another word. She went on to the other junk shops . . .

Antique-Secondhand-Memory Distributor and Antique-Useful-Goods Broker.

. . . and took her box and her long face through the same routine, even at Max's. Not just because she missed her young man dearly.

A little fool pining for a great fool.

She came round investigating exactly as he wanted.

Though it was much too late.

No, birdie. *Because* it was too late. Remember the console-table concessionaire said they all said at Max's that the Keeper didn't offer any details of her young man, only asked if they'd seen him and pushed off. Only after nobody remembered him did she spill everything to us. What I mean is, she went round to shops as if to investigate his maybe having been cheated, but really she hardly investigated anything. That's because she thought he *hadn't* been cheated, but she wanted to believe him all the same. To believe the worst of someone else would've been easier than believing her beloved would go blaming other people for his mistakes. But part of her knew better than that too. So, you see, she was wanting and not wanting to find the truth.

If only she'd come back to us after Max's meeting. Who knows but that she wouldn't have found some justification for believing him with her whole heart? What if, notwithstanding his dangerous foibles, the young man really had been duped? Suppose the Keeper pooh-poohed his indignation, postponed his vindication, for all intents pushing him away, but all unfairly; and the box wasn't an error of his but someone else's sleight of hand, changeling indeed. Interference almost buzzes from the thing, that paper turmoil of intersections, disorder, agitation.

But that's Max, birdie. Max disordering and agitating, that's what muddled everything.

VI

True it is that the meeting at The Last Stop was transparently a piscatorial endeavor of Max's. We think, with her suspicious turn of mind, Max formulated a theory based on the Keeper's mumbles: someone at The Bend noticed the young man's distracted air, observed him wandering aisles and seeing nothing but his phone, and resolved to take advantage of the situation to sell him, let's say, a very expensive and tiny picture but, in a distracted moment, to exchange it for a cheaper thing. After he'd gone, they'd put the so-called "little picture" back on display and sell it again to someone else. A sort of thimblerig.

So you've got your dark and snowy night. Dingy bulb. Musty smell. Moldy-wood fanatic on top of a potato crate, junk-shop man on a crumbling suitcase, other junk-shop man on someone's secondhand coffin. And Max says, "One of *you*," not meaning us who's not invited, "hoodwinked a customer with a pretty little changeling that birdie keeps telling me couldn't have been made out of a single paper ribbon but I'm telling you *was* made of white paper cut into a ribbon and tied round itself to form a box." And everyone remembers the surly Seeker wanting this same box. And what with all their carrying on about the Seeker's tooth, I'd bet any book you like that nobody troubled to wonder why Max made the accusation and what she had for evidence.

She had rumors and appearances. The apparent frantic fury of the Seeker, the apparent melancholic beauty of the Keeper. Assumptions at which Max leapt, driven by her addiction to petty tyrannies. And the inventories of people's shops. Withal the probability that she's not opened a book since the extinction of the telephone directory, Max probably assumed no valuable edition could possibly be mistaken for such a little box. The Antique-Furniture Specialist, in contrast . . .

Oh, she is devoted to chests of drawers and chiffoniers, armoires, tambours, cabinets and cupboards, secretaries, nightstands, anything that anybody that's likely to be dead might've used for putting other things in long ago.

Max claimed to have heard rumors of scandal. Something about an antique cabinet, some sort of art gallery, and "misrepresentation of value." Whereupon she looked at the Antique-Furniture Specialist.

In front of everyone. All her neighbors except us.

The Antique-Furniture Specialist held to her surfeit of dignity. She looked Max in the eye, chilly as you like, and said she knew nothing of any scandal. She might've lied, of course.

More likely it was Max that lied. Max wouldn't scruple to imagine up a scandal or wave a fleeting mote of gossip in people's faces like it was true. She told the controvertible-cabinet fanatic: "Even if no cabinet of your acquaintance was involved, such a scandal percolating through the secondhand-cabinet community would make buyers even leerier than they are already. 'Course you've other, portable things you're brokering. Diversifying, like."

And really, flower, regarding the thing for which the changeling was exchanged, you must admit that nobody actually *knows*, in the sense of having *seen* . . .

Hush, birdie, I'm narrating. "Card cases, curtain tiebacks, wee figurines. Little things which, wrapped in a bit of white paper, would match in shape and inch for inch that pretty paper-ribbon puzzle box as the Keeper who brought it round said had been given her by her young man but that wouldn't fetch half so nice a selling price as the one-of-a-kind antique minipigeon or whatever he really bought, particularly if it was sold again and again. How many times," said Max, while the cagey-cabinet fanatic sidled up to apoplexy, "how many times would you have to sell a snuffbox to make up for an inventory of cabinets that's not been bought?" And it's a sad fact that the cabinet costermonger said not one of her neighbors rose to her defense. I suppose the shock . . .

Or dearth of shock. Despite the staggering surprise professed by the Antique-Furniture Specialist.

She'd no wish to hang round there to be insulted, only the preposterousness struck her all at once. The Last Stop in the quagmire of night. Max's nasty grin. Insinuations straight out of the stenchy air. The Seeker's awful certainty that amidst the tottering tea tables a little box must lurk. Enough to haunt an honest woman's dreams for years, it was, and suddenly all of it ballooning to horrible proportions in the battered-bureau fanatic's slender mind, which would fit ever so nicely in a drawer of spoons. And then she could do nothing except sit with her mouth open and wonder what she'd ever done to Max and the junk-shop men.

That's according to the Antique-Furniture Specialist herself. Personally I doubt that she'd absorb an insult with tranquility. I've a sense that despite her airs and fancy chairs she's not above much of anything. I feel sorry for her, Max putting her on the spot, everybody looking expectant, trying to hide what they're thinking as though she were a prisoner on trial. But my opinion stands: conceit rather enfeebles her credibility.

Stuck her nose in the air: "I shouldn't dream of such a thing." And Max said, "Well, someone did. And the young lady as had the box said her young man's telephone knew the changeling happened at The Bend." And Max didn't say *changeling*, but you know. Max talked in squiggles to keep the others in suspense: "I wonder what became of her," meaning the Keeper. And the subtext of Max's wondering is so bleeding obvious to me and no one else, including other people who tease me for that I read too many books.

Tell us your special theory, flower. Again.

VII

Behold the love of my life laughing at my special theory. Here it is, then. After the Keeper visited Max and inquired after her young man and Max sent her packing with a sneer and her little box, the Keeper came to us in despair while Max sat down and had a think. And there's nothing Max has that isn't suspect, and I should think her thinks would stink most particularly. She stirred the Keeper's visit into this think of hers. Added the memory of the Seeker like a pinch of lizard's eyeballs. Threw in, like spit-of-jellyfish, the scandal over some mystery cabinet and other malicious gossip as happened to be lying about, flavoring the rank concoction with her daring as a fence and her suspicious instincts as a snitch. And she savored this think of hers, did Max, then went and telephoned some burglars and crooked coppers. And my special theory is she found out something about this box. Something the Seeker also knew and that makes this little thing dreadfully valuable or dangerous in snitchy fencing. Max decided whoever made a changeling of it knew it too, and that's why they wanted it out of their shop even though it was too risky to sell.

This is all but speculation, you understand.

And that's why Max regretted having dismissed the Keeper. Whoever helped the box find its way into that young man's pocket, Max called the meeting to give them a good shake-up. They might drop something. A clue. A scrap of history hinting where the box had gone. What if, for example, this box holds the key to an evil real-estate hoarder's file cabinet full of forged documents saying antiquarian booksellers that cannot meet his evil terms must be terrorists and ought to be turned out? And what if Max found out about it?

She'd be bored to tears.

A little birdie told me Max would ruin anybody for a lark. She's no idea the box has been under her nose all the time, right here at her friendly neighborhood booksellers'. She just knows she has to find it before the Seeker, whom we know is wrong in the head. She could have a fit and set the box on fire or drag it back to the evil landlord. But if Max got it first, Max could squeeze landlord and henchman for anything she liked, maybe even squeeze us too.

Flower, the Seeker isn't our landlord's henchman.

How do you know?

"Too much snow and associated stress, known colloquially as snow-strain, may cause self-interference in sufferers' imaginations."

Found that in the funny pages, did you? Why we persist in renting from an evil real-estate hoarder is beyond me. Why you let them tell you this place is "the best they can do": honestly, it's baffling.

Were you baffled before it started snowing? On second thought, never mind. We'll defer that discussion to another time, when we'll also discuss paranoia. I take it you believe the Seeker's evident desperation, wherein I see a creator's despair over a lost creation, to be a mask for ruthlessness.

And desperation can't be ruthless? Nor ruthlessness desperate?

Your leaps from one fantastic supposition to another . . .

You're one to talk. Who's the one as actually suspects the very person who popped round in the first place to tell us about Max and her suspicions?

You don't find that peculiar? Accused of fraud before her peers, a deleterious allegation potentially devastating to her reputation, what does the Antique-Furniture Specialist do but pop round to spread the word? Fairly foaming at the mouth she was, adamant that we should take her side when we learned how Max was smearing her. Might she have been adamant because she was guilty? Perhaps she sold that young man some small expensive thing, the trinket which, later on, was alleged to have been a "little picture" . . .

Nobody else has said it wasn't.

Be so good as to wait your turn, please. As I was saying, perhaps the Antique-Furniture Specialist sold some costly trinket to that young man, switched the trinket for the box, and then, prim as you like, hiding behind the venerability of some gilt-footed dressing table, *lied* to the Seeker and the Keeper too, pretending she'd never seen the changeling in her life, and went on to lie at the meeting.

You just don't like the woman, birdie.

Her motives mayn't have been malicious. Possibly it was a species of accident.

Just because once in a blue moon, she comes round to sniff at our poor old sagging bookshelves and their cozy blankets of dust and says if we're to have a hope of being taken seriously we need queen-so-and-so-era mahogany bookcases. And I daresay, birdie, that under the influence of literature you've let yourself be taken in by the junk-shop man.

Max ruled out the Antique-Furniture Specialist on none but the shakiest of grounds, you must admit.

Once she'd had her fill of tormenting the weary-worktable fanatic, Max said: "But you're unlikely to do a nasty turn like that to anyone who put you in mind of the son that never visits you." Poor dear with all her empty duet benches, she'd never said a word to Max about her son. "Your boy and that young lawyer would be nearly of an age. I expect he brought back memories, stranger though he was." Mean old Max. Brought tears to the hat-stand hobnobber's . . .

Brought out her handkerchief, you mean, and a spate of nose dabbing.

Which wasn't half as dodgy as what Max said next: "Nostalgia tends to activate the best in people, not their baser impulses."

Which nonsense Max considered as good as a verdict.

Which, birdie, though she came to it through nonsense, was really the right conclusion. Shadier by far is the junk-shop man who calls himself "Antique-Secondhand-Memory Distributor."

VIII

A fellow needs an angle. It's a bright one, that.

Whoever heard of antique secondhand memories? What's so profound in my remembering what you did yesterday now that you've gone and forgot it?

Well, flower, there do exist antiques which were made to remember the city. Little ceramic riverboats. Playing cards shaped after government offices.

Those bulbs with tiny cities in. Glitter swirls over the buildings like it's snowing when you shake them.

Once he had a three-dimensional model of the city made of multicolored paper. You could fold it up along the seam of the river. Too unwiggly of a river to be accurate, but it's the sentiment that matters. In the folds of its body, the paper remembers the city as it might have been. Straightforward, bright, and colorful. Craning one's neck out of the upstairs window, one sees no longer highlights of the skyline but a wall of cold and dirty flakes.

You are not to hang round windows! How many times do I have to say it? Cleaning spongy walls and windows is to be left to me.

Our walls aren't spongy.

There's mold. Since some snow is melting while new snow carries on snowing, the humidity is constantly ideal for mold. In our old shop, mind you, mold wouldn't stand a chance against the beautiful air conditioners. But down here it's like the Dark Ages, isn't it. Being near the river makes it worse.

We're managing all right.

Mold makes the walls go spongy. It's worst round the windows. That's why birdie's not allowed . . .

I have to do something. You keep hiding the shovel, so I can't . . .

Tried haranguing our evil landlord. Just ignores us, he does. Owns dozens of places. Luxury apartments, holiday rentals, shops. The Bend just isn't on his priority list. Or her or their priority list. We've no idea really. We've never spoken to the person. If they really are a person. They do their business through a website, so it's impossible . . .

Now who's working themselves up.

And mold is horrible for books. For shelves as well. It's a disease.

You could at least let me clean some of the books. It's really all right, you know. We can manage mold. We can at least do something about it. It's the snow we can't get rid of. Have you noticed even the fanciest buildings no longer wear their lights at nighttime? All their beautifying energy goes to heating. And there's the pigeons.

You and your pigeons.

When was the last time you saw one? They were everywhere, all over the city. They couldn't survive forever in this snow, but where have they to go? Apropos of our discussion, my point is that the city isn't what it was. Not even what it was on this very date last year. As to that, can you remember how the city was last year? Can you genuinely remember what it should be like to be here? Not only how it looked, the smell of sunshine, how streets moved before snowplows overran them. I mean how the city felt in your bones, in the unheeded depths of your self, those parts of you that always know when you should be afraid even when you're too obtuse to think so. In my opinion, the answer's no. You can't remember it even if you think you can. Because you didn't pay attention. You didn't expect to need to. You expected to see spring again this year, not to have to ransack your brain to find a sparrow. Those objects known as souvenirs, provided they were made *before*, to remember the city in a bygone time, in other words only if they are *antiques*: those are the sort of object to which you'd look in times like these, when it seems time itself has lost its way in the snow. Stranded with no view at all except of snow and half-misremembered fragments which you must dig out of yourself; as succor to your shocked and straining memory it stands to reason you might wish for a humble object, a trinket which a long-gone visitor might've bought as a memento of a lost-forever day. A thing that with its very body remembers how the city used to be, remembering on our behalf: we who are not visitors but . . .

Lost in our own home. Our spongy little tomb of mold beside the river.

Leave that alone, can't you? We'll discuss it later.

As you like. I still think "secondhand memories" is a gimmick. And I think that man's more apt than anyone to scam a customer. And if you've finished your tragic aria, here's some evidence. He may traffic in old ashtrays and cigar boxes, outdated guide maps and little plastic dogs wearing hats with the city's name on, but he also sells more jewelry than any other shop round The Bend.

How does such a happenstance qualify as evidence?

And despite everything he said, and remember you're the one, not me, who thinks everything he said at the meeting was a lie . . .

Who wouldn't lie at such a meeting?

. . . "What sort of little present," pondered Max, "is a young man like-liest to want for his young lady on their anniversary? A heart-shaped pendant with a squiggle on to represent the river? A necklace with beads spelling out the city's name? A dainty watch with hands shaped after famous buildings? One could imagine any not-too-tiny bit of jew-elry, arranged in an appropriate box and cloaked in paper that isn't quite this shade of white, conveniently left behind to be resold while another, whiter box made all of paper ribbon got taken away as if by ac-cident." And what had your junk-shop man to say to that? "Never seen any such box," he said, "nor any such young man. For lips that speak knowledge are better than loving little presents," or some such rubbish.

I still don't believe he did it. He doesn't need to. For reasons of sentiment heretofore described, the Antique-Secondhand-Memory Distributor must under present circumstances be The Bend's most successful aboveboard retailer.

That's an assumption, birdie. Just because you've fallen for his gim-mick and romanticized it.

He's therefore the least likely to alight upon such stratagems as sell-ing the same thing twice but more likely to fall victim to Max's envy. Max could've organized that meeting with the sole objective of cast-ing undue suspicion upon him. Just to see the rest of us wrinkle our noses at somebody else for a change.

He's also likeliest to have paper puzzle boxes in his inventory.

True. A secondhand secret sealed in paper which could well stay sealed forever. But as you demonstrated, flower, the very concept of secondhand memories is ripe for disparagement by the likes of Max. Yet according to the Antique-Furniture Specialist . . .

Who you said is your prime suspect.

. . . it was Max herself that said, "I should think you'd go about it differently *if you*," meaning the Antique-Secondhand-Memory Distributor, "had it in you to risk a thing like that," indicating . . .

She didn't mean necessarily "switching someone's purchase for a changeling." She probably meant "having a *thing like that* in inventory," a thing that's posing as a puzzle box but that's really too valuable for a junk shop. Referring you to my special theory . . .

. . . indicating that, despite her sneering, Max didn't believe in his culpability. She only wanted to embarrass him. The Antique-Secondhand-Memory Distributor is after all a dignified and quiet sort. The sort whose humiliation gives bullies the greatest pleasure.

IX

One thing you won't gainsay, birdie. Nobody embarrassed themselves worse than the other junk-shop man.

Antique-Useful-Goods Broker.

From the moment he walked in . . .

If the Antique-Furniture Specialist may be credited.

. . . he refused to be happy on his buckling beverage crate, and instead he went stamping up and down and blustering. "Outrageous, this is blackmail, you lot have nothing on me." That Max ever got round to insinuating anything is a bit of a miracle really. First she tried describing the toothy, scowly Seeker, whom everybody remembered, but Mr. Dull-Bladed-Egg-Beater says, "What's that to do with anything?" Max brings up the Keeper and he interrupts again. "What's that to do with me?" Like everybody else, though, Mr. Broken-Backed-Book-Propper had to admit he remembered the young lady. Tried selling her a shawl with half a toggle that wasn't only useful but of great sentimental value to a long-departed stranger.

What came of all his blustering but that it made him look the guiltiest?

"And who sells playing cards," cried the rotting-settee fanatic, "who sells Tarot cards, secondhand socks and breath-mint tins, key rings with someone else's keys on!" Things which, emparceled whitely, a careless hand could easily mistake for my box.

The Antique-Useful-Goods Broker bellowed, "You, madam, have a great deal more to gain from inflicting a medieval napkin holder on half a dozen fools than ever I could get for a thousand antique napkins!"

I don't think Max was counting on a shouting match. She rather thought she'd intimidate everybody.

Well, by gathering them together, she implied that all of them could be capable of fraud. Finding themselves on the defensive, not only before Max the snitch but before their most proximal colleagues, drove everyone to the limits of composure . . .

Of which Mr. Bent-Baking-Pan had little enough to start.

And with Max having attacked the Antique-Furniture Specialist about her son, then gone and sneered at the Antique-Secondhand-Memory Distributor as though he were a perfect dolt, the nervous tension inside The Last Stop overboiled. The Antique-Furniture Specialist pronounced herself duty bound to point out to the assembly that if anyone would sell you the decapitated chewy toy discarded by a stranger's mastiff, it would be that good sir, the Antique-Useful-Goods Broker.

And Mr. Greasy-Government-Issue-Shoehorn said if that was a genuine whatsit-dynasty tea caddy in her window, he'd swallow one of Max's genuine antique garrotes. And the reclaimed-room-divider fanatic wagered the roof over her head that his selection of antique so-called leather gloves were full of maggots as had eaten holes enough to make them stuffable into white-puzzle-box-sized parcels.

Things rather escalated.

"My good madam, how dare you!"

Not even Max could get a word in.

"How dare *you*, you fat, impudent scoundrel!"

It's quite funny as long as you weren't there.

Truth is, Mr. Just-Use-It-As-A-Paperweight isn't likely to have done it. Mostly what he sells is clothes. And we had it from a friend who's a librarian that she had it from a friend whose husband collects mini-funiculars that the souvenir shyster is serious about religion and persuading Mr. One-Footed-Galoshes to like it too. But you can't get started in religion if you're a swindler. If you're in it already, that's another thing.

Leaping again, my flower.

"If you think anybody would consign to you good money for the sake of a dead man's commode, you're barmier than you are ugly!"

At which the Antique-Furniture Specialist accused the Antique-Useful-Goods Broker outright.

"He did it!"

With pointing. Not even Max could stop them.

And what about good old Max?

X

Nobody would think, just because Max named herself hostess and magistrate, that she is above suspicion. But if there's one thing we can be sure of about Max, it's that she pretends to be nothing other than the crook she is. Max may relieve you of your midnight spoils and come morning deliver a rhapsody to the first policeman who asks for you.

Or rat out the policeman if you're more useful than him.

But she won't cosmeticize her affairs. She won't go bellowing her innocence, for she knows she hasn't got any and the rest of us don't either. Do we not all relieve desperate people of their things so we might profit from them? People who bring books often have no wish to sell them. It's only that they're terribly strapped. Having visited distinguished antiquarians only to learn that their dear volumes aren't quite so dear to unfeeling market forces, down they come round The Bend. Their grim looks say clear as clarions that if only they weren't themselves, they'd buy their books back in a trice. But really they lack the courage to return to things they've abandoned. Abandonment that we pawnbrokers facilitated.

We're not as bad as all that, birdie.

Max understands we're in the business of betrayal.

Betrayal of things? Things ordinary people made?

Didn't people make this city? Haven't its pollutants, people-made, in-fused the planet's body at its essential depths, for all intents remaking it into this deranged thing which may well have forgotten it needs sea-sons? Haven't we betrayed everything that exists, including the city and other beautifully made things, and things turned on us in kind, things we supposed incapable of living? Max knows we're perfidious. She's bloody evil because she embraces it, takes it to extremes, and doesn't care who or what might suffer for it. For Max, everyone's merchandise. You or a policeman, a parrot or a padlock, they're all the same to Max, all objects. And that's not where she goes wrong. Max's crime is treating *objects* as inferior to herself, putting them up for sale, forcing them to betray one another, and doing her utmost to rob them of their dignity so they've no recourse except to surrender to her power. As though she's not one of them herself. She knows it. She won't deny it. She won't paper over her greed in niceties.

You're saying she's above switching a bought thing for a changeling.

I think, in her disgusting way, yes.

If I agree, will you calm down?

You'll agree because it's true.

There, now, we've ruled out everybody.

Because you know as well as I that the Antique-Furniture Specialist has ever been a faithless, presumptuous rascal. Furthermore, despite yourself, you know there is one more conspirator. The persistence of your special theory proves how well you know it. As I said, there is an odd number of sides.

I agree Max couldn't have done it, birdie. Because Max got someone to confess.

XI

Very well. It was the row that did it, really. But as you say, the row was because of Max. If you and I had wished, perhaps for the good of The Bend's seedy repute, to establish who among us had defrauded a customer and to admonish the malefactor against future chicanery, we wouldn't have brought the neighborhood together after the fashion of a police roundup, summoning everyone with insinuations reeking of blackmail.

"He'd sell you rat traps with the rats in!"

He was first to tire of it, that's all.

"She'd sell you the paper from under yesterday's fish and chips and expect you to believe it's all the rage in decorating!"

I'm speaking of the Antique-Secondhand-Memory Distributor.

"Enough!" said the noble peddler of decrepit pennants. "You're both innocent!" And then he started talking.

You mean he started lying.

Why the deuce would the man lie, birdie?

To bring the sordid evening to a close.

Wouldn't the truth have managed that? Everyone shut up and looked at him. And according to the demi-lune-table fanatic, he looked them all right back. And he said, quiet and dignified, that he remembered the customer concerned. The Keeper's lost young man.

But to the Keeper he'd said the opposite. He'd told her he'd never seen her young man before. He'd said the same, remember, to all his neighbors that very night at the start of Max's meeting. When the talk worked its way round to the Keeper's drooping about from shop to shop, the Antique-Secondhand-Memory Distributor stated clearly . . .

According to the wormy-wardrobe fanatic that you think is untrustworthy.

. . . that he'd said he was sorry to be unable to provide assistance, but he didn't recall any young man or recognize the box.

Which was a lie.

It wasn't.

But at the *start* of the meeting, he wasn't to know it'd degenerate into finger-pointing as made everybody panic even though they knew nobody believed any of it. He just thought what we thought when the shivery-chandelier fanatic started telling us the story: everybody'd deny all knowledge and they'd go home. So he joined in. He denied. Only in his case it was a lie.

That denial was genuine, flower. Only *later on*, when others erupted in panic, did he falsely retract his denial in hope of putting a stop to it.

No, birdie. That was his confession.

But flower, only look at it. At the outset of the meeting, the Antique-Secondhand-Memory Distributor denied having seen the box before the Keeper brought it round. I'm saying that's the truth. You're saying it's a lie. But *after Max had ruled him out* and the discussion had veritably imploded, *then* the Antique-Secondhand-Memory Distributor resolved to contradict himself and plead guilty? You'd take the latter for a true confession. But I'm convinced it was a lie. Precisely at the moment when the whole charade attained the summit of wearisomeness, the Antique-Secondhand-Memory Distributor suffered an inspiration. He saw in a flash the image of a misremembered customer. Details flooded back, a miracle of timeliness. A man, yes, rather young. He *was* distracted, come to think of it. And it was he, it must've been, how *could* the Antique-Secondhand-Memory Distributor have forgotten: it was that young man who bought the expensive little picture. A miniature oil painting that could fit in the palm of your hand or even in that box of yours, fancy that. A picture of the city in the spring. And the sky was never so blue, the river never so sparkling and tame in the embrace of lush green trees. To look at such a day, one would never believe it possible that the air between one's eyes and the lenses of one's spectacles would clog with shards of gray in a bombardment without end. A cloud streaking across the blue, a dash of white paint by someone anonymous and departed, means that even this bright day will pass as seasons should, that reprieve is ever the horizon.

I take it you don't think that picture ever existed.

Transported by his opportune apprehension, the Antique-Secondhand-Memory Distributor told the gathering he'd wrapped the picture in ordinary packing paper. Standard, whitish, newsprint sheets. He laid the parcel on the counter. Which, being a convenient display surface, had other things on it. One such thing, amid the clutter, was the box we've called *changeling*. Now consider his description of the customer. "Distracted. Hardly a word to say for himself. Caught up in his phone even as he's browsing for his little present." In brief, the Antique-Secondhand-Memory Distributor echoed without embellishment what everybody else already believed. Now the young man pays for the picture, thumbing at his phone the while. It appears he'd used it to order a taxi, for just as the shopkeeper is printing his receipt, the customer's phone is making a noise, a taxi splattering the snow. The young man startles, for what taxi manages promptness in this weather? He grabs the box and scarpers, leaving his parcel on the counter, and the Antique-Secondhand-Memory Distributor, absorbed in watching the credit card machine drool out receipts, is just too slow stop him.

What's implausible about all that?

He put the wrapped-up picture aside, believing the customer would discover his error and return. Time passed. It snowed. The young man didn't return. One morning, a little old woman and her little old man blew into the souvenir shop on a gust of crotchety argument. The proprietor recognized the pair as frequent browsers who, although their pension wouldn't countenance the purchase of antique second-hand memories, came round often to reminisce in the company of absent strangers' abandoned things. That morning they were at odds, he said, because they'd found they couldn't remember what grass looked like on the riverbank, when it was allowed to meet the water and be caressed by it without asphalt driven between. If these people exist, either they suffer from the same temporal confusion that causes the Antique-Furniture Specialist to imagine the gradual lowering of her ceiling or they are very ancient indeed and must be ghosts. Nobody alive could possibly recall the esplanade without its wriggling roads.

Maybe they'd seen it in a book.

The Antique-Secondhand-Memory Distributor claimed to have had no idea that these irregular, nonpaying customers were passionately enamored of the alleged "little oil painting" he'd sold to the young man until they each let out a cry and nearly collapsed with sadness to find it gone from his display. How could he not be moved, he said. Had not the young man taken something for his money? How could he hem and haw over a customer who hadn't noticed his own purchase and mightn't ever return to put it right when here before him was a chance for giving without gaining as befits a man of faith? Without ado, the Antique-Secondhand-Memory Distributor tore the wrapping from the ever-so-expensive "picture" and presented it to the couple with charity and blessings.

And you don't believe any of this.

All our dubious neighbors acquitted of all charges while Max is made to look unkind, cynical, and foolish, and as a bit of a bonus the Antique-Secondhand-Memory Distributor acquires an aura of saintliness? It's far more likely that until the Keeper brought it round, he'd never seen the box in his life. He pulled those penniless old people out of the air.

All right, fair enough. He dreamed up the sweet old couple. But don't you see, birdie? He dreamed them up not because he's innocent but because he switched the box for the picture on purpose, and Max and all the shouting made him realize the game was up, and so he put a nice charitable twist on his confession. Why risk a changeling at all, you ask? See again my special theory. Your beloved junk-shop man bought the box off some idiot not realizing it was valuable.

It isn't valuable, my flower. It's paper.

Then why mustn't I try to open it?

You can't have it both ways, you know. You can't say "It's just a box" *and* "It's a dangerous enigma that's worth millions."

But birdie, that's exactly as the junk-shop man saw it. Not on account of the box but how people behaved. Yes, he saw it's just a little box made of paper ribbon. But he also saw the Seeker, on the hunt, invade his shop with sinister scowls. Alarmed as all the rest, he wanted nothing to do with her, and so he lied and said he knew of no such box. He admitted it to everyone.

Except ourselves.

If the box was stolen from the Seeker and found its way into his shop, he wanted nothing to do with it. If the Keeper got it through the negligence of her young man, he wanted no part of whatever might come to pass between the Keeper and the Seeker. He didn't want the trouble, so he lied to both! But Max isn't afraid of trouble. Max knows it's worth it.

He didn't do it, flower. Neither by accident nor on purpose.

'Course he did. Boomerang-desk fanatic just pretended to be shocked.

I expect she was relieved.

She refused to apologize to the other junk-shop man. He wasn't about to bother with contrition either. And she said Mr. Handle-Free-Garden-Trowel looked daggers at the self-styled man of faith. Which means Mr. Old-Cat-Litter didn't believe the changeling was an accident any more than the rest of us. And now here's our lovely visitor wondering how the little rectangle of paper silence that wrought such a to-do came to be mine. Well, we bought it off the Keeper!

You bought it. Against my better judgment.

But you said that librarian wants to buy our books off us before mold kills them all.

I said I am considering whether we might ask our sympathetic friend to lend temporary shelter to certain of our valuable volumes in the humidity-controlled library at which she is employed. I did not say I'm prepared to sell our entire stock, give up on our livelihood, notwithstanding any amount of snow.

All right, I said all *right*, birdie. Well, the Keeper wasn't really interested in money. Her price was more than reasonable.

And not at all what I was getting at. As you know very well.

XII

Ever so tired she was, poor child, from carrying her sad story and truncating it for people, cutting it down to just one word, *distracted*, a word that seemed so innocent, only to hear time and again that nobody remembered her foolish young love, as if he'd never existed. We gave her a cup of tea and let her have her cry. And so much was building inside of her that she had to let it out.

No matter how he acquired the box, that young man of hers was no mere innocent. Crawling round The Bend she came, no place at all for a young lady, because he broke her heart over a trifle.

But as she relived her sad story again and again, the story itself, in its retellings, slowly taught her that she needn't punish herself with it. So when she got round to us, she was brave enough not to trim the story anymore. And when she'd done *that*, she realized without realizing: she was ready to start trying to let the story go.

She brought the box out of her coat. My flower was wildly taken with it. Its being made of paper wrapped up tight in itself, so full of stories without sounds, without markings, wrapped in all their seams . . .

I still don't understand why you're afraid I'll open it.

Some things don't want to be pulled apart and unraveled down to their blood vessels. Anyway, we wouldn't have thought she'd take money for it.

"How does such a little thing bring out the worst in someone?" asked her weepy little voice.

The thought of selling it had never before entered her mind. She thought she wanted to cling to it. Like a ghost, she thought she needed to understand it now that it's too late. But this crisscrossed memento remembers not only her lover and their love. It recalls his breaking point and theirs as well. Which brings me, flower, to what you are trying not to ask yourself. When is an accident an affair of chance occurring without reason? When is it the result of swarming energies and aspirations colliding, conspiring . . .

Nobody aspires for their things to end up at The Bend.

But to what do *things* aspire? Things like that box of yours. There's the extra point of view, you see. There's the odd one we've left out.

XIII

Birdie. It's a box. It does what people make it do.

You're certain of that, are you? If, per your special theory, the box has some sway over people, luring the Seeker to come after it, the Keeper to attempt laboriously to trace its history, and all the people of The Bend, save your lovely and intrepid self, to disavow it with all their vehemence; is it entirely impossible that the box might have ways of directing its own fate? Ways of catalyzing events in cooperation and competition with humans? Even if the Antique-Furniture Specialist—or whoever, have it your way, the Antique-Secondhand-

Memory Distributor—even if some hominid swapped the young man's purchase for the box, who are we to say *the box* didn't in some manner cause or encourage whoever it was to make the switch?

So it's my box to blame for everything.

No, no.

Because it's magnetizing people. Perhaps you'd better go to bed, birdie.

Only think about the meeting. Now that it's all over, who's come out ahead? The Antique-Furniture Specialist wishes to install a panic button. The Antique-Useful-Goods Broker wants to sue for defamation. The Antique-Secondhand-Memory Distributor means to quit The Bend forever. Max has yet to make her move, much to everyone's consternation. The Seeker rages unknown through the city, seeking perhaps an inhuman fragment of herself, while the Keeper droops heartbroken through identical gray days. Who has won?

Certainly not you. What with mold sickness making you dizzy all the time so you're having to pull an oxygen tank . . .

You're sidestepping the issue, flower. Very well. Let us not argue. As for the tank, it is on wheels. Hardly inconvenient.

. . . blaming the snow for that you're queasy and wheezy so you can join in the city's tragic aria. What you need, birdie, is to quit this dreadful midden of a place that the evil real-estate hoarder dug out of his rubbish bin to throw like rotting fishbones at his untrendingest tenants.

Any opportunity to criticize our shop and make me out to be an invalid, you jump at it. Only listen to me: I'm all right. We're managing.

There you go again.

Remainder

La Blue Boite

Listen. I'm a remainder of a dead woman. The Boite is everything to me. I do everything I can to take care of La Blue Boite. I clean the Boite's toilets and ovens. I serve its meals. I paint its walls. I'm the Boite's bartender. The Boite stores my remainder. The Boite is all I have. You are all I have.

I didn't mean to upset the chair. I'm drunk because I'm afraid. Look. The chair is safe. Your chair is safe. Your chair is your bar is you but not all. I disinfect and polish this chair's seat, back, legs because they're of you. You: the Boite. You are La Blue Boite.

A letter came last night. My letters are yours because they bear your name. I don't know who's sending these letters. They say they're written by my child. I don't have any children. I don't understand what they want. I don't know how they know your name. The man who killed me doesn't know he left a remainder.

I failed to hide from the Boiteuse that I'm a shred. I weakened and told her I had to disappear. The man who killed me mustn't find my remainder. The Boiteuse says I'm a survivor, not a remainder. She doesn't see I'm just a leftover of a night. A remainder isn't even a ghost. A remainder falls off a life and is left. A remainder can't come back. Nothing is haunted by a remainder. Everything haunts a remainder. I've not left the Boite in twelve, fifteen, seventeen years. I'm never drunk. The Boiteuse renamed me. She pays me cash. The authorities think I'm not here. I'm nowhere. I've no phone, computer, television. I'm a double negative.

The Boiteuse is you and yours because the Boite is hers. I found the first letter in the Boiteuse's office. I was emptying her garbage. She'd thrown the letter in the garbage. She'd found it in the lobby on the floor. She'd not recognized the name on the envelope. She'd assumed it was someone who'd meant to stay at the Boite but was unable. It was a big envelope. It had no postage label or return address. It came by unseen hand. The Boite's name and another were on the envelope. The other name wasn't mine or the sender's. Mine is the name the Boiteuse gave me.

The dead woman's name was on the envelope. The Boiteuse knew it from looking at my face. I said I'd burn the letter. The Boiteuse said we should read it first in case it warned of trouble. I'd never want trouble for the Boite. I must've done something wrong. That's why letters to the dead woman keep appearing in the lobby.

I never know when a new letter might appear. They're brief letters without signatures on small papers in big envelopes. He killed me because I wasn't strong enough to escape. He wouldn't pretend to be a child. He's not mentioned in the letters. The Boiteuse knows I have no children. She knows the dead woman can't be traced to the Boite. She says we must wait and see. We can't tell the authorities. They'd write down a connection between the Boite and the dead woman. It'd be my fault if trouble came to the Boite. It'd be my fault for being afraid and begging refuge in this small hotel.

❑

The Boite's bar is closed at night so I can care for it. Four chairs and this table are now clean. I'm putting the chairs on the table. Chairs on the table reaching for the ceiling with their legs form a thing like the bud of a sleeping flower. The chairs are legs-up on the table so their feet won't scratch it while I'm cleaning underneath. This is my taking care of you.

You deserve to know. A remainder is haunted by itself. It's haunted by the division that severed it from itself. A remainder's only history is that division. Its former self no longer exists. Its former self doesn't exist as the memory of a dead person exists. I'm a trace of a night of violence. A trace of a night is a nightmare or symptom.

The Boiteuse and all the guests are in bed except Mr. Six. His room is number six on the top floor. Mr. Six isn't the man who killed me. Mr. Six isn't behind the letters. The Boiteuse would know. Mr. Six is someone else. I'm afraid of Mr. Six. I wish you'd tell me what you think of him.

I'm talking to the Boite. I'm drunk. What you think may not be tellable. Your thinking may not be thinking. You are a hotel. I'm maybe not in my right mind. Mr. Six is out there. I'm afraid. You are La Blue Boite. You deserve to know about Mr. Six.

Mr. Six shows respect for the hotel by looking presentable in the bar and dining room. He brought a few days' worth of clothing. He's stayed over a month. He pays for our in-house laundry service. The Threes tried wearing sleepwear to the dining room. They got angry when the Boiteuse forbade it. She invited them to present themselves appropriately or pay for their stay and leave. The Threes didn't leave. The Boite is full. It has a waiting list. The Boiteuse says there's not been a waiting list in years. She gave the Threes an ultimatum because of Mr. Six. He came to the city just to stay at La Blue Boite. The hotel isn't at its best. It's fallen on hard times. Its heyday was long before I was born. Mr. Six knows all about it. He's no older than I. It's his first visit. The day he meant to leave was the day they gave up on the airport.

It's because of the snow. Snow makes it hard for pilots to see properly. Snow makes runways unsafe. Airlines are afraid their planes will skid. They refuse to land their planes in the city or make them try to leave the city. The city's snowplows are overworked and breaking down. Trucks carrying new snowplows can't get into the city. Snow hampers the highways. Snow makes it hard for boats to manage the river. Sailors can't see properly. The river's bloated from too much snow. The city will flood when the river overflows.

A big hotel stands between the river and the Boite. Rumor says the river's sneaking into the big hotel. Its bulk should stop the river from getting to you. The big hotel belongs to a global hotel chain. They built it when I was a child. The chain hotel's guests should've been yours. Aging gracefully is hard enough without competition. Guests talk about you as if you're a crone of a hotel.

The Boite is full because the chain hotel is full. It's because the airport's closed. The river port is unreliable and may close. The highways are at a standstill. People stranded in the city can't sleep out in the snow. They must pay what the hotels demand. The Eights came to the Boite from an apartment building across town. It's been cold so long a central pipe in the building froze and burst. The building flooded. Its plumbing cannot function. The Boiteuse and I tend your plumbing day and night. We learned plumbing from books. The Eights came to the Boite for its plumbing. The Eights are a pair of adult couples. The Boiteuse lets them share a room because the Boite is full and there's nowhere else to go. The Eights have to pay as if each couple had a separate room. The city's hotels are all at capacity. They're full of stranded foreigners and locals with damaged plumbing. The situation forced the Boiteuse to institute policies. Guests must settle their bills weekly even if they cannot leave. We need money to feed the guests. Mr. Six has the best room. He could see the river if the chain hotel fell down.

Mr. Six thinks the snow is Earth's rebellion and trauma-induced breakdown. He calls it a disintegration event. The snow is dead-cold particles of everything disintegrating. The Boiteuse said the authorities are covering up the facts. They've done nothing except measure. We know the same amount of snow falls each day at the same speed. We know the melting speed is the same each day but slower than the falling speed. Mr. Six said that's what worries him. He said stable measurements are wrong reasons for snowing. The Boiteuse said the Threes won't let their children catch the snowflakes on their tongues. She and Mr. Six were here in the bar. I said the snow won't harm the children if they're not evil children. The snow falls in a constant pattern as a punishment. The city is an evil place. The snow is proof that the Deity sits in judgment.

A customer said the snow is from a vast thing cracking at the seams. She said we live in the vast thing. That's why we don't notice it. She said the thing we live in is a thing of things. Blizzards, springtimes, snowflakes are some things that are the vast thing. She said it's like rooms, chairs, stairs, ceilings are things that you are. Head, eyes, heart are things that are the thing I am.

□

I shouldn't talk about that customer. She isn't here. The room, the bar, all the things in it are you. I've not felt so much *you* in your presence before. I almost don't want to say *you* to you, the Boite. *You* are whom I'm talking to whenever. *You* changes its meaning. The Boite is always the Boite. This hotel is where I am. The Boite must be for me to be. You are you and it. You are the Boite is.

That's why I must explain about that customer. She will never be a guest. She was a regular at the bar. Mr. Three called this customer the boxer because of her front tooth. I said nothing because Mr. Three's a guest. You shouldn't tease somebody for having been beaten. The Boiteuse calls that customer the local assuming she lives in the city. She has very black hair like a veil. She never spoke till she was drunk beyond intelligible. I sensed she was foreign everywhere. That's why she liked drinking in hotels. Some great lack set her apart. The local drank at the Boite till late then disappeared. She was like a darkness the snow emitted and absorbed.

I saw the lack in her look. I've developed that ability. It's a safety precaution. The local's look trapped her in it. It was the look of finding out that the thing she was looking for wasn't what she'd thought it was. Mr. Six says the thing the local's looking for possessed her. The thing possessed the local by not being hers. I didn't know the depth of her possession. I couldn't have known how strong the thing was. The thing pulled and pursued her all the time from far away. We think the thing the local was pursuing is a box. Desperation to find the thing intensified when she drank.

I don't know how long the local was a regular. Steady snow unsteadies time. Snow not stopping makes movement feel like stillness. Mrs. Five thinks it's been snowing for four months. The Boiteuse thinks it's been ten months. I'm adrift between times. I'm no one's remains. My presence is without essence. My night of origin is a hole in the forgotten. My feeling of time's pace is the Boite's pace. A moment passes to the next when the Boite needs new light bulbs in the laundry room. A moment becomes a new moment when a stain appears on the floor in the lobby. I change your light bulbs, do your laundry, mop your stains. You experience time as changes in your body. I'm one of the Boite's ways of taking care of itself. I am part of your immune system.

The local became a regular at the bar when boxes overran the Boite. Guests were in an online-shopping frenzy. The Threes and Twos were scared because the airlines recanceled their homeward flights. They bought crazy things like inflatable toys for swimming pools. The Eights bought rugs and cookware for their abandoned apartments. Snowstrain makes people crazy. The Boiteuse feared the Eights would start a fire in their room. She confiscated the cookware. She threatened to make them leave. She took pity when they begged. Guests' purchases arrived in big strong boxes. The boxes stacked up inside the Boite's storeroom. The boxes would go moldy if we left them outside. Sometimes garbage trucks don't come. Snow makes things difficult for garbage trucks. Mold would cause trouble if it infected the Boite.

The Boiteuse asked CytyBox to take back the boxes and recycle them. CytyBox refused. She asked Garden SuperCenter to take away the hothouse palm trees the Fives ordered. Garden SuperCenter's truck driver's helper didn't refuse exactly. The truck driver said his helper was thinging with the trees. The helper couldn't understand the Boite's not being a home for things like trees. He linked his arms with the trees' trunks and didn't move. He was silent and not moving.

Mrs. Five refused to pay for the delivery. She entangled the Boiteuse in an argument with Garden SuperCenter. The Boiteuse asked the guests to restrict their online shopping to necessities. The guests refused. The Boiteuse had to institute a policy. The Boite will refuse large deliveries unless the purchases were made by the Boiteuse.

□

Mr. Six started frequenting the bar when the airport closed and he realized he couldn't leave. He didn't stay late. He didn't acknowledge the local. She didn't acknowledge him. He didn't speak unless the Boiteuse paused in her dashing, scrubbing, cooking, plumbing, budgeting, cajoling to chat with him. They'd speak about the Boite, snow, airport, other hotels, television. They spoke often about you.

Silence is safer than speaking. Keeping to the background is a useful safety precaution. The Boiteuse and Mr. Six didn't push me into the foreground when Mr. Six started coming to the bar.

Last night was different. The local and Mr. Six outstayed everyone. She was at the end of the bar nearest the window. He was at the other end near the sink. She was drunk and talking to herself. He had a full glass and didn't speak.

The Boiteuse came to say goodnight. Mr. Six reminisced about La Blue Boite's boxes. I hadn't known about these boxes. The Boiteuse enjoyed Mr. Six reminding her about the boxes. He said an artisan used to weave beautiful little boxes for the Boite in the Boite's heyday. He said each guest received a box on their last night. The box sometimes had a gift inside like chocolate. The box sometimes was the gift. He said his director had given him a Boite box to show appreciation. The box was an expensive collector's item. Mr. Six said he treasured it. The Boiteuse was moved. She said Mr. Six gave her hope for the future.

I listen between what people say. It's a skill I've developed as a safety precaution. Mr. Six knew too much about the Boite.

He saw that I distrusted him. He asked quietly if he'd offended me.

Mr. Six is an important guest. He shouldn't care about offending me. He hadn't offended me. He'd frightened me. Mr. Six spoke too tenderly about you. He spoke as though he had a personal stake in you. I'd just received a letter. Being frightened makes me angry.

Mr. Six is the brain behind a famous television show. It's about hotels. A famous former athlete pretends to stay at hotels. He tells the audience what he thinks of the hotels. Mr. Six researches and visits the hotels. Mr. Six tells the athlete what to say. Everyone thinks the athlete is a hotel connoisseur. Mr. Six could be the most important guest we've ever had. Mr. Six could buy any hotel he wanted. He spoke tenderly about the Boite as if the Boite would soon be his. I suspected the former athlete wanted to start a hotel chain and name it after his television show. I suspected Mr. Six was scoping you out for the new chain.

I wanted Mr. Six to know I'd seen through him. I asked point-blank if he was scoping out the Boite for a buyer. Mr. Six looked astonished. He said the Boite wouldn't be the Boite without the Boiteuse. I said his interest in the Boite was too personal for a connoisseur. I've seen him looking tenderly at your doorframes. I've seen him gazing at upholstery in your booths. I've watched him stroking the bar. I've wiped his fingerprints off it. Look. This is your citrus press. I disinfected it after Mr. Six stroked it when I moved it to clean underneath. Mr. Six strokes banisters, glasses, cutlery, walls, barstools, doors, fiberglass orchids. It shocked him that I'd seen. He clutched his hands as if to stop them getting away.

I thought I'd ruined everything with your important guest. I thought I'd betrayed you by bringing ruin. I decided to kneel before the Boiteuse. I decided to beg her not to make me leave you. I'd endure any other punishment.

Mr. Six finally spoke. He apologized. Mr. Six looked at his hands and apologized. He said it's true hotels interest him personally. He said he hadn't meant to throw his weight around. He hadn't come to steal or harm the refuge that's La Blue Boite.

He used the word *refuge*. He didn't know anything about me. I'm the bartender. A bartender's a stranger behind a solid border. Customers don't need to apologize to bartenders. Customers unburden themselves to bartenders because bartenders are furniture.

Mr. Six ordered another. He drank it then looked at me. He was measuring himself and me.

He said he pays attention to every hotel's things. He looks for things that pass unnoticed. He takes things personally because he can't help it. He said it's because of his twin brother. I listened between. I thought I listened between what he said. Customers are always their twins in their own stories.

htl-esc

Mr. Six's twin brother got entangled in some conflict seventeen years ago. I don't know what kind of conflict. Not knowing people's conflicts is a key safety precaution. Mr. Six's twin brother refused every compromise. His obstinacy cost him everything. He felt like everybody except Mr. Six thought he was worthless.

Mr. Six's brother found a job in a hotel called htl-esc. I'd never heard of htl-esc. Mr. Six said people didn't know if it was hotelesque, hotel escape, or hotel E.S.C. His twin had never worked in a hotel before. He'd never been a gardener. htl-esc chose him because he was young, strong, homeless. Mr. Six's twin pretended he'd known he'd get the job. Mr. Six felt his twin's relief in his own chest. Mr. Six felt it even from afar.

htl-esc was far away. It had a river behind it. They'd cleared most of a great forest to build the hotel. They'd tamed the rest of the forest to make the maze. The maze was the only way from the guarded gatehouse at the huge gate to the hotel. Cars couldn't fit in the maze. A guard took Mr. Six's twin from the gate to the hotel in an electric cart.

htl-esc was a renovated mansion. Legend said a mad naturalist built it. It had terraces and turrets and hidden corridors in odd shapes and places. Mr. Six said the decor was modern and old-fashioned.

The bar could've been glass with verses engraved in it in ancient alphabets. Sconces could've been like orchid snails, elephant snails, stivaconchs. Decorators competed to work for htl-esc. They consulted mystery writers, painters, moviemakers, sculptors, safecrackers, magicians, circus artists. The lobby had five staircases. A metal staircase spiraled through a hole in the ceiling. A wood staircase came down through a trapdoor and folded up into a hidden pocket.

htl-esc's famous wine cellar had a soil floor. Mr. Six said the cellar was where the hotel rendezvoused with Earth. They rendezvoused inside each other like twins. Mr. Six said he and his twin lived inside each other from the moment they were born. Each brother felt the other's feelings because that's the way twins are. Mr. Six said they were two bodies of one mind. They were two bodies of one body like the cellar and Earth.

Mr. Six apologized for talking about rendezvous. That made two apologies.

Mr. Six didn't know what the hospital said fifteen or thirteen years ago. They'd never seen an arm pulverized like mine. They'd never seen shattered ribs or a concussion like mine. The authorities would think I'd misunderstood a rendezvous. That's what they said.

◻

The day manager explained htl-esc to Mr. Six's twin. htl-esc canceled your bill if you solved a riddle. You had to pay your bill if you couldn't solve the riddle before the end of your stay. The riddle was how to get from your room to the gatehouse. You had to turn up at the gatehouse alone on foot. A cart would take you to the gatehouse on your checkout day if you failed. The authorities found no reason why you should be unable to get out of htl-esc once you'd got in.

htl-esc's rooms had names instead of numbers. The rooms had wallpapers inspired by the names. A room called the indigo eel's cave had indigo eels, flicker coral, sparkle-ringed octopuses painted in the wallpaper. You'd find your way from the room to the nightclub by looking at the wallpaper and connecting what you saw with things in corridors and whatever you learned about the nightclub. Clues about amenities were in all rooms and common areas. Some things were easier to find than the nightclub. Things like the baccarat lounge were difficult. Directions to one of the hotel's restaurants were obvious somewhere in each room. You'd find a ceramic monkey eating ceramic fruit in the jungle room. The fruit was hollow. Directions to an on-site restaurant were in the fruit. The pharaoh room had a bowl of glass grapes instead of a monkey. The grapes gave you directions to a restaurant when you put them in the proper order. You might also find a crossword puzzle, blacklight torch, pressed fern, color-swatch book, combination lockbox, magnifying glass, archaic poem, lockless key. The things pertained to clues to finding other restaurants, spas, bars, casinos, pools, lounges, terraces, galleries, cafés, libraries, movie rooms inside htl-esc.

htl-esc's operating principles were escape-room principles. An escape room is a game. The game is you're locked inside the room. The room is full of riddles. You solve the riddles to find clues that show you a way out of the room. You win if you escape within a certain time. The manager unlocks the room if you don't win. Mr. Six said htl-esc was an icon of the escape-entertainment industry.

□

Mr. Six's twin was htl-esc's first indoor gardener. The day manager gave him a phone with an app that showed him everything he needed. Escape-entertainment principles, the legend of the naturalist, a map of hidden corridors, instructions about doors that were not doors, mirrors that weren't mirrors, how to tell which room a figurine or plant belonged to. The new indoor gardener had a week to study the app before it deleted itself. He couldn't use it to help guests find the gatehouse. The day manager wouldn't tolerate bribery. The camera department discouraged cheating. The hotel itself discouraged cheating from succeeding. Cheating undermined the escape-entertainment industry.

The day manager gave Mr. Six's twin a riddle to keep in his pocket. Mr. Six's twin wrote one day to Mr. Six that a guest had brought him a glassblown flower. The guest said an urn on the terrace said to take the flower to the indoor gardener and ask its name. That was the signal for the indoor gardener to give the guest the box in his pocket.

Mr. Six's twin told Mr. Six that the box looked like a box but was a knot. It was a large paper folded crisscrossing into itself. The indoor gardener said the box looked plain on the outside. He unknotted it into a sheet and found drawings of plants. The plants lived at htl-esc in urns, vases, mazes, paintings, books, carpets, wallpapers. They were the finest drawings he'd ever seen. Some needed a magnifying glass. One rip in the box would make several drawings unrecognizable. The indoor gardener was to give the box to anyone who brought a leaf or flower and asked its name.

The guest with the glassblown flower was the only one who ever did. That's why the indoor gardener thought his box was a valuable clue. The guest must've been advanced in his search for the gatehouse. The indoor gardener thought his clue might help the guest figure out the maze or find the lobby. The mansion had so many staircases there was no point in all of them going to the lobby. The indoor gardener said all guests forgot how to find the lobby after a night in the hotel.

□

The indoor gardener's job was to address irregularities. A hole was digging in the cellar. Nobody saw or heard anything digging. The day manager consulted engineers, contractors, plumbers, exterminators, outdoor gardeners, geologists, seismologists, silvologists, volcanologists. None found any problems except the hole. Guests who knew there was a hole would've told the world htl-esc was unsafe. The cellar was dark and quiet. The hole was in the floor. Mr. Six said the hole was big enough for a small tree to take root in. The day manager arranged for a shovel and bag of soil. The indoor gardener filled the hole with soil.

The indoor gardener was htl-esc's only live-in employee. His room was an extra corner sticking out of the attic. A lamp stuck out of the wall above his bed. He didn't think the lamp tapped him on the head. He thought he'd had a dream. His phone made a sound. It delivered his first message from htl-esc. The housekeeping department's manager wanted him to address a guest's concern.

Mushrooms stuck out of the water holes in the guest's showerhead. The mushrooms were tiny, pink with yellow star-shaped speckles. The guest said there'd been no mushrooms that morning. The indoor gardener was no plumber. He called the maintenance department. The maintenance manager asked if it was really plumbing or an irregularity. The indoor gardener looked at the mushrooms. The maintenance manager told him to discharge the irregularity and text-message the room's name to the maintenance department. The message system would schedule the room for a plumbing check. The indoor gardener plucked the mushrooms from the showerhead. He put the mushrooms in his pocket. He turned on the shower. Water came out of the showerhead. The guest was happy.

The indoor gardener's phone had another message. The nightclub manager had heard about the mushrooms. It was the nightclub's policy that all found mushrooms be brought to the nightclub. She said guests loved escaping to the nightclub for dream-making mushrooms. Wandering mushrooms, hammerhead mushrooms, mermaid's footstools, indefinite mushrooms, apeironyx vitalyx, xerioneirics. She also asked the indoor gardener to fetch a certain wine from the cellar for the nightclub.

The cellar had a new hole in the floor. It was as wide as the old hole if not as deep. It was in the same place exactly. The indoor gardener had filled the old hole just hours before.

La Blue Boite

The Threes wanted the latest on the trains. I said I know nothing about trains. I said the same thing yesterday. Parents Three are going crazy from room-sharing with Children Three. Parents Three tried to hide in the Boiteuse's office. She sent them to the bar. Their phones are hunting escape routes. The latest route has them walking to the underground, riding a train to Central Station, catching a train from Central Station to a city with a working airport, flying on a plane to their home city. Mr. Three thinks it sounds easy. Mrs. Three foresees an ordeal.

The Boiteuse doubts they have the courage to go anywhere. She says route plotters can't cope with irrationality. She says the snow's a serene tempest that's uncovered the irrationality of all existence. The Boiteuse doesn't notice the Deity in charge of justice.

The Deity is punishing the big chain hotel. The chain hotel has a riverwalk entrance. Ducks would waddle from the river to the hotel's restaurant across the concrete riverwalk. The ducks are gone. The snow is too much for them. We hear the chain hotel's snowblowers and snow brushes working day and night. The river swells in all directions. It's swelling underground. Rumor says the river sneaks into the hotel through the floor. Carpets are sodden, tiles slippery, plumbing and wiring destabilized on the ground floor. Lobby, sports bar, coffee shop, gift shop, hair salon, fitness center, business center, three restaurants, four kitchens, concierges' station, housekeeping facilities, administrative offices are all on the ground floor. Rumor says carpet blowers and wet-dry vacuums operate around the clock. The hotel bulk-ordered noise-canceling headphones. The snow is preventing any headphones' arrival.

The chain hotel has a long waiting list. Guests who complain must leave. Guests who spread bad rumors must leave, according to the chain's new terms of service. Rumor says guests fabricate impossible amenities to post online. They spread rumors that the snow is a rumor, the hotel is fabulous, the top rooms are all celebrities', the hotel chain should rule the world. The Boiteuse heard the guests want the chain hotel's computers to overhear their rumors. They want the chain to offer gratitude discounts. The chain hotel's rates are even higher than the Boite's. The Boiteuse says it's snowstrain that makes guests think the hotel's computers spy on them. Paranoia is a symptom of snowstrain.

Mr. Six says hotels shouldn't be able to blackmail guests. Hotels shouldn't be able to use fear to control what guests say. Fear that guests will leave should be the hotel's burden. Fear of homelessness as punishment for mentioning sodden carpets shouldn't be guests' burden. The guests have no alternative but to cling to the hotel because of Earth's rebellion.

□

I was wrong about Mr. Six. His work took him to hotels around the world. The indoor gardener's work kept him in one hotel. The indoor gardener couldn't be Mr. Six.

Twins live together in closed boxes with private views. Mr. Six opened his brother's story to me. Mr. Six can't understand the indoor gardener's story. It hurts him not to understand. He didn't know when he stumbled and dropped silences. Mr. Six said his twin looked just like him.

He said guests went to htl-esc to escape themselves. They escaped to secondhand dreams of the hotel's owners' dreams of escape entertainment, their dreams of the legendary naturalist's dreams, the decorators', mystery writers', moviemakers' dreams of a mad naturalist's dreams and of a hotel. Escape rooms dream they're sealed off from the world. People escape to escape rooms to escape from them. Mr. Six said escape rooms are doubly conscious of themselves as manifesting dreams. He said dreaming is escaping to imprisonment in your own mind. He said htl-esc materialized the paradox of dreaming.

He said hotels are unsettled. A hotel isn't a home. A home's things are possessions. A hotel's things aren't anyone's except the hotel's. The person who doesn't use them is the one they belong to. The Boite's things belong to the Boiteuse. The Boite's things still aren't her possessions. She must replace things if they displease guests. Mr. Six said belonging is powerful. He said possession is even more powerful.

Belonging is one-way. Possession goes both ways. A hotel, box, or ghost can belong to you but can't belong you. A hotel, box, or ghost can possess you. A possessed thing loses itself to its possessor. Things retain their memories. Their memories can possess them. Mr. Six said buildings have the strongest memories. He said a hotel's guests surrender to the hotel and its things.

I've surrendered to the Boite. The Boite remembers to protect me by being solid and almost forgotten. I think Mr. Six thinks you remember your violent becomings. You remember care. You let me massage your bar to free it of condensation. You notice when I clean your sconces, doorknobs, washing machines. Your carpets know my careful tread. Your floors lap up in silence the Boiteuse's loving footfalls. Your staircase groans under the Threes' stampedes. Your beds feel strangers throw their bodies down and must submit. I'd not noticed the Boite noticing. I notice now because of Mr. Six.

Mr. Six said everything carefully. He was here more than a month before he spoke to me of anything besides drinks. He was here more than a month before I spoke to him.

htl-esc

The indoor gardener loved htl-esc. He loved the carpet, maze, walls, unexpected corridors, secret staircases. He loved his attic room. He loved irregularities. His phone sent him all over the hotel. His co-workers messaged him night and day with odd smells, staticky telephones, strange noises, unresponsive computers. Guests sometimes caused stains. Leaky faucets were sometimes just leaky. The indoor gardener referred them to other departments but had to investigate them just in case. He'd no time for other phone calls. He emailed only Mr. Six.

He was busiest at night. The night manager wanted nothing to do with irregularities. The day manager said htl-esc was a stepping stone for the night manager. That's how the indoor gardener learned htl-esc belonged to a consortium. It operated hotels and escape rooms. The indoor gardener felt no loyalty to the consortium. The consortium paid his wages, but he belonged to htl-esc.

Mr. Six thought htl-esc was good for his twin. He wrote to Mr. Six about things being alive in their own ways. Things understand in their own ways. Hotels understand differently from stools, bars, humans, consortiums. htl-esc understood it was the dream of a riddle. htl-esc let people solve the riddle to varying degrees. Being htl-esc meant being lots of different things. Instructions encoded in a dessert menu. An anemone in painting after painting. A coin-sized mirror embedded in a railing opposite a bookcase. Each thing was itself and was htl-esc.

Mr. Six said thinking that things have different ways was good for his twin because it loosened up his mind. It loosened Mr. Six's brother's habit of insisting on his own opinions. Mr. Six said his brother dug his heels in where he shouldn't. He refused to listen to alternatives, got impatient, entangled, quarreled. That's why he changed jobs often.

Mr. Six was a postgraduate student while his twin was an indoor gardener. That's why the indoor gardener asked him what consciousness felt like to a mushroom, a door, a hotel. Mr. Six said thinking about consciousness is groping in the dark knowing something you can't name is groping in the dark beside you. The indoor gardener said he felt like that all the time. He said htl-esc was an escape that couldn't escape.

The indoor gardener started seeking irregularities instead of waiting to be called. Night was the best time to check the pool, spa, restaurants. He had to keep the corridors clear of diablo orchids, leaping lamps, carpethuggers, socket mushrooms, evil-eye mushrooms. htl-esc had lots of polyester plants. It had some living potted plants. The indoor gardener found a living plant with a polyester flower. A live plant with a fabric flower was an irregularity. Nobody else noticed the hybrid plant. The indoor gardener named it Robin. He put Robin in his secret garden in the attic. He told Mr. Six he never would've dreamed life was capable of so much living if he hadn't found htl-esc.

Mr. Six thought his twin's emails were playful. He used emoji to show they made him laugh. He told himself later that the indoor gardener took his responses too much to heart. Mr. Six thought it was because they were twins.

□

The indoor gardener visited the cellar several times a night. The hole was a hole again every time. The indoor gardener filled the hole with soil. He left and returned to find the hole back where it started.

He stopped refilling the hole. He wanted to see what would happen. The hole grew wider and deeper. It stopped widening but became too deep for him to see the bottom. He duct-taped an electric torch to a broom. He lowered the broom into the hole. Roots didn't protrude from the soil walls. Animals weren't tunneling in the walls. Darkness swallowed the broom-shine. Darkness devoured the bottom of the hole. The indoor gardener felt distance brushing his eyelashes. He returned with a bigger torch on a chain of extension cords. Darkness had taken root at the bottom. Darkness had grown up into a tall tree with leaves of darkness. The bottom was no longer visible through the growth of leaves.

The indoor gardener plugged his phone into the extension cords. He started the voice recorder app. He lowered the phone into the hole. He heard air and soil brushing the phone on the recording. He listened to the hole with his own ears. He told Mr. Six he heard wind sighing, branches creaking. Mr. Six said he'd listened an imaginary forest into the hole. The indoor gardener wrote maybe the hole listened him an ancient forest. Mr. Six responded with laughing emoji. He suggested the hole was hungry. The indoor gardener wrote the hole wasn't something growing but the opposite.

Robin made the indoor gardener not want to eat vegetables. He already wouldn't eat animals. He wrote to Mr. Six that Robin was a lot of history. He wrote that history is Robins, vines, holes, candle snails, fevermosses, carpet dreams, mad naturalists.

Mr. Six's story was a briar. Things snagged on the story's thorns. The story fought to stay inside him. It fought to emerge. He said his research hit a wall when he tried to learn who'd really built the mansion. It might've been a wealthy madman. It might've been the consortium.

□

The indoor gardener complained of insomnia. He'd no time to sleep between discharging irregularities, listening to the hole, checking public areas, making videos of the hole, checking service areas, pouring water in the hole, making rounds of guest rooms with the housekeeping department, informing the day manager he hadn't heard a splash, checking hidden corridors, looking after Robin, the carpethugger, his secret garden. He wrote that hotels inhabit people. People inhabit hotels but differently. He wrote he didn't have insomnia anymore. He thought his dreams weren't all his. He thought he was evolving into an emaneater.

The indoor gardener wrote that every chair and shelf and doorknob emanates what it will do and wants to seem and cannot bear. Napkins, cellars, bartenders, carpets, everything emanates histories and potentials. Everything's emanations blizzard all the senses all the time on almost secret wavelengths. We ignore things' secret wavelengths unless we can use them. They'd be too much otherwise. The indoor gardener thought he could no longer ignore emanations. htl-esc teemed with emanating things.

The indoor gardener wrote that he no longer needed sleep. htl-esc's crackling dreams energized him. He wrote nightstands dream of forests because that's what nightstands used to be. He wondered if the trees in nightstands dread or emanate their destroyers. He wondered if we're just furniture's dreams. He wondered if a tabletop's memories of treehood were nostalgic or nightmarish.

He thought something was happening to the world's seams. Something made him sense that seams were never where he thought they were. Something stepping forward was showing the indoor gardener that people imagine seams in the wrong places. He asked Mr. Six if we're just nightmares of a traumatized Earth. Mr. Six said if you don't know where the seams are between things, you don't know whether you're anything anywhere.

He congratulated the indoor gardener for broadening his perspectives and exercising humor. He praised the indoor gardener for not letting his mind rot. He applauded making the most of menial work that wasn't what anybody wanted out of life. Hindsight made Mr. Six shake his head at his own words.

□

Mr. Six didn't hear from his brother for a while. He assumed the indoor gardener was busy with irregularities. The indoor gardener finally wrote that htl-esc had made the hole as a sinkhole in a wound in a pit in a night in a split in a bottomless pit in a hole in an endless night. Mr. Six sent emoji that laughed till they cried. He complimented his brother on turning a janitor job into a creative self-education.

His twin didn't reply. Mr. Six missed him. Mr. Six emailed to ask what was keeping him so busy. He asked his twin if he'd caught explorer ferns guzzling wine. The indoor gardener wrote that crushed rotten grape corpses are unpalatable to plants. He asked whether Mr. Six ever read his emails. He took offense at being called a janitor. What shocked Mr. Six the most was what the indoor gardener didn't say.

The indoor gardener didn't say he'd expected all along to be believed.

Mr. Six shook his head like he was at a loss. The shock and shame were still fresh. They subdued his voice to whispering. He'd never doubted his belief in his twin's impressions before. He'd never doubted because his twin's impressions were his own. That's why Mr. Six thought his brother had to be joking. The indoor gardener and Mr. Six were born of the same cell. They were one mind split in two.

Mistaking his twin's impressions for idle jokes was the same as mistaking his own impressions. That meant his feeling that the indoor gardener felt his own twin didn't believe him was absurd. Thinking pink mushrooms were just a dream of the indoor gardener's was the same as thinking he, Mr. Six, had only dreamed the bartender who was listening to him.

Mr. Six started doubting every judgment he'd ever made. He doubted that his hand was his, that his desk was a desk. He doubted his sensations. He wondered if his twin was doubting, if his disbelief had mangled his brother's sanity. Mr. Six started disbelieving his own sanity.

The effort of summoning his story consumed Mr. Six. I watched him struggle not to disbelieve what he was saying. The story chased his voice out of whispering. The story made him wring his hands. Feeling like he'd done something awful out of stupidity made him shut his eyes like a fist was coming for him. He fell into a pause like he'd been running for his life and tripped and tumbled into silence. I knew not to look at Mr. Six while he composed himself.

Mr. Six said the long silence between himself and his brother was unprecedented. The silence was a gash in their twinship. Ignoring a gash means letting it get infected and spread out deep inside you. Mr. Six remembered falling ill with a fever.

La Blue Boite

I've been listening for emanations. Nobody could survive if things didn't communicate. I might feed the staircase dog food instead of keeping up the varnish if the staircase didn't let me know it's not a dog. Woodworm would get to it if nobody kept up the varnish.

Mr. Six was looking at his glass. It wasn't because it was empty. He was looking at the glass. I topped it up because it's my job. Mr. Six said nobody knows what life is. He said it not for me but for the glass. He said life isn't a force that's bestowed. Life is just each thing.

Mr. Six didn't want the intensity of his words. He didn't say they emanated from the indoor gardener. His look and intensity made his words ask and not just say. His intensity asked me to agree with his words. His look begged me to scoff at them.

I'm not interested in what life is. I already know what life isn't. I didn't want to tell what I know. He didn't mention what has to die for every life. He didn't mention remainders. A remainder isn't a dead leaf falling off a tree. A remainder is a chair's nightmare of men with power, contempt, weapons killing the tree it used to be. A remainder is an arachnipestibloom. Nobody inside the Boite wants to think of you as a remainder.

Mr. Six's silences were sinkholes in his unfinished past. I didn't want him to hear my silence. I felt him watch. I was angry. My glance flew like a dart all by itself. It made him wince because he saw it was a wince itself.

Mr. Six said he'd been observing my listening. He said my listening is different from his. His listening grabs fun facts. My listening attunes to potential while repelling it. Mr. Six said when he whipped out fun facts about the Boite he sensed me attuning to what his voice and words could do. He wished he'd known how to listen for secret dangers in the indoor gardener's emails. He wished it'd occurred to him to try. He thought I could identify what went wrong if I heard the story from the indoor gardener himself.

I don't know why I let myself speak to Mr. Six.

I said people are most apt to overlook the truth when they know the price of overlooking will be agony.

Mr. Six's silences were efforts not to feel what he remembered and what he'd missed. They were efforts to punish himself by feeling what he'd missed and not trusting his feelings. That's how Mr. Six handled this story that wasn't his.

The indoor gardener's story is a remainder. Mr. Six's silences were remainders of the remainder. He didn't recover from his tumbles into silence. He was only half in his voice when he resumed his storytelling. His other half sometimes tried to climb out of the silence, sometimes stood at the bottom staring up. He was fighting and not fighting the will of the story.

I didn't want the memory of when I met the Boiteuse. I didn't want to remember fighting and not fighting the dead woman's story. I can't risk remembering the dead woman gouging her own scalp in pain. I never allow my feelings to be moved because to be moved is to be baited. I was angry because Mr. Six's storytelling baited me to wish I didn't need to fear him. I'd not meant him to catch me listening through his fun facts. He knew I'd misheard his tenderness for the Boite. It wasn't greed. It was regret.

His brother could've worked at La Blue Boite. He'd ended up at htl-esc. Every hotel makes Mr. Six relive the story. He tries reliving it differently because he's uncertain. He's searching for certainty in this story that's not his. He's searching all over the world.

I don't want to believe his story. I don't want to believe what I heard between it. I didn't want to hear it to the end. I didn't want to feel sorrow or his quiet voice. I didn't tell him to stop talking. I didn't listen to myself while listening to him. I didn't take proper precautions. Mr. Six didn't anticipate his telling shaking us and provoking silent echoes. He looked at me as if something about me could fill the gaps in the story. He looked like he thought I'd hear what he needed to say and couldn't. He looked afraid of how much he'd said already. He asked why I didn't tell him to stop talking. He told me all the shards he had. He kept asking why I didn't call him a liar. He asked what my furniture tree was. He didn't want to tell the story. Possession means there's no choice.

htl-esc

An email came for Mr. Six while he was ill. The indoor gardener wrote as if there'd never been a hole between them. He went back to describing his adventures with flowering colanders and castaweed anthuriums. Cutthroat cornflowers jumped out of a drawer of frying pans. The indoor gardener called this behavior diablo. He cleared the drawer of plant matter but couldn't find the roots. The day manager confessed her stapler had been diablo for years. Handheld showers curled their hoses into rosettes. Keyboard mushrooms, light-bulb mushrooms, towel mushrooms.

The indoor gardener called artificial plants emaneaters. He thought they fed on emanations. He called regular plants lighteaters because they fed on light. He named them visitor allium, marguerite-at-midnight, wandering muddlewort, oneirian creeper, beauty's spindle. Mr. Six was overjoyed by his brother's emails returning. They gave him strength to recover from his illness.

The indoor gardener's words weren't like before. Something had happened to them. Some were sharp. Some felt like arrogance instead of wonder. The indoor gardener wrote as though carpethugger vines were common knowledge. The indoor gardener reviled Mr. Six for calling him a janitor. Mr. Six wearied of the indoor gardener's conceit. Mr. Six indulged his brother anyway. He asked the indoor gardener what the carpethugger was.

The plant started as a lighteater. It lived for years in htl-esc's biggest restaurant. A decorator had brought it in a pot. A trellis covered the wall behind the pot. The vine grew up over the trellis. It grew down to the floor. Years passed before anybody noticed it had put roots in the carpet. The carpet sprouted shoots. The shoots were too strong to uproot. They sprang up all over the restaurant. The day manager ordered the carpet torn out. This was before the indoor gardener's time.

The day manager told the indoor gardener to monitor the carpethugger. She said if they tore the carpethugger out, the wall would be full of holes and could fall down. The indoor gardener was to keep clipping the carpethugger so it couldn't reach the floor.

He felt bad about dismembering the carpethugger. He told nobody when he found another in a hidden corridor, another keeping Robin company. He wondered if they were all one carpethugger that had started in the restaurant and suffused the whole hotel. Carpets' reds and purples appeared in the leaves. Greens of leaves seeped into carpets. Color sharing was symbiosis or violence.

□

Guests attempting to watch television saw machines killing forests, smashing wood chips into particleboard, assembling microchips and chairs, drilling for oil, injecting animals with fluids, vomiting rivers of plastic, screaming orange smoke. These images appeared where porn channels should've been. The indoor gardener said htl-esc misinterpreted the television company's secondhand stories. He chastised guests for complaining. He said everybody misunderstands others sometimes.

A guest said they'd found a key to the trapdoor in the lobby at the bottom of a pool. The guest said they'd watched the pool dissolve the key. A guest claimed a crossword puzzle vanished from their room. A guest accused the housekeeping department of switching a painting for a mirror. The housekeeping department accused the guest of switching the mirror for the painting. The indoor gardener said possessiveness was part of being an escape hotel.

Mr. Six said the indoor gardener shouldn't chastise guests. He should only talk about management-sanctioned fantasies. The indoor gardener said Mr. Six had no right to call his observations fantasies. Mr. Six thought the indoor gardener enjoyed pretending to know htl-esc in ways nobody else could learn. He thought the indoor gardener misconstrued his possessive feelings about htl-esc for htl-esc's feelings about its guests. He thought the indoor gardener's possessiveness sprang from the combative obstinacy that'd cost him every prospect except janitor work.

The chairs in one of the restaurants formed a circle. Their arms fused together. Their backs curled over the center and fused together. The indoor gardener called it a sleeping flower. The dining department refused to operate the restaurant until the maintenance department removed the thing with chain saws and wheelbarrows. A massage table fled the spa for a corridor. It stood on its short edge. It changed color to match the walls. It blocked the corridor. The indoor gardener argued against its removal. He said it was guests' responsibility to understand htl-esc's expressions. He said the point of visiting htl-esc wasn't to solve riddles that humans imposed on the hotel. The point was to discover questions that the hotel asked itself.

The housekeeping department suspected a wall of nibbling a linen press. They complained about the indoor gardener. They said the indoor gardener existed to prevent irregularities. The day manager asked why he wasn't keeping up with the irregularities. She asked if there were more irregularities than there'd been when he'd arrived. The indoor gardener saw the increase in irregularities as an achievement. Her offer to find him an assistant offended him. He said nobody who hadn't listened to htl-esc should touch it.

The indoor gardener dreamed about the hole. He didn't describe his dream to Mr. Six. He didn't visit the cellar anymore. He didn't explain why. Mr. Six thought it was because there'd never been a hole in the cellar. He suggested the hole was the indoor gardener's symbol for his own emptiness. The indoor gardener said Mr. Six had no idea what fullness is.

□

The indoor gardener quarreled with the day manager. She said he'd misunderstood his job. She said his job was to guarantee guests' safety and satisfaction. He said his job was to support htl-esc as it endured being itself. He said without someone to care for it a hotel cannot overcome the traumas that made it. He said a hotel is born of ravishing the ground. A hotel is a golem cobbled from dismembered bits of murdered trees and stones. Melamine, oils, excrement, animal bones run through a hotel's veins. Its bones are plastic, brick, glass, polyester, steel, dead vegetable. The indoor gardener said every tile, pipe, cushion remembered. The day manager said she hadn't hired him to indulge htl-esc's pseudopsychology. She'd hired him to conceal htl-esc's quasi–nervous breakdown. His duty was to protect guests and coworkers. She shouldn't have to spell out this basic fact.

Mr. Six told the indoor gardener the day manager was right. Mr. Six told me the day manager was wrong. She was wrong not to realize the indoor gardener was crying out for help. The indoor gardener didn't realize he was crying out for help. Mr. Six didn't realize until it was too late. Hindsight hinted that overwork, hostile colleagues, loneliness, stewing over past conflicts could've driven the indoor gardener to a breakdown. The indoor gardener refused a visit from his twin. He wrote he'd no space-time for visitations. He refused holidays.

Things disappeared from htl-esc. Drawer pulls, teacups, figurines. The day manager saw a guest with a huge conch shell from the spa. The guest didn't know the shell was in her bag. The day manager received gold snail shells in the mail from former guests who didn't want to be accused of stealing. They'd found the snails in their luggage when they'd unpacked. The maintenance department found gold snails in sinks and vents. The indoor gardener called them hitchhiker snails. He said they were expressions of htl-esc's desire. Mr. Six said guests pinched souvenirs and felt bad later. He told the indoor gardener to stop pretending htl-esc was more than it was. He'd gone too far by quarreling with guests, coworkers, managers. The indoor gardener said he'd never thought he'd hear his twin call him a liar.

◻

I shouldn't feel anything. Not feeling is a crucial safety precaution. It shouldn't hurt to imagine Mr. Six's twin lying down beside an empty pit that he'd stopped trying to fill. It shouldn't matter that Mr. Six's twin looked just like Mr. Six.

The indoor gardener emailed that he'd woken up beside the hole. He didn't remember lying down in the cellar. Mr. Six was angry with his twin for believing he'd turn against him. He was angry with himself for losing patience with his twin. He didn't believe the indoor gardener slept in the cellar while the furniture tree grew.

Nobody saw it grow. Everybody saw its terrible maturity. The in-door gardener said it was a break between reality and knowledge. Mr. Six told me it made the break between himself and the indoor gardener undeniable. The furniture tree illuminated their mutual distrust. Distrust meant the twins no longer shared a mind. The indoor gardener wrote in capitals as if he knew he'd be unheard. EVERYBODY SAW IT. Mr. Six wrote that the indoor gardener or-chestrated the catastrophe to prove something.

The furniture tree appeared overnight in the biggest restaurant. Things came from all over htl-esc. Things climbed one another, knotted, fused, conjoined their bodies in the shape of a grand tree. Chair backs were leaves. Legs became boughs. Eggbeaters, blenders, pillows, showerheads, cutlery, cushions, trowels, security cameras, pipes were foliage. Tables, chaises, rugs, desks, trays, lawn mow-ers were the trunk. Veins were computer cable, television cable, garden hose. An ooze flowed through the veins glowing magenta. Carpethuggers snaked between bookshelf bark, barstool boughs, fabric flowers. Carpethuggers plaited through the trunk, swirled between branches, sank roots into the floor, thrust roots into the ceiling. Carpethuggers glowed magenta.

Department managers stood at the bottom of the tree. They shouted at the indoor gardener. The indoor gardener was ecstatic. The furni-ture tree was the most magnificent thing he'd ever seen. He wrote the tree appropriated the managers' shouting as a forest appropriates breezes to make its voice. Guests gathered around and marveled. They put pictures of the tree online. The indoor gardener challenged Mr. Six to see the pictures. The indoor gardener dared Mr. Six to wonder if a human or covert human team could've built such a tree.

The day manager was incensed. She said the catastrophe was due to the indoor gardener's overindulgence. She ordered him to oversee the tree's immediate dismantling. She ordered all departments to as-sist. The indoor gardener was appalled that she'd kill the furniture tree. She asked him where the restaurant's guests were supposed to sit. The indoor gardener said chairs weren't only for guests. He said chairs existed for themselves. He said a tree was a chair's dream and ancestral memory. A tree was a dream and memory of a hotel. A tree was the potential of a hotel and a chair. The day manager said the indoor gardener must discharge the irregularity or leave htl-esc. The indoor gardener said he'd defend the tree with his last breath.

La Blue Boite

The furniture tree rose up from the depths of a memory that didn't belong to Mr. Six. The furniture tree as the indoor gardener's memory rose up from far away. It hurled Mr. Six into a pit of silence.

Mr. Six slumped like a used napkin. He told me in a used-up voice that to this day he tries to listen for his twin. He tries to feel between them for the truth. He feels deep silence like a black hole in a dark ravine.

Mr. Six said he dreamed the indoor gardener climbed the tree. The indoor gardener linked arms with chairs. He parried chain saws with his body. They rang out like metal against metal when they struck him. Mr. Six dreamed the indoor gardener didn't climb the tree. He stood in front of it, shouting, till they took him away. Mr. Six dreamed his twin was back where he'd started but run through with holes. Mr. Six dreamed the furniture tree lay in wait for the indoor gardener. Mr. Six dreamed the furniture tree collapsed on his brother. htl-esc rained down in pieces on its beloved indoor gardener because the world couldn't fit them. They perished together.

Mr. Six didn't believe any of his dreams. He knew of no reality with which to compare them. He knew he'd never again believe anything that looked to him like reality.

□

The indoor gardener never wrote to Mr. Six again. He answered none of Mr. Six's frantic messages. htl-esc's receptionists said a manager would call him back. Nobody called back. Rumors about htl-esc didn't appear online. htl-esc continued winning good reviews. Mr. Six was sure his twin was safe at htl-esc. He was sure his twin was homeless, banished from htl-esc. He dreamed of htl-esc fusing chairs, confusing transmissions, severing corridors, drinking colors. He dreaded that his twin was lost even if the indoor gardener was safe.

Mr. Six decided to book a room at htl-esc. The hotel's website was gone. The consortium didn't list htl-esc among its holdings. Nobody answered the telephone. Mr. Six flew to htl-esc's city. His taxi driver said he'd heard from another driver that htl-esc was closed because of problems with floors and ceilings. The driver said htl-esc must have negligent managers. He said problems requiring major renovations don't pop up overnight. I don't understand how htl-esc's closure didn't attract attention. Mr. Six suspected the consortium of a cover-up.

Memories of visiting htl-esc damaged Mr. Six. Needing to tell them damaged him. His telling was broken and scattered. He said htl-esc was a ruin. A ruin is a remainder. Nothing holds a remainder to itself except itself.

I imagine Mr. Six riding a long way in the taxi. The river runs along the road on one side. A big wall runs along it on the other side. That's wrong. Mr. Six said the river was behind htl-esc, not in front like at the Boite. I have trouble not imagining htl-esc with the river boxing it in. I have trouble not imagining htl-esc as a lockbox made of crisscrossings with a riddle for a key and all-blank faces so you can't tell what the riddle is. The gatehouse was empty. I wonder if Mr. Six had to climb the gate. He didn't say how he got through the maze. Contractors maybe tied orange tapes to trees. Bulldozers might've flattened the trees to make a path. Trucks could've dragged the furniture tree to the road.

I couldn't ask Mr. Six. He was staring into a hole with a gap in it with a night in the gap and a hole in the night. I topped up his whiskey. It was all a broken bartender could do.

htl-esc

They said the indoor gardener climbed the furniture tree. He climbed till they couldn't see him. He didn't come back down.

Mr. Six didn't say who they were. He spoke as if he'd been alone at htl-esc. He wasn't alone. Somebody showed him things. He didn't say whether they mistook him for the indoor gardener or his ghost. They didn't say whether they worked for the consortium or someone else. Mr. Six was too afraid to ask if they'd seen the indoor gardener. Mr. Six spoke as if he'd stepped out of the taxi into a world like a dream where there were only interiors. He said they took him to the furniture tree.

It wasn't the spectacular thing he'd seen online. It wasn't a ruin. The furniture tree had overshot the ruin phase of its destruction. It just wasn't anymore. It was a pile of indistinguishable rubble. They'd built scaffolds through the ceiling. Hammering noises cluttered the air. It took time to reduce the furniture tree to rubble. The rubble must've meant the indoor gardener hadn't been at htl-esc for a while. The rubble must've meant he'd come down from the tree.

Mr. Six didn't say so. I had to suppose. Mr. Six didn't say he suffered nightmares of his twin absorbed by htl-esc into the tree and ground up with the tree into rubble. He didn't say discovering his twin had vanished felt like waking to discover he himself didn't exist. He didn't need to say. I knew because I've done that kind of waking.

Someone showed Mr. Six the indoor gardener's attic. It wasn't a dwelling. It was a storeroom. Garden shears, pliers, watering cans, stethoscopes, telescopic pruners, shovels, microphones. Wrenches, buckets, paintbrushes, dental mirrors, pipettes, ophthalmoscopes, spanners, hand rakes, hatchets, pots, lengths of wire, bags of soil, ropes, tubes, hand mirrors, tuning forks, floss, screwdrivers, carpet knives, otoscopes, magnifiers. A mess of dead plant matter was on the windowsill. Flowers blue and purple were in the mess. Mr. Six's nose knew the rotting leaves were leaves. His fingers knew the flowers were polyester. They had frayed edges like old clothes. His eyes knew the fake flowers and real leaves were one plant. Something made him feel the flowers were alive. The leaves were dead. The plant wasn't dead and wasn't living.

Mr. Six fled the attic. He decided the indoor gardener must be hiding in htl-esc. The indoor gardener wouldn't abandon htl-esc to be gutted. The indoor gardener would've felt abandoned by the twin who shared his mind. Mr. Six decided the indoor gardener was nursing rubble in some corner. Mr. Six ran through corridors screaming his brother's name and not seeing the corridors, carpets, paintings, doors, mirrors, stairs, cafés, wallpapers, glowing nightcrawlers, dreameating clematis, eye-of-vampyr mushrooms. He was hurtling through an impossible forest. He was tumbling through somewhere that didn't exist. Mr. Six felt an angry listening stinging him. He forgot whether he was questing or escaping. He remembered forgetting to look in rooms. He thought maybe he was looking for the cellar. He remembered a synthetic chemical smell. It kept growing stronger. He ran into a gray door with a push bar.

□

He was in a grotto with black boulders, dark grasses, greenriver milfoils, deep-space mosses, mora vitulium, cobblersbane. A swimming pool was in the grass in the grotto. Trees closed in overhead, mood indigones, cotazuris. The sky was leaves. The pool was in half-light. It was a hotel-quality pool made to look like a grotto.

It looked like it had never known a maintenance department's touch. The water was brown. It was full of giant lily pads and reeds, nightswimmers, veratrum konterfei, saturn mushrooms. Vines were everywhere, hemp apocybane, midnight chanteuse. They clutched the trees. They seemed to be at one another's throats. The pool smelled like a swamp. The synthetic chemical smell lay under and over the swamp smell. The chemical smell was strong. It was trying to lure Mr. Six into the forest. The forest was a black wall beyond the pool. The forest was black as a pit. Mr. Six shouted for the indoor gardener.

A jackhammer started inside the hotel. Mr. Six went into the forest. He didn't think his twin would hide in the forest. He realized he didn't know the indoor gardener. He thought maybe the listening followed him into the forest. He couldn't remember for certain. He said the forest was sullen. Plants tangled with one another. Everything seemed bigger than it should. Mr. Six thought he remembered violets ten times the size of violets, vines glowing blue with red and purple thorns, mushrooms like octopuses. He didn't trust his memory. He didn't trust his senses. Darkness and the chemical smell overwhelmed everything. The spiteful stink infuriated Mr. Six. It bullied him through the forest. He went thrashing through the forest. He said he had no objective. He just lashed out at the forest. He threw himself at the smell.

The forest ejected him onto the riverbank. The smell hung over the river in an invisible fog. The smell was in the river. Mr. Six couldn't remember the color of the river. The smell almost knocked him off his feet. His eyes recoiled from the withdrawal of the trees. The light and the river were maybe tough silver.

He remembered a boat on the river. Two people were in the boat. One of them pulled a thing out of the water. It was a dipstick with a test tube on the end. The people in the boat wore yellow hazmat suits. The light ricocheted from their uncontoured plastic faces. Mr. Six saw a factory on the far side of the river. He saw grimy cisterns and smokestacks without smoke.

□

The taxi driver had never heard of the industrial complex by the river. Mr. Six didn't trust his own mind. He felt ill. He wasn't himself. Mr. Six researched fertilizer, chemical, electrical, petroleum plants, pharmaceutical, plastic, furniture, paper manufacturers. He found no record of any factory behind htl-esc. Nobody at the consortium would speak to him. The authorities told him not to pester the consortium. Mr. Six no longer trusted his own eyes. He spent years looking for the factory. He spent seventeen years searching hotels around the world for the indoor gardener.

A great denial had taken place, a great effacement. All that's known of history is counterfeit. That's what Mr. Six said. I didn't want to say violations are victorious when smothered by denial. I didn't want to say most violations are victorious. That's why I cling to the Deity and fear the Deity. I wasn't drunk as I am now when I said those things to Mr. Six. I felt so much like myself that I was frightened.

La Blue Boite

Mr. Six's life is a remainder of htl-esc. He made a career of visiting hotels so he could search for the indoor gardener. Mr. Six built his life around that search. Every hotel terrifies him. He's afraid his twin might never have been there. He's afraid the indoor gardener might be there. He's devised tactics for gathering information about hotels' employees. Offering managers a shard of story is one tactic. The shard says a man who looked just like Mr. Six went to work for a hotel and was never seen again. The shard says this damaged man might seek refuge in other hotels. Every shard unleashes the story's full force on Mr. Six. htl-esc pursues Mr. Six through the story as Mr. Six pursues the indoor gardener. The pace of his pursuit decides the pace of his life. Each hotel is a long moment of anguish. His brother's absence drives him on and drains his will to go on.

Mr. Six lacked the courage to lay his shard of story before the Boiteuse. He knew after one night in the Boite that the indoor gardener hadn't been here. He sensed anyone seeking refuge in a hotel would stay with you forever. His story was useless here. It needed unleashing. The story's need flogged Mr. Six like a stone in the throat. He needed a listener who wouldn't scorn its hopelessness.

Listen. Mr. Six didn't tell me just because the story flogged him. Mr. Six told me about the hotel that stole his twin because I was afraid Mr. Six meant to possess you just like the indoor gardener

tried to possess htl-esc. Mr. Six wanted me to know he's no viola-
tor. He said he'd never wanted to tell his story for that reason before.
He'd never wanted to tell out of worry for someone who isn't the indoor gardener.

The force of the story frightened him. The story drove him
through itself as punishment. It absorbed and emptied Mr. Six. Mr.
Six's story made me well up in me and drove me through me. The
dead woman rose up like a zombie and chased your bartender through
me as she tried to chase down her story. I still don't know which
words were mine. I heard myself speaking about violation and denial.
Mr. Six looked at me speaking about violation and denial. I couldn't
stop speaking. I couldn't keep up with the story that was chasing me.
I didn't want to want to speak for the dead woman emanating me almost like the indoor gardener emanated the despair of Mr. Six.

I don't want to believe Mr. Six. I don't want to believe he was listening to me. I don't want to feel I understand him. I've betrayed
his confidence by telling you his story. I did it because I don't want
his confidence. I did it because you're the Boite and I'm drunk. I'm
drunk because I'm afraid of Mr. Six. I'm afraid of myself and Mr. Six.
I'm too much like the indoor gardener. I know his yearning for the
love of htl-esc. Mr. Six doesn't want to be missing. Mr. Six wants to
be present to someone. He's not used to not belonging to anyone
even after seventeen years of being alone. I'm a remainder of errors. I
want to stay missing. That's what Mr. Six couldn't understand about
the indoor gardener. He suspects it now he's told me the story and
I've told him too much.

I shouldn't have wanted to say anything to him. He didn't stop
looking at me while I was talking. Mr. Six's look wasn't a lie. He wanted
me to give him permission to be vulnerable. He looked at me as if I
could help him survive truths. I shouldn't have let him see we're both
exhausted from being afraid.

Mr. Six is wandering the city now like a lost dog. I'm drinking on
duty. We're afraid of counterfeit senses. He's out in the snow. People
fall down in the snow. Everyone has poor visibility. Somebody who

wants a victim could mistake Mr. Six for the one they want. I'm afraid of him returning. I'm afraid of him never returning. Last night Mr. Six reached across the bar in anguish. I gave my hands to Mr. Six in anguish. Mr. Six spoke the name the Boiteuse gave me. Mr. Six asked me what my furniture tree was.

□

I don't have a furniture tree. I have the man who killed me. I have letters from somebody claiming to be my child. The letters want to possess me. You're the Boite. I'm your possession. That's why I'm talking to you. Your being the Boite must've drawn me to my surface. The will in my words even then could've been yours.

I wasn't drunk when I told Mr. Six about the beating, goring, gouging, soiling, searing pain, pain that hurls me into nightmares, shocks me out of nightmares. It was my fault for not escaping. My escape wasn't escape. Running, bleeding, fainting in the street, finding myself in an ambulance, not knowing how, were all just half a moment in an endless night.

The man who did it left his waste in me. The waste grew into a thing I hated. I thought the Deity would punish me if I expelled it. The Deity punished me for not expelling it. I told Mr. Six how it ate me, battered me, hated me from inside me. It gorged on me till it was too huge for me to carry or expel. Pain almost stopped my heart. I fled the result as soon as I could walk. I left it in the hospital. The man who killed me doesn't know he left a remainder and result. The result isn't my child. It's my agony and death. I'm not the woman who died and ran. I'm furniture of La Blue Boite. I belong to the Boite and the Boiteuse.

I told Mr. Six because I wanted to repulse him. I told it to the end because I was terrified that Mr. Six would be repulsed. Mr. Six wasn't repulsed.

Mr. Six is angry with the man who killed me. He's angry at the person who's attacking me with letters. The Boiteuse thinks Mr. Six went out in the snow because of me. She thinks Mr. Six is prowling around the Boite. She thinks he's trying to see who'll deliver the next letter. She said a quest will be good for Mr. Six. She doesn't know about the indoor gardener. She said a rich man who clings to the Boite must be disappointed in himself. She thinks it'll be good for him to focus his feelings elsewhere.

She said it was good for me to tell Mr. Six my story. It's been eleven or eighteen years since I came to the Boite. That was the last time I let my story unleash me. I told the Boiteuse she shouldn't say such things. Mr. Six is a guest of the hotel. The Boiteuse said the snow is changing what it means to be a guest or a hotel.

Mr. Six is watching for the local too. The Boiteuse and I are watching. The Boite watches with blue glass windows. Mr. Six and I were fools. We forgot about the local.

The local broke into the story. She asked what else went missing from htl-esc. She asked what disappeared besides hitchhiker snails.

□

I don't think you'd wrap your walls around me if I needed to never be seen again. I wish I believed you would. I don't know if you care. I don't know if I'd defend you to the death. I'm not the indoor gardener. You're not htl-esc. You're my refuge or you're just the box that holds the feeling that there's listening inside the hole in the night in the emptiness of me. You're the walls that block the snow but not the letters. You're my present moment that keeps out the past and future. You were a steady moment till Mr. Six revealed that I don't know you. I don't know how to know if you're listening. The feeling that someone's listening could just be a memory of the local. You are the door that let the local in.

The thing the local is pursuing must be a white box.

I'm uncertain. I don't care. I don't care what the local wants. The box if it's a box reaches across time and space to interfere with other things because that's the way things are.

Mr. Six said this morning that the box drained the local's strength from far away. Her quest to find the box drained her energy to go on. Mr. Six said that deprivation drove her on. That lack is a break in the seams that hold her together. Mr. Six says this weakness is her energy. Vulnerability is her power. The box also has that power. It's vulnerable because the local is looking for it.

Her breaking into our stories felt like being hit by a truck. My story and Mr. Six's story were raw. The local didn't care about our anguish. The local eavesdropped. She grazed in our stories like they were fields and she was a wild horse. She swallowed our stories and inside her broke them down to feed her anguish. She lay in wait until nothing was left of us except remainders of stories. I gave Mr. Six my hands because there was no other way for us not to disintegrate.

Mr. Six didn't answer the local's question about hitchhiker snails. She started asking questions about the furniture tree. Mr. Six and I were too shattered to pay attention. Mr. Six asked her to leave us. The local said Mr. Six didn't understand. She said she needed to understand how hitchhiker snails hitchhiked. She needed to know if they were really snails. She needed desperately to understand the furniture tree. We think she was asking because of the box.

Mr. Six and I believe the box possessed the local. She's afraid of it because she's drawn to it. She's drawn to it because she's terrified of it. I think the box is like the letters. The local needs the box to disguise what she wrote. It unfolds like the indoor gardener's knot into a book of names or the local's final will and testament. Whatever she wrote includes a secret she shouldn't have known. She found a secret and tried to tame it with understanding. The secret found a gap in her understanding. The secret escaped through the gap. The local realizes she has no right to that secret. Her writing down the secret was a violation. She wants to find the box she wrote in so she can drop it in the snow. She wants to finish her violation and deny it. The snow will cover it forever. She thinks that means she can escape it.

I neglected to take precautions. I didn't tell the local that she had to leave the Boite because the bar was closed. Mr. Six held my hands.

He told the local we were having a private conversation. He knew there was one more letter. He knew I hadn't told him about the letter that had come that very night. It said the letter writer had robbed a shop at knifepoint.

◻

I don't know why a stranger would confess a crime to me. I don't care. I want them to disappear. The letters try to use the crime that was left in the hospital to cover up the crime that was done to me. They try to cover their own crimes by pretending my escape was criminal.

Last night's letter said the writer robbed a shop in the city's foulest armpit. It didn't name the shop. It didn't say what kind of shop it was. The shop had a white box made of crisscrossings. The criminal made the shop people play switchblade blackjack for it. The criminal took the box away and then wrote me a letter.

The letter said the criminal didn't know how to open the box. It said the box had too many crisscrossings. I shouldn't have told Mr. Six. I told him the letter said the criminal saw one way to open the box. It said they were going to break it open with the switchblade. The local leaped over the bar. She grabbed me by the throat. She slammed me against the sink. She demanded to know where the box was. Mr. Six dragged her away. The local demanded to know who the criminal was, where the letters came from. Mr. Six was shouting to make her leave. I was shouting that she'd better not come back.

What I said about the local was a contradiction that wasn't. She needs to save the box before the criminal stabs it with the switchblade. She needs to destroy it in her own way. She needs to see the snow soak through it. She needs to see readability bleed out of the secret. She needs to be the sole witness to the drowning of what nobody should know.

The Boiteuse came running. Mr. Six told her about the local. Mr. Six saw my head was bleeding. Bottles from above the sink had fallen on my head. Blood and liquor were in the sink. Things on the bar were broken. Liquor fell on me and on the floor. Liquor is expensive. The bar was a mess. It was my fault. The Boiteuse said it wasn't. I said there would've been no letters if I'd escaped. Mr. Six said the letters are insane. He said a box you can't open is a pit in a night in a hole in a bottomless pit.

Mr. Six and the Boiteuse made me lie in a booth. Bartenders aren't supposed to lie in booths. Booths are for guests. The Boiteuse cleaned the bar. You didn't make the bar stop the local. You wrapped me in a booth after as if you'd changed your mind. You are aloof as if you're not listening. You've heard everything. You're La Blue Boite. You must be listening. I don't know. I don't know. Mr. Six made an ice pack. Mr. Six held the ice on my head. Mr. Six didn't slap me for sobbing. Mr. Six put his leg under my head. Mr. Six only held my hand and stroked it to try to make me feel safe. He sat still. He was gentle.

Icon

Of course you want to know about the murder. The noise has died, the noisemakers moved on to the devil knows what new atrocity, but anyone with half an ear knows the noising off only skimmed the heart of the matter, the noisemakers refusing to concede the dubiousness of their "witness," simply noising off to the whole city, which paid little attention, having other problems to worry about including other murders, and what's the use of paying attention to noising off that admits no useful information? In a way the story itself is inadmissible because it isn't a "whole" story, even involves "partial" people, and nobody cares about misfits killing misfits because their refusal to get on with it and *function* like other people makes them useless except as curiosities, and in the present emergency who has time for curiosities! The events themselves tell us nothing about anything, not even about themselves, beyond the fact of their occurrence, as in "It happened, so it happened" or "The fact that this occurred means that it occurred," meaning the occurrence has no meaning, meaning there is nothing to be gleaned from it, it's of no use and is therefore irrelevant. The only salient aspects of this murder were its location in physical space and the fact that Civilization, even the human condition, is built upon corrugated fiberboard boxes of undented perfection, which contain, secure, convey, even symbolize that which enables the city to exist and the reason for which it exists: in short, the very soul of the city. This indoor shopping mall through which we stride is among our city's greatest features because here the city's soul is alive and cherished—Commerce!—engine of progress, sire of growth, dynamo of the Civilized spirit. And what do you see here all around us? Boxes! Boxes in boxes within boxes. And do you think anybody notices that boxes are where and what they live and wherefore? *Never in their lives* unless they're privileged to have an inside view. And you know, even most people with an inside view are idiots who don't so much as glance at what's in front of them. Or at the opposite extreme, fools who drive everybody cuckoo with useless questions about nonsense. The worthlessness of usefulness, the unfairness of Civilization, the future of democracy or some such nonsense, the purpose of Commerce as if such a thing requires questioning, abstract consequences of this or that which nobody understands and what about the penguins? Maddening. Superfluous. When everybody knows that time is money therefore wasting time with useless questions betrays the city's very *soul*! Here in this shopping mall, which is itself a perfect rectangle, other rectangles function as nests or pistons of Commerce wherein manufacturers make offerings and desires, trends and futures.

Only look at this shoe shop. Here citizens discover the joy of being accepted by Civilization because they fit into Civilized, flawlessly homogeneous, democratically mass-manufactured shoes. And the rectangular aisles of the rectangular shop are delineated by walls built to average-shoulder height of which the very bricks are boxes; boxes enabling all shoes of the same style to line up one above the other in a pedestal, the crown of which is an exemplar shoe of average size. In place of that efficient pedestal, what would you have there without boxes? Chaos! Only look at that ridiculous, lopsided shoe with the elevated backside. You can see from here it's a shoe for old women. Now, I ask you, if there were no boxes to contain such a shoe, how could other shoes stand upon it without toppling? Impossible! It's too crooked to hold up anything! You wonder what could be the point of such a shoe, and well, it is itself a kind of box, informative packaging that enables you to categorize a woman just as the boxes here, their ability to follow and build up to the exemplar in orderly fashion, and of course their markings, their brand names, enable you to categorize the shoes; and because categorization is meaning, is actually the meaning of meaning, there exists nothing more meaningful than rectangular classificatory packaging, just so, as the means by which things are rendered capable of meaning ("meaningfulness" and "utility" being synonymous, as is doubtlessly self-evident). And so let us walk on. I come here every day, you know, for the stimulation of vigorously circuiting this shopping mall. Executive HQ permitted my fitness-club membership to lapse, but the error shall be shortly rectified and in the meantime I must remain in optimum condition. My reinstatement as Sub-Executive Supervisor of CytyBox 3937 is *imminent*, as is a *battle* to preserve the metropolitan way of life from useless terrorists who'd threaten Freedom. Those who battle shan't have time to carry unproductives into the future; the *future* is the *survival of the fittest*, people embodying perfection, devotion to Commercial vocations *including organized fitness*; in short, people with the wherewithal to *stamp out weakness* are *exclusively* worthy to fight for Freedom against anti-Commercial elements: the future has no room for old women, wishy-washy intellectuals, nor indeed anybody who is not a *true metropolitan*, a man who *in himself* is nothing more or less than the soul of the city! After all, why pretend the basic constitutive principle of the city and even of Civilization has ever been other than exclusion? Especially when vital systems are disrupted from without (and disruptions of a system always originate outside the system, never within, for otherwise there'd even be no such phenomenon as a system), the citizens of a true and proper Civilization rise to its defense by rallying *together as one* against the enemy and the useless: our union is *by definition their expulsion*, and only as a union can a Civilization survive, as a union *committed* to *perpetual motion, production, and expansion*, to gathering even the remotest deserts under the unflagging wing of Commerce, mobilizing the empty-seeming dunes in Capital's unending battle against emptiness, wherefore I say Civilization constitutes *by definition* the operational logistics of Commerce, the living logistics of Freedom itself! But we're talking about noisemakers. Morons. I would not disrupt my training for their convenience. I made them scurry through these corridors as quickly as their legs could carry them, for a Sub-Executive Supervisor is *beset* with vigorous responsibilities: one may be called upon to pack or load any manner of thing and often enough it's only supervisors who have any idea how a thing ought to be managed. Those good-for-nothings forbore to print a word I said, simply babbled without regard for the facts, so even if you pored over everything that was shouted out and scribbled about this murder, you'd have no idea what happened or what was at stake. You'd have a head full of rumor, which is as good as nothing at all. I warned them, I personally advised them to consider that although the victim appeared to be an unproductive nobody, what sort of person is an enemy agent most likely to be? Obviously someone who, from the point of view of the city that is *her* victim, contributes decidedly nothing, the aim of an enemy agent being sabotage. Of course, this is only one hypothesis of the victim's identity, regarding which there exist only hypotheses, which is not to say the murderers are justifiable, certainly not: egregious moral degeneracy is rampant in all of them and they have only themselves to blame. But the truth is, well, nobody would mistake the victim for a damsel in distress. If you've seen her unfortunate picture in the news—a sketch, of course, for no pictures were found of this person as a living being, nobody's come for her remains, it's been too long now for anyone to want the bother. She carried no identification, her nose and teeth were crushed, her skull caved in. The artist had to reconstruct. And you know artists err on the side of generosity but, in short, this was not a pretty or even normal woman. She had a certain tooth. Unfortunately it was in the front of her mouth, where it was, one has to say, revoltingly prominent. This tooth, even before the beating, was marred, broken, twisted not at all in a becoming way. She'd more black hair than the artist knew what to do with. And her eyes weren't real eyes but sort of placeholders for eyes, the flat eyes, open but closed, which result from an artist having no idea what expression to put in them, this official artist having known the woman in question only, well, inertly, as a thing in a refrigerated drawer. The noisemakers nevertheless did agree on certain details. First: *she* arrived at CytyBox 3937 around midday. I wasn't there, nobody was supposed to be there, 3937 as you know is closed. HQ saw fit to suspend its operations as a concession to the "snow," a concession that shall at any moment be revoked. As to why *she* turned up at 3937, that was not reported. The detectives reasonably supposed that I, as Sub-Executive Supervisor with intimate knowledge of 3937's qualities, would have some idea regarding her intentions; but my hypothesis that she was an enemy agent who'd infiltrated the city only to be infiltrated by it, consequently going rogue and cracking up, permitting her search for something useful and sabotage-worthy to degenerate into a pointless pursuit of something meaningless, seemed not to satisfy the august champions of the law, who put forward no better ideas. She managed to gain ingress not entirely because, unbeknownst to me, 3937 had snagged the attention of some sort of residual children, adolescents from that public school, the one that closed, for which again we must blame "snow." Continuous "snow" for months on end is enough to overwork many a boiler, and you should note that it is happening all over the city, it's what happened to the school. There was no disaster, it's all temporary, but the school remains nonoperational and has unleashed all sorts of young persons upon the city without anything to do. The public libraries are launching some initiative. You know all the schools have doddery old boilers. But children don't want libraries; children want computer games that let them play at wreaking havoc, and where they cannot have computer games (if for instance their inane progenitors subscribe to the ludicrous rumor, surely instigated by the enemy, that electricity must soon be *rationed*) nowadays even the most inflated bullies are too indolent to endure the cold, the wet, and above all the loss of face which, courtesy of the snow, would result from their inevitably public slip, slide, and smack onto the sidewalk were they to attempt wreaking havoc in the streets. Thus and so, we must contend with gangs of children hanging about in shopping malls. You see them there, fourteen or seventeen years old, draping like cobwebs over coin-operated baby rockers. Security forces here are diligent; bored children tend to shoplift. I've seen several apprehended, and so far this mall has seen only a knife attack or two. But some of these dispossessed creatures contrived in the weeks prior to the murder to break into CytyBox 3937. I had no idea. As I say, HQ, with Commercial prudence, had rendered "redundant" 3937's employees until such time as objective conditions call for reinstatement. I've made it known that I stand ready to remobilize at any hour, at an instant's notice to throw open the doors of Outpost 3937 of the global Commercial movement known as Metropolitan Professional Packing and Express Shipping, also known as CytyBox! The final snowflake could descend *at any moment* as soon as the enemy is unmasked. A public accusation by the city would bring the enemy to its knees, it couldn't possibly be otherwise: when cries of outrage bear their name across the world, they'll no longer have the strength to hide behind this mockery of winter, and the last snowflake will fall, the roads, river, and sky will clear, and Commerce will cast off and take wing once again in professionally packed corrugated fiberboard! HQ, farsighted in all things, must know I'm correct that things will come to pass just so, because far from stripping 3937 of the materials required for springing into action they instructed me to seal 3937 with its inventory intact, doubtless in anticipation, despite the claims of certain people, that Freedom's enemy shall be foiled and with that victory our city will have seen the last of this odious so-called "snow"! Thus I sealed 3937, confiscated every key, secured *all keys at the bank* in a safety deposit box because of course HQ is in another city, and here, you know, the snow, the roads, the post office, the devil, thus and so, it had to be the bank. I must've been here at my training when the residuals invaded. The school, you know, identified them as *the* most undesirable of all the undesirables who'd no interest in learning anything beyond how to establish savage hierarchies that prevent terrorized children from learning and teachers from teaching. The noisemakers reported that this undesirable quartet, two boys, two girls, "used" 3937 during the day, returning to their parents' dens at night, and what insolence! For weeks, those wicked squanderers—to this day, I can hardly bring myself to speak of it—at least a certain "witness" gave me to understand that these invaders constructed towers (towers!) from the biggest, *most valuable and precious fiberboard boxes in inventory*, built these horrifying structures *to the ceiling*! And then as if in contempt for everything, the vandals climbed the towers to the summits and *threw themselves* therefrom, their worthless hides crashing into polystyrene peanuts, polyethylene air-cushion film, brand-new boxes of paperboard, fiberboard, *essential and expensive* materials, which the villains gathered into a perverse sort of swimming pool. Everything was ruined, so they did it all again, rebuilt towers and pool, climbed and flung and crashed, rebuilt; and when they tired, they attacked every surface with markers, obscene sentiments, hideous glorifications of themselves, nasty vilifications of everything else. In short, terrifying devastation, indiscriminate destruction. And you know, if they who call themselves metropolitans can *destroy* organs of Commerce with contemptuous glee, then what counts as a true metropolitan must be reconsidered and enforced, and it should hardly surprise anyone that whether or not they perceived some threat in the unidentified stranger they—on this point, I'm afraid there is no question: one of the vandals stabbed the woman with a switchblade, which she, the killer, just so happened to have on hand; another stabbed her with a Premium Spring-Assisted AllPurPRO knife he'd unearthed at 3937; a third knocked her down from behind, breaking her skull with a fire extinguisher; and the fourth, a girl who's with child by one of the boys, stood on the victim's head and throat while she lay suffering. These horrors, just so, were forensically confirmed. And then the "witness" whom the killers in their frenzy somehow forgot but whose credibility is partial at best and who in any case witnessed only some of the brutalities, leaving the rest to be deduced by the coroner, this "witness," also known as a "giftwrapper," fled while the murder was ongoing. Fled by the rear entrance where vigorous trucks of the CytyBox fleet once traded unpackaged merchandise for the beautifully packed and insured boxes that with expert skill and devotion I had made ready. Well, and so certain screaming, stabbing, and beating she claims to have been privy to firsthand, but of the denouement she has no notion, having bolted at a whiff of danger. She telephoned the police when she'd reassured herself of her personal security; but she's a slow sort, she took almost too long, the killers absconded before the first responders could respond. Fortunately the police had a dossier on one of them from a past offense, and so his fingerprints, you know. And the public school, the teachers, named his usual entourage, produced addresses, everything. The quartet was arrested within hours and within hours released again, pending trial, without any consequences save their passports' confiscation and their expulsion from school. And the noise, of course. My god! It was proposed that the murderers claimed to be innocent purely out of spite. It was proposed that they *were* innocent even though they'd killed somebody whom they didn't even know. It was proposed that the victim brought it on herself. It was assumed, given the highways' and airport's incapacitation, that the victim wasn't a foreign agent but a resident, even a sort of "uncategorized citizen," however oxymoronic, of our wronged city (and we must refer to her just so, in deference to the detectives, who as ministers of the law are caretakers of Civilization). It was propounded that our great city failed the victim and the killers both, the former because she lacked categorization, documentation, and employment, the latter on account of a tax-funded boiler. But really all these "psychosocial commentaries" are beside the point. I would not call 3937 a "house of art," but it is surely a piston of culture. What else moves the things of culture, phones, computers, wines, medications, vital organs of automobiles; by what means other than professional packing and shipping are the *things* of life disseminated, the things big and small, clanging and fuming, that make the city roil and glimmer, the things in short that make the city *the city*? I won't say it's an art, Commerce hasn't time for art, but the *skill* of packing and shipping requires so many special attributes which intellectuals would call *talents* that even such gratuitous persons must know my work for a kind of genius. The foremost special attribute of a professional packer is *unquestioning respect*. You might have at your workstation the stupidest object imaginable. A woolen cactus. A miniature sofa that makes your phone appear to be a spaceship captain. I tell you, I've packed everything. I've personally handled the most vacuous and extravagant objects that even have no business going about in boxes, things you'd never believe it possible to box, not even if you were the brainiest intellectual in the city; however, unlike a supersaturated smarty-pants, did I waste time wondering why such objects fell to me, why such inveterate nonsense should require professional packing and transmission, what reasonable purpose could be served by a pair of goggles that trick a person into believing they're a gun-toting cartoon? No! My business was to *believe* someone had a rationale for flying a secondhand history of pigeons across the globe in bespoke packaging. My business was to *find* that perfect packaging; and if the ideal box for, say, a floor lamp shaped after a giant zigzag didn't exist, it was my responsibility to make up the difference between the intemperate thing and a sensible box, which, though it may lack certain qualities of a zigzag, has the advantage of being extant and the vital virtue of rectangularity. The rebellion of the thing must be put down! Irregularity, nonconformity, resistance to containment must be smothered in polystyrene foam, polyethylene-encased air bubbles, ink-and-acid-free newsprint! Because, you know, I'll let you in on a certain secret: when a box cannot be found to suit a thing, it's never any box that is imperfect but the thing itself, the thing's insistence on excessive slipperiness or angularity, quite so, without exception, so that *if there is no box that can contain whatever thing, it follows that the thing should not exist*, for that there exist boxes for all things is a natural law of Commerce, *order* is alone the natural state of Commerce, and indeed Civilization exists *to stamp out disorder* wheresoever it appears in citizens or in things. Enforcing things' obedience to boxes is thus a vital responsibility to which, for example, giftwrapping is uncompromisingly subordinate. Giftwrapping *undermines* things' integrity by causing them to masquerade, making uncalled-for things seem necessary, but the professional packer is in a singular position with respect to gifts or, more importantly, purchases: I must take a thing that is not mine and prepare it for someone to whom it doesn't yet belong, having been sent away by someone else to whom it belongs no longer; I am handling a thing that at the moment is nobody's possession, a thing in a moment of absolute liberty, without any idea about the sender and recipient or what they hope to gain by sending and receiving this particular thing, without, in short, any insight on the thing's secrets, which I must nonetheless believe in and faithfully transmit to strangers. In contrast to giftwrapping, professional-quality packaging materials, homely though they appear, *preserve* a thing's integrity by enabling it to fit in a prefabricated container which elides the thing's physical ambivalences so that, in stacking well with others, moving among them without initiating or incurring disruption, the thing may function as a productive member of society. The container, that is, the box, relieves the thing of needless jutting, reducing its redundant irregularities to the smooth conveniences of the fiberboard rectangle. And when you think it through, the box *just so*, the box *as such*, emerges as an unsung but remarkable instrument of democracy, a vigorously democratic structure that *equalizes* every thing right down to the most superfluous, ridiculous, amorphous, and ambiguous into a constructive and dynamic Commercial organ! The Great Equalizer, a foundation of all that is democracy and Capitalism, *that's* what a box is, and the fates of thousands of them passed directly through my hands. Well, and so, that a woman was killed over a box is neither insignificant nor surprising. As the "unclaimed citizen" needed somewhere in which to belong, the undesirables desired the very arbiters of belonging to belong to them; hardly understanding what it was they wanted, having been proudly obtuse throughout their entire lives, they wanted to possess the very paradigms, in their most commendable and practicable material forms, for categorization and exclusion. What's truly egregious, however, is that because the superfluous lives of both killers and victim were empty of meaning; because, having no wish to contribute to Civilized progress, they had practically cultivated a lack of discernment: they clung to and even debased themselves in violence over a thing that in their ignorance they *misjudged* as an exemplar of the democratic structure that excluded them, or more precisely from which they'd excluded themselves. What could resound a more plaintive, exigent plea for the *immediate* reinstatement of CytyBox 3937? The enemy must be stopped. The roads and so on must reopen. If metropolitans are not to lose all sense of themselves, what's necessary and essential is the affirmation of the vital structure aforementioned, the vitality of which is instantiated by none other than the free and liberal movement of *things*. The desire to make and consume as many things as possible and even to invent things for people to desire, *this* is where the city's elemental momentum originates; this is what those misfits, who after all were citizens, murdered for and died for *even though they knew already* that they had failed their city. The killing at CytyBox 3937 manifests the clear and present danger that, if this debilitating "snow" is permitted to persist, the city will destroy itself. Only consider: from my workstation, equipped with my computer, wherein I maintain impeccable records of *every* incoming and outgoing item along with exhaustive documentation of *every* operational adjustment to which this obstinate "snow" has obligated CytyBox 3937, from my installation of SnowConqueror doormats to the termination of excess truck drivers, I could tell you *exactly* how long this so-called "snow" has besieged our mighty city; upon the instant of my remobilization (the computer, like the network whence it harvests information, being the property of CytyBox and not, you understand, my personal property) I'd prove to you *exactly* the duration of our city's torment! And yet people do exist, proof that the weak and stupid are already beginning to crack and go too far, morons not insignificant in number, who'd sooner put their faith in "snow counters": widgets that neither measure snow nor know how to count but, without warning or apparent cause, *pop up* on your screen brandishing up-to-the-millisecond accounts (rows of numbers separated by colons and inanely color-changing as they increase too rapidly for you to see) intending to quantify the monotony, the suspense, the uncalled-for protractedness of our condition which to the shortsighted seems interminable and to the timid seems hopeless. To this perfect torture instrument people with nothing better to do *voluntarily* subject themselves, thereby affirming what they would deny, namely that snow counters' appalling popularity and pretensions to exactitude are but symptoms of a general crack-up of which the pervasive *and unchecked escalation* is the *stupidest* and most unnecessary corollary of the unjust, unsporting, *unmeteorological deception* that this "snow" is practicing upon us! For what reason other than proliferating madness would these "snow counters" in any given moment *each display a different count!* Numbers, mathematics, "experts" who swear by numbers and mathematics are simply propagating madness, blindly following those fools who give themselves up to torment, as if conspiring to erode every last crumbling toehold left to rationality; for the question "How long have we endured this vile persecution?" has no bearing whatsoever on "How long must we *continue* to struggle *under siege* against the enemy's vile persecutions?"! Counting bygone moments, or in this case piling arbitrary numbers one atop the other in a great trash heap, offers no resistance and is even counterproductive. What citizens should be doing is marshaling their resources, vigor, electricity, *and brainpower* in readiness for the *imminent* moment that shall call upon all metropolitans to come together and with the might of our combined superiority *crush* Freedom's enemy forever! It is in short the supreme duty of every citizen *not to surrender* to the pestiferous crack-up! First the noisemakers giggled about snowmen and snowballs, then it was snow castles, snowstrain, "snow studies," *snowmadness* now becoming the favorite excuse for laziness, stupidity, arbitrariness, and forgetting not to go around barefoot out of doors, and what nonsense will they think of next? Snow worship? Snow activism? Snow gangs? Perhaps crimes against snow? Snow rights, I suppose, once everyone has gone irremediably cuckoo: "Citizens are snowflakes too!" and vice versa. Idiots. Do you see that woman? Look! I call her

Princess PowerPack. Isn't that clever? That store sells nothing but batteries. Vintage batteries, designer batteries, big and little batteries, any of which, had the "snow" not grounded the valiant CytyBox fleet, could've been purchased and delivered instantaneously to her door in safe and economical packaging with but a swipe and a tap. But alas, every day Princess PowerPack, not so surreptitious as she believes, visits that redundant store and buys what I call box-batteries, namely battery packs that look like ordinary boxes, cigarette cartons, boxes of playing cards or medication, so they will not tempt thieves if you have them on the table while patronizing the food court; and I've little doubt she visits *all* purveyors of box-batteries as often as she thinks she can manage it covertly, driven by old-womanish terror of unsubstantiated rumors of electricity rationing. (Come now, keep up the pace; the future won't await the dawdler's pleasure.) And this is the sort of deranged, superfluous conduct that's become rather too noticeable throughout the city, I'm sure you've observed, and that could certainly overwhelm the feebleminded demographic that, ample though it is, mustn't be permitted to overrun the sane. Princess PowerPack is a relatively benign example, but that may be only for the moment. Having forgotten death and children and that which nourishes the city body and soul, certain noisemakers are scampering in droves to the ZV building of all places; that art institute, or whatever it is, where some disgruntled profligates are supposedly holding some sort of sit-in. Of course, I don't believe a word. A sit-in outdoors in the snow? Ludicrous. Superfluous. Nobody would see them. They'd have to be perfect fools. Running rampant nevertheless is the rumor (what else can you call such deranged nonsense, even televised and broadcast?) that nobody can get into the ZV building or get out unless they are prepared to sally forth and *ram* a human barricade formed of unhinged artists, who believe the city at large, especially people with working brains and metropolitan priorities, to be sacrificing "art itself" to the "snow"; their puerile argument being that the government has yet to repair the district-heating system in the neighborhood of excessive galleries where the artists' works are freezing, moldering, cracking, disintegrating, and so on. Those with resources enough to shelter these superfluous objects have a *moral obligation* to do so, if you please: this is what the cuckoo "creatives" (who are supposedly all women) wish to impress upon the moneyed "uncreatives" running the ZV place by besieging the latter in their luxurious building. Thus the institute's disinclination to buy or rent and store *every last one* of these nutcases' mad creations is an ethical failing on the part of the cruel, irreverent, uncharitable museum or institute, whatever, which if you ask me is no less superfluous than the artists. This too, just so, is a relatively harmless example of the material consequences that could indeed result if the population's vague but increasingly unstable instability remains unmastered: this sense of too many minds scampering all at once unto the brink of their personal precipices—already certain people claim to feel it as a scentless sharpening, invisible growing, grinning shadow in the city's very air. But I was saying about the murder: the noisemakers failed to acknowledge the dreadful unreliability of the sole "witness," namely another partial, superfluous person, a parasite in fact. At the height of her career, she was one of my lowest subordinates, a packaging and customer support associate. She worked at CytyBox longer than I have lived, yet she never advanced beyond her entry-level post and even never wished to, remaining nonetheless "at large" far longer than reason dictated, HQ having formed an impression—well, and so to explain objectively: HQ rebranded Metropolitan Professional Packing and Express Shipping as "CytyBox" when its operations expanded onto the internet, then called "cyberspace"; and even today a customer may lodge an online request for some item to be collected from their residence or office, professionally packaged at one of those happy Outposts that yet thrive in foreign cities, and sent on to the customer's chosen destination with, should they desire it, appropriate giftwrapping. The last, I'm afraid, became an inordinately popular service among busy people who want to seem to care and so on, but with online services came online reviews, and 3937 was acclaimed above all for its giftwrapping, in other words for the mindless furbelowing which, demanding no mental exertions, was for a long time delegated to the subordinate aforementioned, and—well, to the devil with her! Miles of expensive fake-velvet ribbon, sparkly paper that falls to bits when you so much as look at it, and what for? Sentiment! Foppery! Well, and this *subordinate*, a vile old woman who excels at nothing so much as work that is no work at all, possesses a sort of mania for giftwrapping, a passion that other subordinates have been pleased to admire and that customers the world over have praised as "beyond exceptional"; and HQ even lost their heads over her "internationally acclaimed" giftwrapping, they sent a little trophy for her workstation, and then nobody would hear of permitting her to retire, never mind she's old enough to have spawned the Earth itself (only she didn't, of course, she's some sort of spinster or widow, wrinkly and measly as discarded food packaging). The one worthwhile result of 3937's provisional abeyance is this "giftwrapping specialist's" being finally made redundant, and at her age she's no right to sue for reinstatement. Lacking initiative and even bodily resources, she even refused to meet me at my shopping mall when I demanded an interview after the police. She insisted *I come to her* and subject myself to some odious cafeteria on the ground floor of the block of flats where she squanders her days. There I learned that although she and I and all of us had for some time languished in redundancy, that stupid little crone had *never stopped turning up* at 3937 *even after* I'd sealed the facility! How she infiltrated I've no idea, never had she been entrusted with a key, all keys being in the safety deposit box to which *never in a million years* could she gain admittance. She and the residuals weren't even squatters in the proper sense. Lacking the tenacity of those unwashed drunks of whom the trains, train stations, and even this, my shopping mall, are forever having to be cleared, the "giftwrapper" returned at night to her own home, returning again next morning to 3937, and the "children" witlessly imitated her superfluous back-and-forth. Yet as if it were the most natural thing in the world, she informed me that she'd gone there daily with her "work basket" because now that it was empty of people it was a nice quiet place for "spinning notions and fancies." Well do I remember this "work basket." Other subordinates liked to call it her "knitting basket," which set them to giggling as though that vile person were their sweet little granny. This basket, corpulent enough to bear a picnic for a dozen, had nothing to do with knitting, working, or even anything at all. It housed the things she concocted from stolen and discarded bits of paper, ribbon, tape, even costly paperboard. Right under one's nose she'd filch the bits and twist them, cut them, bend them, braid them, poke them, bringing forth from a perfectly reusable envelope, for instance, some little giraffe or warthog, flowers, miniature mermaids, "fey little things" she called them, stars, planets, abstract shapes that were even a bit arcane and creepy, but it's all nonsense! One shudders to imagine the *miles* of adhesive pressure-sensitive polypropylene tape squandered on affixing paper flowers to the heads of tiny paper elephants! If only you could see the twinkle in her eye that says, "I know something you don't know and I shan't tell you because it's too obscure for you"; the twinkle of *up-to-no-good*, that's what it is, and *nobody else noticed it*, not even the detectives! Sweet little granny, that's all they saw. Well, not a day went by but that I caught her twisting paper into squids or belladonnas and her evil twinkle gave me shivers. Not fearful shivers, never, I'm after all a man, but the shivers everybody gets when faced with the unnatural. She knew I saw through her; she turned her twinkle upon me with a twisty grimace that in her boundless insolence dared to *mock her Sub-Executive Supervisor.* And if you think twisty grimacing is no evidence of contempt, consider: that little witch infiltrated 3937 *on the very morning after I had sealed it!* The instant my back is turned, back she goes to her crimpy little corner. The electricity is disconnected, but scissors and tape, order forms, staples, envelopes, boxes lie all unprotected, ripe for scavenging. Back she goes to fabricating frippery as if I'd done nothing at all, as if my orders and even her termination papers were nothing to her! She even disdained to say how she got in, the devil. The main thing is 3937 was already compromised, betrayed *from within* before the killers ever got—well, here we are at the shoe store! We've accomplished a circuit of the shopping mall. And look! Not one snowflake on our heads. A refreshing state of affairs, wouldn't you say? Walk on! Pick up the pace!

There we are in the greasy spoon below her flat, the little old crone and I. She asks, "Have you ever spent time in a wasteland?" Our livelihood and vigor, CytyBox Outpost 3937, that horrid woman is pleased to call a *wasteland*. Worse than impertinence, it's even an outrage! And stupid! A wasteland is a wasteland because nobody spends time in it. Yet she even seemed to think this one unfortunate happenstance, the death of a residual nobody at the hands of other residual nobodies, effectively unhappened, invalidated, in a word *canceled* everything 3937 had been to us, to customers, HQ, the city itself. She went on about floating dust specks twinkling in useless half-light and silences on countertops. The stillness of sounds and things was something she felt she could almost gather in her hand "like the potential of a subtle magic," she said. Absolute rot. I always knew her "little things" were no-good instruments of some occult nonsense; what she called "knitting" must've been some ritual, some insane invocation of monstrosities that existed only in the darkness of her mind. Well, and so the undesirables got in too, found her at her useless "papercraft." She said to me (what vanity!) that it seemed the "children," the murderers-to-be, formed at first sight a striking impression of her as a "creature of the wasteland." They were uniformly thuggish: in pictures all four, male and female, seem to cultivate a forced, aggressive masculinity; they tried of course to frighten her with obscene insults. But the little old crone just looked at them, her twinkle glinted, her tricky hands went on with her dark knitting, and she even snickered, "hmhmhm," with her special malevolence— and it frightened them! Cowards! Fools! They never troubled her again, even avoided her. Only now and then, as you'd peep at a crocodile to make sure he's sleeping before you tiptoe by, one of them peeped into her little corner, peeped and ran away like a rascal ten years younger. She thought they regarded *her*, maker of bows, curler of ribbons, as an "enchanted forest creature" like "the sylvan sorceress whom you can only find when you are lost." She said the adolescents feared her with fairy tales' fear of the unknown, which, disdaining rational learning, they'd never supplanted. They stopped trying to get rid of her because, by her own estimation, she was the "guardian spirit of a forgotten forest." I asked by what uncanny feats she'd retained the bandits' misplaced awe. She made her "fey things," she said, and watched the "snow." Well, and so, pray tell, what did her observations yield? I'm even very interested in this "snow." I've made my own observations and naturally drawn astute conclusions. But other views interest me for their preposterousness, particularly insofar as I try to disillusion citizens of my acquaintance, the quicker to incite them to confront the government and demand the truth, immediate action. What are the facts, after all? Matched precipitation rate, matched evaporation rate, the former exceeding the latter by a *fixed* interval, every day the same *exactly*, for months without reprieve, because the air is somehow trapped at a certain temperature, a dangerous chill that is cold enough to explode pipes and boilers *but isn't cold enough to stop the snow*, which accumulates on the ground just enough to slow down everything to a stupid crawl. Traffic jams, the airport closes, docks shut down, everyone's confounded, beginning to crack and so on, babbling that the river is a gluttonous serpent that's going to slurp us all down now it's gobbled vast hotels and stevedore cranes. Talk of serpents only spreads with fear. And it's even about time! Not for fear, of course, fear and going cuckoo are superfluous, but for acknowledgment of the *facts*: this "snow" is not "irregular" but *malevolent*, not an accident, no freak of nature but a *crime*! Villainy! Sabotage! Only think on it. This whatever-it-is, "precipitation," has wrought enough damage to grind the city's infrastructure to a halt in a gruesome drawn-out spasm and thus, in short, to get Commerce in a chokehold. But no more! Forced unemployment, mechanical breakdowns, shortages, traffic accidents, plumbing-induced dispossessions, snowmadness, pneumonia, the virtual state of siege in which the city hangs suspended: import-export, travel, transport, trade, traffic *hanging in suspense*—all of it is horrible but not enough to kill us all and just have done. The thing is clear: this is no snow but an *attack*, no blizzard but a *blitz*; and it's orchestrated just so by some foreign "power," some antimetropolitan enemy of Freedom who attacks our prosperous city out of envy! Out of cowardice and impudence, and because these foreigners know nothing of honor, this cunning enemy chose a weapon that at the same time is a mask and a white cloak, an insidious silent weapon that even melts away like some sort of ghost or demon or a dream masquerading as a thing of "nature" so it seems there is no one to blame. But these days even intellectuals realize there's no more "nature"; Man has conquered everything, even the tiniest weed takes root and survives only where Man allows it. Hence in the matter of the "snow" there is but one pertinent question: *Who is responsible?* Find them, crush them, and all will be well; the metropolitan way of life will carry on towards greater and greater Freedom. But continue as we are, with our government *not* admitting to the facts, not admitting anything, and the gentle little snowflakes shall continue to infect our trucking routes, shipping channels, runways with relentless chills and ice so that, little by little, our cranes, buses, forklifts, boilers, even snowplows shall suffer breakdowns and morbidity, and Commerce, tormented by headaches and hitches, will gradually find itself unable to drag itself along. For corroboration of this grim and final point, look no further than the flooded shops along the river, or alas, look at CytyBox 3937. Sales and purchases must be free to move. Packages must be free to sail, to drive, take wing, and only the stupid and the dead would wonder why. *Commerce is Freedom! Freedom is life!* Purchases *must* go forth with vigor and without inconvenience to the purchaser or vendor! Metropolitans *must* have purchasing power or we will starve! Metropolitans *must* receive their purchases or there will be blood! There was the truck that was hijacked, you remember, in the street, while it was hemmed in by traffic. Armed attacks on packing and shipping outposts whose trucks are imprisoned at the docks in endless queues while freighter captains smoke their pipes and *debate* unloading, reloading, casting off. And this is how the enemy kills us slowly.

Certainly it will seem to be an accident or even as if the city did it to itself; but where there are rapid-fire guns, atomic bombs, unmanned drones, poisoned gases, deadly sounds, what enemy power *couldn't*, from a scientific point of view, engineer a weapon that appears to be an innocent, "natural" phenomenon yet strikes with such precision at the city's very soul? Slowly, silently, they are burying us alive, in the meantime they want the city to eat itself from the inside, and I am telling you this is terrorism. But *she*, that stupid crone, dared to ask whether I really know what I'm talking about, in short, what "terrorism" is. As if anything were more obvious! Terrorism! Foreign fanatics! Determined, because they're useless and abnormal, to poison Commerce and break the hearts of normal, homegrown Capitalists who just want to grow their smokestacks and profit margins in peace! And she asks me what is terrorism. It's just the sort of irrelevant babble in which useless people try to conceal their irrelevancy and hide their faces from the facts. And if you want to know what must be done instead, well, it's simple. The city must stop pretending there is nobody to blame. The government and its useless meteorologists must stop pretending that our suffering is due to some inadequacy instead of simple malice. The government must *identify* the foreign power that's responsible, and if they've already done so they must inform the citizens! We must *fight back* with all the might of Capital! I explained to the noisemakers with precision, but did they print a syllable? Not a one! And that vile old woman scoffed at what she called my "bogeyman," my "persecution fantasy": the old bat believes this "winter" to be just so. Only she thinks it is the "final" winter, that the snow is the beginning of the end and won't stop until the end has done away with everything. Now, of all the ridiculous excuses, and as Sub-Executive Supervisor one hears a great many excuses for downing tools and idling ourselves to death, the apocalypse is surely the most infuriating. Given that these are the end times, that silly old woman saw no reason not to fill her final days with herds of little paper horses in her corner and even saw no reason not to let "the little thugs" do as they pleased! No sooner had they invaded than did the youths run out of means by which to amuse themselves. There ensued in the inventory room, where everything a professional packer might require stood in readiness, the construction of the horrible pool and towers and the subsequent climbing, flinging, crashing. Since the old woman had her corner behind the customer service station, which for efficiency's sake is just in front of the inventory room, she saw and heard a good deal of what transpired within. The little thugs spent their days raving about their poor lot in life, the blame for which fell on teachers, parents, policemen, bus drivers, great aunts thrice removed, everyone, in short, who's old enough to buy liquor. They blamed *every* human being who's ever lived, except themselves, for instigating this mad "winter," and later they even proclaimed it to the media: our city and everyone who's ever been in it caused the problem *directly*. How did we contrive such a dastardly thing? By living in Freedom! Building a society with a Commercial soul marching industrially towards progress! Creating, selling, packaging, transporting, for example, the very electronic toys for want of which the vandals wallowed in ennui and violence against fiberboard boxes! The uninspired young minds even said it is a war: "*They* ravished the Earth so it's gone cuckoo and forgotten how to administer climates and meteorological routines; consequently there's so much snow we can't ride our electric scooters and shan't ever have cars; they've shut down 3937, disconnected the electricity, so we can't plug in our phones and stream pornography and purchase useless paraphernalia over the internet; and now they're threatening electricity rationing because of the climate emergency, and if that happens there'll be no phone charging anywhere and nothing whatsoever to do; and if they were going to bring us into this world, by god, they should've perfected it beforehand." The old woman heard them opine that everyone over thirty should be put out of the way unless they're providing for children, and this seemed so obscene that she confronted them. "Well, and so, young people, pollution generated by manufacturing, transportation, and personal living has stupefied the Earth's sense of proportion, and one of your little science teachers saw online that global warming produces more airborne moisture and warmer winters which, although it's perfect nonsense, bring more snow instead of less," which populist explanation *ignores* the matched precipitation rate, a documented fact; "and so everything's ruined, it's everybody's fault except your blessed own; you want the Earth 'saved' for you, not for the Earth's sake but your own, as if that wasn't humanity's first mistake; you want everything 'sustained' not so the rivers and forests will come back to life but so you can exploit them in your own way in your turn: how does that make you better than the ogres you want put to death? And finally what are you going to do? Cease longing for cars and stop using pollutive buses? Give up your computers, games, movies, all of which burn electricity, and even give up your desire for such things? Will you put away your scooters forever? Because you know they too consume electricity, and where there's consumption there's pollution. Will you stop eating mass-produced and refrigerated foods, put aside your phone and never wish for it again, forbid your parents to turn up the thermostat? You whine that other people are waging war against you even as you lounge here pining for limitless electricity; but if you must have such things, then *you*, by your own reasoning, share the blame for the present crisis! I know of no solution, being a weak old woman, but what do you plan to do? Mama-to-be, papa-to-be, how will you remodel the Earth to feed and titillate your little one?" A more sacrilegious diatribe you've never heard: as if nobody's innocent. Mama-to-be flung out insults, but papa-to-be said "none of that" was his problem, meaning the partial "little one." The crone recounted this exchange to the police and even some noisemakers, inciting discord among the latter, who muddled everybody by contradicting one another regarding who in fact was responsible for the crime. This despite the indisputable presence of certain fingerprints on certain knives and a particular fire extinguisher and of a certain shoe print on a certain throat. Some accounts have the "unacknowledged citizen" seeking refuge from the snow, noticing 3937's open door, slipping inside to receive the shock of her life when her glance fell on the tower, and being set upon by bored ruffians inclined to robbery. Other accounts have the "children" seeking refuge and their "clubhouse" set upon by an invader who seemed to present a threat because she either "appeared confused" or misrepresented herself as someone in authority. But giving rise to a third, most extraordinary account, one of the killers disregarded his attorney and whined publicly: he wasn't about to let any old woman even so much as seem to look at anything of his. He said "They," meaning everyone, had taken every opportunity from him, and he would not allow "Them" to abscond with one more scrap, and clearly, he continued, since the woman wasn't attractive she couldn't have produced children, therefore and in conclusion where exactly was the loss? None of the other killers granted interviews to noisemakers, but this particular boy, who claims officially to be innocent, seeks to justify his actions on the grounds of his preexisting "disadvantages" including the "snow" for which he thinks the entire city is liable. What he fails to consider is that the "snow" is obviously the work of foreign terrorists, provocateurs don't murder their own agents, and if the unidentified woman wasn't "one of theirs" they wouldn't have known that she existed in the first place. Thus connecting the two crimes, "snow" and murder, ameliorates none of the young quartet's culpability. There she goes, Princess PowerPack. Scurrying off to drain her next victim of box-batteries. What could she possibly hope to accomplish with all those little things? You'll notice she never buys the bigger batteries. She couldn't power a refrigerator or electric grill or even a small heater, couldn't do anything more useful than charge her phone a hundred times. Had the undesirables been able to charge their cartoon supersuits or virtual assault weapons, it would not have spared their victim's life, notwithstanding all their whining. The detectives were correct that the "box" for the sake of which they murdered that woman possessed the killers at such depths that even computer games could not have reached, for whatever computer games have to offer are not *things*. The tower, in contrast, was a game of a very different kind: the little thugs played at significance by playing with *things* of significance, at once exaggerating their vitality and destroying them in a manner not unlike the killings of goats and firstborns sacrificed to ancient gods. Though the sacrificial act was useless and therefore meaningless, the sacrificial things' *thingly materiality* made a difference to *their* significance, thus to the kind of adversary liable to interfere on their behalf; in this case an adult female and total stranger ready to hurl herself headlong into a fight to the death. But really it's all nonsense. The detectives would believe, on the advice of "experts," that this "battle to the death" was the apogee of some pseudorational progression, as when an arcane idea seems arbitrarily to exert a kind of magnetism over a growing number of brains to the point that the idea seems possessèd of its own life, energy, will, and the ability, like a demon or the latest trend, to not only attract brains but also *seize and possess* them, turning previously reasonable people into fanatics. But the main thing is, as the bone of contention between victim and killers, invader and thugs, or foreign agent and born citizens, the supposed "box" *appeared* as potent as a dominant ideology but in reality and in every respect fell short of its appearances. Furthermore, there was nothing reasonable about these people; neither the "little thugs" nor the "stranger" who, having left no traces anywhere of her existence, was as if a ghost already, nor even the sole "witness" to their collision, the details of which shall hence remain forever speculative. For among these "citizens" *not a single one* had even *thought* of trying to do their part *as citizens* by resisting the proliferating madness or indeed doing *anything* of any productive value in any rational context! Their uselessness belied their metropolitan exteriors, rendering them *meaningless*, all as treacherously meaningless as the so-called "box" itself. As to the bloodiest events that "little granny" actually witnessed, to the extent that she witnessed anything and didn't concoct it all—Do you know she concocted a spiderweb from packing tape, spinning it with spidery fingers that seemed never to stop fiddling even when her Sub-Executive Supervisor demanded her attention elsewhere? She claimed it was a snowflake. She may even have constructed it on one of our last sunny days as if to curse us all. Curses and lies, that's what she knits. To hide her obsolescence in cobwebs of fear, putting people under her spell with her "forest guardian" aura. She even thinks I'm afraid of her! As though a man in the prime of life could fear an old woman! As though a superior could fear a subordinate! Devil take it, why couldn't she simply get out of the way? God knows I wished for it all those years; she as if bewitched everyone while I alone, day after day, endured her twinkly-eyed mockery and condescension. I even recommended her removal to HQ, a quiet little retirement, because quite simply there's no time for old-womanish dawdling. But she persisted always, *always*, regardless of her disregard for authority, her know-it-all looks, the "inside snickers" she shared with other subordinates at my expense—so that I wouldn't be surprised if she knitted the thing herself! I'm speaking of the thing that started all the trouble, which the detectives brought to show me. That thing is not a box, however boxlike it appears. A box, properly speaking, is a container for other things, but the *tease* of the thing under contention is that there's no way to open it. No coaxing or puzzling will induce it regardless of what "granny dear" might say to you; I saw it with my own eyes, which, remember, are those of a professional. The thing could fit in your palm if the police allowed it, which they wouldn't. I myself was permitted to see but not to handle. A glance revealed that it's unsuitable and that's all there is to say about it. Dropping it in the snow would be the end of it, you'd never find it, and it seemed to be constructed of an altogether too dainty paperish material, appearing to the expert eye to be just that sort of material intended to self-destruct upon contact: *giftwrapping*, in a word, designed to beautify (as if there's any greater beauty than a sturdy and above all useful container), to conceal and dissimulate and then to be undone, torn off, discarded. And though the thing was as uniformly white as unremarkable copy paper, it had the look of a wrapped thing. Not wrapped professionally, certainly not, but an excessive, ludicrous, truly pathetic job of wrapping as of a trainee who'd gone cuckoo. For the thing was as much an agglomeration of layers as it was a thing; layers dashing every which way, crisscrossing as when a place is so thick with cobwebs that you can't make anything out. Notwithstanding its flimsy constitution and diminutive size, which perhaps could fit a packet of small nails or miniscrewdrivers, any pretensions the thing might have to utility are undone by the pointlessness of its design. The "sylvan sorceress" may snicker all she likes, but I give you my word as a specialist: those devilish layers *will not be disentangled*, they'd sooner give themselves up to destruction than relax their coiling death grip on one another. Only by taking a knife to it would anybody have a hope of getting inside. It follows therefore that the thing cannot be a container withal its apparent rectangularity and capaciousness, for if it cannot untangle itself from itself then reason dictates it is manifestly impossible for any other thing to have slipped between the layers to their interior. A thing is no container if it cannot contain. A box cannot be a box if it is no container. Wherefore I say *that "little white box" is no box at all!* Owing to its appearance and the stupidity of people like that futile crone, who insist that if it looks like a box, a box it is, and if it descends from above, it must be snow, the *thing* has been assumed to be just so, as it appears, even by detectives to whom as a result, as soon as our esteemed defenders of law and order overcome their perplexing hesitations, the next recourse must be a blade. But! A true box is a practical matter, a box is *equipment* and—wait for it, here it comes . . .

The shoe store! Tally another circuit! Boost our speed and those ridiculous orange flip-flops shall flare before us once again before I'm through with you! But there's the matter of the strange delusions the thing inspired. There's a sense in which they're understandable somewhat, these fancies, casuistries (as when subordinates squander layers of giftwrapping to trick you, so you think you're getting a set of hand barbells when all the useless devils have given you is a protein bar they filched from your office) that are only mindless, stupid, loathsome superfluity, and what for? An excuse for your inferiors to chortle in your face! However, as is often the matter with delusions, the undesirables' had a basis in reality. This, too, the detectives failed to realize, as if desiring not to, though I even phoned them to instruct them in the right interpretation of events as described to me by the old woman; because the thing is clear, *this is the heart of the matter* even though it seems that everybody couldn't be more disinterested: *a box as such is the vital endo-exo-skeleton of Commerce!* What protects Commerce when it moves? What things are its plumage? What is it that calls to you from yonder across the superstore? Soy nuts? Indeed not! That in which the nuts are packaged, attired, and have traveled, protected, their freshness secured, in short, not the soy nuts but the *box* of soy nuts; the bearer of the logo, the nutritional facts, the herald of the all-important *brand name*. Therefore the undesirables' insistence upon something "transcendent" intrinsic to the fiberboard foundations of their delusions is in its way appreciable though the delusions themselves are not, arising simply from these superfluous persons' groping about for some reason for living, and in fact if that thing is an icon, it's an icon to the last great god, which is Man, and to his soul, which is Commerce. The killers built a church, in short. Though the tower that they climbed and thence went flinging and crashing was not a sacred edifice at its inception, the arrival of the "little white box" changed everything. You wonder, as the detectives wondered, why this "box" above any of the real boxes that all around the killers lay ready to hand? "Because of itself," said the crone. Nonsense. Because, I say, of all the boxes in attendance, this "little white box" was the only one that was a *lie*, that in its futility was *meaningless*, and because the little thugs contrived to persuade themselves or to be witchily persuaded that they themselves had discovered it. One of them turned up with the thing one day. Busy at her knitting, the silly old woman witnessed neither the thing's arrival nor the ensuing discussions. She only noticed when the undesirables began "incanting." Well, and so she went and peeped. Standing before the latest tower, one of the murderers-to-be played at being a sort of priestess, throwing up her arms into the dark and chanting whatever drivel came into her head, which the remaining three echoed in pathetic grunts, the summary effect being a sad and crazed responsory. Somehow the tower was such, its architecture rearranged from the usual, that the peeping hag saw the thing, *"the icon,"* she called it, at the summit, right in the spot to which the hooligans would climb before leaping and crashing. The icon was the priestess's cynosure: babbling, she gazed upon it, and the crone said "her eyes shone" and "danced"; crazed with ennui as they all were, the remarkable thing is all the rest of them not guffawing, deriding, or fidgeting, not in fact making a peep unless it seemed such was required. "The truth of the world, essence of all," intoned the priestess, "is the blank of *thing*, absolutely self-contained; making no appeal to anything outside itself, blessed inertia, it allows" (and if I'm misremembering or inventing, it hardly matters, it's all nonsense) "nobody into itself, perfect and arcane, thinging now and everywhere, not needing" (and maybe stupid "little granny" made it up); "not needing to touch or to be given and therefore greater than all of us, *thing* will survive while we perish and decay (and the acolytes never did leave off climbing the tower in order to fling and crash, endangering their icon, which might so easily have been stepped on or dislodged), *thing* will *repel* itself into the empty future on its pure, negative vigor, the *no* it says to all. *Thing* needs no religion, society, or state, being of itself the secret disorder of orders," and so enough, it's all cuckoo. The priestess shut up eventually and the "guardian of the forgotten forest" tippy-toed to the tower, the altar so profligately constructed of *such good boxes*, which thus profaned were no longer fit for anything; and she plucked the icon from the summit, crowing, "The knitting of the thing! Profoundly exceptional paper knitting!" And the acolytes allowed it. The crone stood at the foot of their cathedral with their icon in her tricky hands looking at it, the acolytes lounged about looking at her, and strangest of all, if the old witch can be believed, was the solemnity of the business. In the immense silence that absorbed the incantations, the silent congregation, not even with suspicion but a sullen sort of fear, with honor, devil take it!, and even perhaps some strange hope, scarcely definable, admitted her into the midst of their weird ceremony as if they'd almost been awaiting her, as if she was the fey demon whom they'd half hoped might hear them but were too timid to call upon. She didn't scold them, asked no questions; she claimed it never occurred to her to wonder where "the paper marvel" had originated or how it might be used to induce its cult of destroyers to abandon 3937 (alas, such a rare affliction is loyalty!). All she cared about was the "*uncanny* workmanship," praising the "little white box" to the skies and even beyond, so of course one couldn't help forming suspicions of the obvious, namely that her ecstatic crowing was not a matter of artless wonder at the thing itself but a matter of vanity: that "uncanny workmanship" was *her own*, devil take her! This is my opinion as a specialist, which she received with indignant sneering as if no human (perhaps only *thing!*) could concoct such an object: the undesirables filched the perverse not-a-box out of her "knitting basket" and designed their occultish ritual out of mockery for the stupid old bag's putting on of "uncanny" airs. But due to their limited imaginations and general overestimations of themselves, the acolytes believed in their own nonsense almost from the start, they bought into the drivel as soon as it dribbled from one of their own. So what began as a derisive game became sacred almost immediately because "snow" and other "disadvantages" seemed to give them an excuse to devote themselves obsessively to bitterness. They decided if nothing else was to be given to them freely, then they would take this "nothing," "not-needing," "repelling," "inertia," and, in a word, worship the illusion of their disadvantage and even that with bitterness and mockery. And the redundant giftwrapper encouraged them, the devil, because she also values herself inordinately. Quite in earnest she told me the "iconic" not-a-box is "an energetic thing," insisting that regardless of who brought it into being and imported it to 3937, the thing's own "vitality" was the cause of everything, the thing "exerted its surfaces upon surfaces to converge with others' surfaces" or some such drivel. Now, the objective of piling drivel upon drivel could only have been vanity: to call attention as if askance to the "vitality" of her knitting thus to the power and necessity of the old woman herself, whose potency acquired metaphysical proportions. It wouldn't surprise me in the least if she not only concocted that deceitful, wasteful, even offensive box-that's-not-a-box, but also, even before the vandals got hold of it, bestowed the name of "icon" upon it and persuaded those bored minions to turn their tower into an altar, a shrine, in fact, to the defunct giftwrapper. For what's that "paper marvel" but a relic of her irrecoverable past? The woman swears she's not responsible, swears she'd never seen the not-a-box before the little thugs enthroned it atop their terrible tower, and, as I say, the detectives trust her implicitly. However, "little granny" also claimed that as she stood before the congregation with the icon in her hand, someone murmured that the thing was "a reification of mystery itself, an embodiment of the absolute unknown"; and the detectives even believed this perfect impossibility, believed, to be exact, that it was a little thug who spoke as such, whereas I'm certain the old woman made it up herself. Multisyllabic concepts are quite beyond the reach of these residuals whose idea of "schooling" involved nothing more than bringing themselves to prominence through bullying and whining, yet by her account she inquired as to their reasoning and even received a response. "Because," came the reply somewhere in the congregation, "you can see it's got some riddle, perhaps a secret code in the pattern of how the layers and seams go crisscross" (my word as a specialist: of patterns there were none), "and if the riddle's answer is the way into the box, then since there seem to be a million crisscrossing answers and no answer, well, the riddle is absolute, the box is nothing more or less than *the* absolute riddle." And then somebody else: "But aren't riddles supposed to *mean* something? If you can't solve it, so you can't get in, you won't find anything that *means* anything." Babble ensued concerning meaning and unmeaning relative to paper and the unknown, also concerning agency, things' capacity for such, the implications of such "*thing-power*" for polystyrene peanuts, bubbly drinks, existence itself, and so on, including the possibility that "manifestations," as if by paper ghosts, of the meaninglessness and emptiness and also the nonemptiness of existence may be the point of the not-a-box and even the only general truths; for even if they contrived to pry the not-a-box away from itself and open it, *still they wouldn't actually see into it* because nobody ever sees the thing in front of them to any degree of "essentiality," the reason being that the thing is right in front of them. And would she listen when I reminded her that according to the natural laws of Civilization all things are objects, thus by definition useful; therefore nothing "right in front of us," nothing that truly *exists*, is capable of secrecy irreducible to utility; therefore and in sum *nothing escapes* the all-powerful tautology that is the Civilized order, according to which useful objects are objects that are used? Of course not, the devil. Her monologue drowned all common sense. In fact you wonder how it is that these undisciplined hooligans never seemed to tire of her babble. Well, the thing is clear: *she* concocted it all and "remembered" it *post factum* in the mouths of babes! She looked at the not-a-box. She wiggled it, claimed to hear "whispering as if it had thoughts of rattling." Well, she's a liar! Hadn't she herself babbled of emptiness? Haven't I, an expert, demonstrated that *there could've been no such rattle?!* "But the way in is just there. It's even obvious," she told the thugs, and she twisted her shriveled little hands around the thing as if to accomplish the impossible. I tell you she could've managed it not by unlocking some nonexistent riddle but by brute force alone. Yet when I pointed out that her "way in" could only have been violence, the woman became offended! "You're just saying that because you couldn't puzzle it out and the detectives couldn't either!" And this is how I suffered all those years for duty and honor, for CytyBox, the soul of the city. *Any* reasonable person would break a box they cannot open, yet for proposing such an eminently normal solution I must endure abuse. You yourself, when a thing you've bought arrives entangled in carelessly and wastefully applied packing tape that won't admit even a fingernail, what do you do? Do you enshrine the thing as an unanswerable question? I defy you to pretend you do not keep a steel or ceramic retractable multiblade, popularly known as a box cutter, on your person in case of just such an aggravation! In fact, how that thing could've survived a *robbery* is beyond this professional specialist. The detectives claim to have records: the fingerprints of one of the killers match certain fingerprints discovered at the scene of an armed robbery during which the victims claimed a "little white box" was taken. Only imagine that flimsy bit of frippery and then convince yourself that it would emerge unscathed from a violent altercation. Naturally you'll find it's impossible, and that's why reason necessitates that the crone's *entire story*, every word and detail, be called into question! I put it to the detectives that "little granny," who after being made redundant broke into 3937, knitted the *thing* out of mad bitterness, bewitched or otherwise caused the undesirables to consider it a sacred object, and then *disavowed* her "uncanny workmanship," her "paper marvel," and her "guardian spirit's" influence when the thing and little thugs got entangled in that murder. The situation is clear! Nevertheless the detectives believe so wholeheartedly in this "armed robbery" that for them there's even no question: the woman denies knitting the "little white box," and if this "box" was allegedly stolen from someone else, then the old hag couldn't be lying on this or any other point. Our honored detectives even claim that other than myself *no one* suspects any connection between the murder and "sweet little granny." One detective made so bold as to suggest that I must harbor a grudge against that piddly subordinate, that driven by my "little grudge" I even *wished* for her involvement in the murder, disregarded and "disdained" any evidence beyond my own suggestion that the vile old trickster isn't what she seems—as if testimony should be required beyond a Sub-Executive Supervisor's! The detectives preferred to hang on *her* every word. But enough. Whether she meant to rend the not-a-box or had genuinely "solved the riddle" of the "way in" if such existed, we'll never know; for when she made as if to open it, the undesirables sprang into action—"It's not yours! It's not to be opened! Unhand the sacred icon!"—and snatched it away from her. She mocked them with "hmhmhm" and a witchy warning. "The thing with which you are so bold as to make free is not a toy, and you understand it very well, for all your ignorance and stubbornness: *things are more than they are.*" Rot. With that, the "guardian spirit" faded to invisibility in her corner while "hmhmhm" lingered behind her like an evil familiar, as if to spy on the undesirables while they stood cringing. The next day's ceremony was a protracted affair, which became more protracted the next day and the next longer still, each time following a special silence, which the little old crone described as "somehow fixed" and "somehow wary" like the silence of a forest that precedes a stalking tiger wherever he roams. Each evening honored a different acolyte with the icon's overnight stewardship, a superfluous exercise that according to the detectives meant to minimize the probability that the "stolen goods" would become traceable to anywhere in particular. And the thing even survived its vagabonding in smelly pockets and sticky teenage bedrooms without injury, so when the detectives brought it to me its condition was pristine. It says a great deal for the spell under which they'd fallen that four murderers took such care to preserve this "little white box" while passing it from hand to malevolent hand. Then one day the steward failed to turn up with the icon. The inventory room writhed with impatience; the old woman claimed to feel the tension "sprickling" (going so far as to invent a word as though her "sylvan" sensations exceed any experience accessible to mortals). The steward was delayed by the "Snowflake Suicide," the idiot who flung himself off a skyscraper in order to "match precipitation." His body landed in the street, the bus on which the icon rode to meet its worshipers became trapped in the resultant traffic jam, and in spite of the steward's relentless messaging, how they cursed him! Kicking things over in a rage, the three residuals were convinced he'd betrayed them and kept the icon for himself, and after a while—oh, it sickens me to think of it!—the old woman began noticing a smell so vile and pungent that it beckoned her from her corner to peep into the inventory room. The leftover acolytes and priestess had destroyed their church. This in itself was unremarkable, the edifice being prone to frequent toppling during the leaping and crashing following the daily ceremony; but the ridiculous occasion of the moment was neither aeronautical nor ceremonial. Instead the villains sprawled amidst the rubble like corpses. They smoked cigarettes, gazed at the lightless ceiling, strange grimaces on their sweaty faces. Sometimes someone loosed an incongruous giggle or snort; or a grotesque twitching came on for no reason, a foot jerked, a hand batted, a weird facial spasm sent one eye rolling while the other looked stonily on. The crone suspected hallucinogens, looked closely at their "cigarettes," and saw that these were not rightful cigarettes but constructed impromptu from—from strips of fiberboard in which, as she surmised from the smell, the villains had stuffed an evil mixture of polystyrene particles, polyethylene air-cushion film, paperboard particles, melted adhesives—glues, you know, and perhaps chemicals from undersides of tapes or flaps of envelopes, the devil only knows! Nobody can imagine a viler perversity than a trio of useless persons *grinding down the vital wings of Commerce into nothing*, into chemical toys, *deliberate delirium* and titillating madness, to no purpose at all except to make themselves *more partial*, more superfluous, extravagant, useless, and stupid! After the remaining boy depleted his abominable cigarette, he stood over mama-to-be. She seemed not to notice, grimacing as if beatifically, until he plucked the squib from her fingers and she jumped up, knocked him down, threw him to the ground, a boy much larger than herself, gave him a kick or two, even drew back her fist to strike him! But at that moment the steward arrived with the icon. The acolytes' bleary eye-balls rolled to him as one. Mama-to-be lost interest in pummeling and hauled the boy up by the scruff of his neck, an indignity that surely neither he nor she ever forgot and that transformed the group's dynamic, as if with a switch and shooting sparks diverting the un-desirables onto an unfinished track to an unbridged ravine even as nobody spoke of the resentment curdling the air. Everyone was wide awake, everyone crowding the icon. The timid little crone dared not show her face, but she heard the ceremony. With the icon in its place of honor in the tower, the congregation was in ecstasies, the intoxi-cated priestess completely carried away; and with that, a new inhu-man influence born of chemical destruction crept into the depraved bullies, beguiling them ever nearer to the point of no return. What will become of us, my god? What's to become of Civilization? I'm not saying we should be afraid, I am in fact never afraid, fear is nothing more than ludicrous and even disgusting: to admit to fear even for a microsecond is to invite snowmadness in, and what the city needs are the fearless Capitalists that all its citizens were born to be, unafraid of usefulness and sacrifice. Ah, CytyBox 3937! Why, in our hour of need, do they imprison you in slumber! I find it impossible to imagine the deterioration of the atmosphere, I'd even say the feeling of CytyBox 3937 for itself: from brisk, air-conditioned, halogen-enlightened vigor to the stench of inertia and darkness, noxious hallucinogens, sizzling resentments, and most horrible of all the wrongness which even that vile old woman sensed but out of sentimentality did not heed. Such was the atmosphere in which the undesirables' bitterness fermented into paranoia. Murmurs of a plot reached the "guardian spirit" about getting rid of her, "purifying" 3937 with the "no-ing" of the icon; and such was the climate in which the stranger who by now is naught but nonidentity made her unfortunate appearance, demonstrating thereby the indisputable fact that when the people of this city find themselves facing the void, *they turn to CytyBox 3937*; and the lure of this haven, this vital piston of Commerce, is like a fire in a barrel *irresistible to everyone* from dispossessed fanatics to displaced witches and desperate hunters. Of the warmth, the buzz, the promise which, before this damnable "snow," drew our erstwhile customers to place their thousands of dispatches, purchases, and presents in the hands of the professionals at 3937, remnants obviously remain. Perhaps you'll say it's impossible, you believe objective conditions to be nonconducive to reinstatement due to enemy machinations, and you'd even be correct. But are objective conditions any reason to sit back on our laurels? Is a bit of precipitation, biological warfare, or something the matter with the Earth, which if you ask me is starting to look all too old-womanish, is that reason enough, I ask you, for 3937 to be tossed aside, vitality itself thrown out like so much tissue paper?! *Nowhere* is less deserving of the blemish of that murder, that ridiculous excursus in its illustrious history; the enemy agent *herself* would've appreciated this had she not been cuckoo. No foreign power in its right mind would've deployed a covert operative for the sake of that not-a-box, wherefore I say the saboteur, this "unknown citizen," must've intended to sabotage something else, something possessed of utility and therefore *meaning*, only she too was driven cuckoo by the rampant crack-up instigated by snow terrorists of which she herself was one! But even if the detectives had not themselves gone cuckoo (the law synonymous with madness: what is to become of us?!), if they had seen that woman for what she was, the anti-Capitalist malevolence scrawled all over her skew-toothed face, it would've made no difference since, far from offering clues to her commanders' whereabouts, the not-a-box led precisely nowhere, the twists and turns of its "knitting" leading only to themselves, connoting nothing. Thus and so, *she*, the victim, as if contrived to materialize out of thin air; the "witness," nestled in nostalgia in her corner, contrived not to hear anything until the shouting started; and for the killers by this point nothing more was needed than the fact of the stranger's unfortunate existence, daring to appear before their eyes, to bestir them to detonation. The little old crone said one of the detectives said to her, as together they superfluously muddled their brains over the unresolvable question of why the victim did as she did (as though reason plays any part in madness and as though the detectives hadn't proper experts at their beck and call): the detective read, in fact, to the "witness" from the official statement of one of the killers who claimed to have been struck by the stranger's "utterly exhausted" gait and carriage upon arrival. "She leaned on the air," the little old woman said they said. The "unexplained citizen" was, I understand, almost physically crushed by her own emptiness; "her head hung as though it would fall off any minute." And a metaphor was even proffered for this head, "a leaf that's gone through too much wind," as though the neck might be coaxed to produce fresh heads come springtime. It's even likely that of all comparisons only the most absurd are possible in this case: the case of a huntress hunting a thing inanimate, which, as anyone can see from its intractable comportment, defines itself by its uselessness and like the most ludicrous tautology has within it, behind it, has *to* it nothing and nothing and makes as such a reasonable quarry for the huntress who's gone cuckoo and for her alone. And now as I've already drawn your attention to the metropsychological consequences of putting Commerce in fetters, I'll say no more on the matter beyond that the degeneration of such a hunt into a pure expression of desperation was inexorable, the desperation of this impossible huntress having attained the maximum level possible for human beings and spilled over into insanity. In her condition she could've done no more, had she succeeded instead of perished, than set her pointless prize upon a pointless pedestal, there to be revered as a symbol of her hopelessness. The main thing for the little thugs was that they were only just beginning to resolve to conquer 3937 once and for all, only beginning to find the courage to banish the witch at last, and now there was this interloper, an envoy of the perfidious and antiquated *Them*. And most egregious of all, from the killers' point of view absolutely unforgivable, so pathologically possessive and possessed had they become: the invader meant *to take the icon*, abscond with their favorite toy! Regardless of her being outnumbered and of a certain age, being in fact of no significance so that for all eternity she'll be unremembered as nobody at all, *she* (whose inexplicable rashness won her the box, a real one, wherein she'll be incinerated), she outshouted the whole band of worthless thugs; the little old crone heard her shrieking in "the voice of someone driven beyond her limits": "*It doesn't belong to you either!*" and "*Perhaps not, but I've a better idea than you!*" and then it's believed she *leapt* at the tower, meaning to snatch the paper-knitted not-a-box and make a run for it. But, well, the switchblade and the rest. An absurd death. A stupid death. A waste. And meaningless. As meaningless as the *thing* itself, the killers' absurd icon, deified for its absurdity. And the worst of it is: CytyBox 3937 will be stained forevermore by the pointless rage and empty horror of that disgusting violence. An insult, I tell you! To Commerce itself and its grandest institutions!

Medium

[AYJ]: Email 1:
To puppymama37@mymailboxrightnow.free]

~~Dear R. No. Hello, R. No, please X that out.~~ Dear R. It's been a long
time. ~~I realize you may think. No. All right, deep breath. Oh, you
typed that too. Everything, yes, I understand. It's just difficult. Put this
please:~~ I know you think I should've stayed. Solidarity with our family. ~~Solidarity? Slippery but solid-seeming. Sorry, X that. Why do you
write a full-stop if my pause only. Sorry, yes. No time.~~ I can only say
I'm sorry and hope. ~~That's for my sister.~~ I've little time. Much to explain. I'm at Central Station. Waiting for a train. To exile me from the
city of my exile. And bring me back to you at last. If you'll allow me.
Even if not forever. Typing this email is the Socket Medium. She's very
important. Emails, online searches, articles on request. Because not
all of us in the Queue are near a socket. And it took me a long time.
To find courage. Saving my phone to keep in contact with my husband. During the journey. Battery packs are expensive because of rationing. Because the snow. So for a small fee the Socket Medium. Her
steno keyboard with her tablet computer. She's very fast. Each person
can take twenty minutes of her time. Every twenty-four hours. She'll
even help make your will. Lots of people here are. You must've heard
about the snow ~~but have just been too busy to. X that.~~ Can't wait for

you to meet my husband. He'll come later. He's a physician at City Hospital's Emergency ~~so for now. You're right. It's too hard. Someone who's never dictated. Words want to go where they want not where I. I'll try your way. Queue them up to sit them down. I have one. Thanks. In my job I made notes often. I'll try again tomorrow.~~

[AYJ: Email 1 cont.:
To puppymama37@mymailboxrightnow.free]

[. . .] ~~notebook, thanks, it helped. See my punctuation. Now where we left off.~~ The Queue.

Rippling thrumming through the long room's lace of spaces. The Queue, long benches, long walls, still staircases, frozen escalators to fabled platforms, and the spaces between things twining like living wicker.

Between the only ends, street-level revolving doors and platforms below, the Queue clutches itself, in and out of itself in all directions. No one can discern no one needs to learn the way. When you join the Queue you know where to go and how to be. Just like that. The Queue goes down to the platforms to come up again and down again, an organism shivering in fever that comes and goes. Sometimes with delirium that comes and goes.

And the waiting room long and deep as a landfill, towering as a theater of worship. All the long benches face one way. As if in worship of the digital timetable enormous as a cinema screen but off. Giant rectangle of empty. Hanging as if prostrate because it drank too much of time.

Tops of the long benches shaped like ends of scrolls. Calculating the number per bench, a bench so long, so wide a queuer, therefore the Queue is so many, you'd miss things. Suitcases. I'm wearing two sweaters. My husband gave me one, my children the other. The sweaters can't go in the suitcase, which is full. R, my distant sister, I'm not making this up.

Each member of our group is permitted one suitcase. So baggage is no excuse. For them to turn us away. Maybe the woman with the potted plant is on her own, but if she's with us she has a plant instead of a suitcase. I gave our dog to our son. Group and journalist are for another email. I get only twenty of the Socket Medium's minutes.

Another rule. Another queuer may save your place for three hours. Then whoever's behind you may move into your place. Maybe pressured to do so by whoever's behind them. So the thing that hasn't happened but may happen has you by the throat.

Some people go crazy with waiting. Some hope others will go crazy and give up. Hope their homes are waiting. Rumor of a woman feigning narcolepsy, snoring night and day to make people in front of her go crazy. Since I joined the Queue, it hasn't moved. No trains yet. More people behind me every day. And a feeling now and then.

Suddenly the feeling that a train is almost here, a slap of certainty, I'm so sure it's true it hurts my eyes. Certainty like something burns when you shouldn't drink it. I can't help it, I jump up, grab my suitcase. Standing quivering in my place, sure I'm going to see a bright light. The train's cyclops light piercing through the floor just for us.

People around me, our eyes meet almost asking. No words and that scared silence shade the abstract sketch of lace joining the corners of our eyes. The white and silver truths of chemical blonds and auburns. Veins swollen like the river in hands joining without touching across space and time from bench to wall to dirty corner. So we know not knowing each other we're together. Hand on suitcase I'm standing, looking at pity in their looks. Nobody else is moving.

Gray light, settled dust. The Queue is. Still is. Still. The feeling gone, I sit back down.

Queuers near sockets can charge their phones in daytime. Sockets are in the far wall with the restrooms. The Socket Medium spends all waking moments fetching news and sending messages for the socket-less. Her Messengers tiptoe over legs and suitcases between her socket and the far reaches of the Queue. Other socket people sit with their sockets behind their backs. They wear headphones, stream movies, ignore everyone. At night AERS turns off everything.

Rumor from the sockets. People crossing the city in the night on foot with suitcases. Because underground trains still run. Erratic, unreliable, everything depends on AERS, but underground there's no snow. People walk through the night to where the underground begins. To queue for the first train to Central Station. Long-distance trains come and go from Central. The only mass transport out of the city.

Long-distance trains travel overground. Underground trains go partway overground. What the Socket Messenger said about over-ground: In wintry conditions, a train's deceleration when approaching a station or railway intersection compresses the snow on the rails and turns it to ice. Ice fuses the rails together. Trains cannot run on rails frozen together. City officials said: Snowplows, deicing round the clock, Central Station top priority. Other officials: Fuel rationing must apply to heavy equipment including snowplows and deicers. What the Socket Messenger said the Medium said some news site said: Long-distance trains crowded, slow, track conditions uncertain, possibly dangerous, delayed.

Another rumor. Underground trains bypass Central because of the Queue. To join the Queue you must walk to Central Station. Or risk a skidding bus or find a fuelless car. Or ride in an ambulance with your husband, who's bribed the EMTs to look kindly upon you.

Rumor. Underground trains going back the way they came in-stead of emerging overground as scheduled. People riding the under-ground as far as it will go, climbing into the stinging gray when the train will go no further. Those people, their suitcases in the snow. They're not even in the suburbs. Wherever the train drops them, they put their backs to the city. Rumor. Those people just start walk-ing. [. . .]

[CWL: Will & Testament]

I am Citizen-Watchman Lucrez of the Transit Authority Reserves. I've had many mothers and fathers and in consequence possess no name other than Lucrez or Big Lu. Besides my clothes and malacological texts, I own almost nothing in the world. I have one bequest, and it is small.

Enchanted by this small thing, the Socket Medium invited me to set its story down. It's an unusual request, for like a bright lamp in a thick night the Socket Medium attracts more stories than could possibly interest her. Potent feelings convince her that the story of my bequest should be stored. Storage will take the form of this digital document which the Socket Medium will upload to her archive. It will be clearer then that the story is an entity distinct from and constitutive of moments and convergences.

Because writing is slower, I prefer it to dictating, which means speaking. When it comes to speaking, I'd rather not. People tend to rush speaking, not giving anybody time to think. The story will come to you via a process of: (1) story inscribing itself through me onto paper, (2) paper via Socket Medium transmitting story's words to keyboard and computer, (3) computer digitizing and conveying words via algorithms to online archive, (4) computer retrieving words from archive via decryption algorithms, (5) tiny printer inscribing words onto paper, (6) hand of Medium or Messenger conveying paper to you. Note that the paper on which the story appears to you will not be the paper that gives the story to the Socket Medium.

All this puts the Socket Medium in an interesting position. She is and isn't this story's narrator. Without her socket, computer, ethereal archive, this woman would be no Socket Medium; what we call "Socket Medium" is rather a composite thing, a cybernetic hyperobject that's all kinds of separate things. Insofar as when you read my story it shall issue directly from this thing-complex, the Socket Medium is its narrator indeed. She isn't its narrator insofar as she didn't live it and didn't organize its narrative.

The story will be stored in the Socket Medium's collection of Final Wills and Testaments. It ill suits her other collections, being neither email nor article. And though I don't expect to die soon, I may not be on shift if and when whoever receives my bequest wishes to learn about it.

I'm in the odd position of not knowing who my legatee will be. The box will let me know in its own way and time. As legatee, you'll be called "Courier" throughout this document.

You're entitled to know something about its provenance, that is, about me. I became a Citizen-Watchman when the Transit Authority Reserves (hereafter TAR) formed as an emergency law-enforcement supplement. The wages are lower than Garden SuperCenter's, but when the latter declared bankruptcy the TAR was better than nothing. I like watching trains and passengers. "Officer" is better than "Bigfoot" even though I'm not an officer. And few are willing to join the twenty-four-hour patrols at Central Station, where lots of old women are waiting.

Everyone's supposed to be afraid of them. Yet it's these women who are queuing up to flee the city. A journalist whom they regard as an organizing authority asked me quietly whether I, in a hypothetical altercation with actual police, would side with the women of the Refusal in exchange for a place on the train with them. I agreed, and she said I'm the "one safe watchman." I'm "safe" because other watchmen say I'm "not quite right." Asked to define "not right," colleagues, instructors, social workers, and foster families have said "slow," sometimes "closed." You should know this, Courier, should you find yourself disinclined to believe me: You wouldn't be the first.

The Socket Medium advises me to give you "a sense of [my] perspective and priorities." I longed to be a malacologist but was unable to complete the necessary education. Given a green space, I'd start a pesticide-free sanctuary where snails could grow old without fear. You won't find many snails, if any, in the city now. Snails like to sleep in secret. A snail's priority is peace. A snail is a package that wants never to be opened, couldn't survive being opened: because a snail's inside is the outside it creates. The packaging is the packer is the fragile cargo that is packed. In that wonder of a box, that marvel of torsion weaving itself above itself from underneath itself, spinning out of its own fluids the spiral container in which it already lives, a snail could slow its life-rhythms down to the verge of death—and sleep through the snow.

Snow seems to be a given now, a premise on which rests the conceptual order of things. The age of the premise seems incalculable because our hearts beat quickly. But imagine a dormant snail. At five heartbeats a minute, a winter is but a day. Now imagine a being that needs no heartbeats.

Let's begin with self-evident examples and coax ourselves beyond the obvious. To say a snail is animate and its shell inanimate makes no sense. Although it's made by and of the snail, the shell's rigid constitution is very different from the mucilaginous snail, almost a contradiction. Yet the shell carries the snail as the snail moves the shell. To say humans are animate and trains inanimate similarly makes no sense. Although trains are made by humans, their rigid constitution contradicts our softness, yet the train carries humans as humans move the trains. Shells also begin new lives after their snails are gone. They become jewelry, hermit-crab houses, limestone, cement, sidewalks. Can it.be that one thing is so many species of life? The answer is yes.

[Retrieval: "Trust Your Housecleaner? Think Again," *MAN OVER MATTER: REAL PEOPLE, REAL NEWS:* Messenger Delivery]

"[. . .] Well, and so you have cleaning women stealing boxes out of kitchens. Never mind that the so-called box in question was supposedly in the garbage, which dubious claim is nonsense and instead of noising off about it people might as well admit it. The main thing is, stealing is sabotage regardless of the nature of its victim; to take without reciprocating is a criminal subversion of the system of exchange that is our city's very soul! A citizen who was a thief would be the vilest of deserters! Wherefore I put it to you that the burglar who violated that beleaguered family's kitchen was no citizen but a *foreigner* of the dirtiest and dullest sort, namely a *cleaning woman*, one of those superfluous hangers-on who, lacking brains and general vigor, not only don't object to our city's besiegement by meteorological weapons but even purport *not to believe* in the existence of such weapons so that disbelief may disguise *their responsibility* for the overall mess, for our shortages of everything, and for simply running away in fear of shortages, leaving our city in the lurch in a decisive moment when every hand and heart must pull its weight."

"Have you listened to yourself, sir? Or are you too loud for yourself? First you want rid of us because of where we were born. Then you want us out because of our age. Then you complain we're leaving you in the lurch by resigning our jobs as your lackeys and getting out of here just as you said you wanted! And whose fault is it in the first place that most housecleaners are women 'of a certain age' whose every path to an income is barred by prejudice [. . .]"

[AYJ: Email 2: To puppymama37@mymailboxrightnow.free]

Dear R,

My last email must've frightened you. I'd no right to expect a reply. Let me try again. Installments. Because the Socket Medium's schedule. Why after all this time, out of the blue.

Snow is traces, covers traces. So much white you can't see anything. Canceling hue and shade. "Matched precipitation rate." A term stolen from agriculture. To rationalize unmatched irrational phenomena. Precipitation rate and evaporation rate separated by a constant interval. Absence of spring and summer. History of seasons converging in a climate. And born of the vast thing that is a climate.

History of the climate converging with fossil fuels like a forest falling to conquerors. Silence. From people who should know. Convergences where people don't want them are truths. Secrets are the truest things. Things people try to unhappen but the things rebel. The depth of their footprints. The street where marchers fell.

What snow's done to the city: Everything dangles on a verge. Tip of an iceberg melting ready to fall. On the edge of becoming the city that sleeps for a thousand years. Every building yearning to lie down. Every street almost about to crumble underfoot. Or dangling in the instant before exploding. People flee the edge like it's a monstrous maw. People scramble to reach it before it gets to them. Navigation by snowlight feels like marching in place.

"Citywide crime wave." A form of daring the edge. They want to blame the Refusal, marching, fleeing, dying, but that's another email. Sister, no matter what they say, this "wave" began before. Some say with a random killing committed by children. Or before. Before "crime wave" started trending they were rationing firewood, gaso-line, propane, coal, oil, natural gas, testing Automatic Electricity Rationing Systems. Putting on AERS. Because everything combus-tible must heat. Because nobody knows when fuel shipments will come, if. What rioters said: All this time begging alternative ener-gies, you wouldn't listen. What power plant bigwigs said: The snow will go away, climate can't collapse, it's a wave.

Riots against rioters. Rioters burned things that mustn't waste. Organized hoarders robbed all the supermarkets all at the same time. Turned out the supermarkets' employees were behind it. They knew trucking companies were giving up on the city. Trucks stuck on highways running out of fuel, better send them somewhere else. More robberies, fast-food places, clinics, hospitals, unprovoked as-saults, the March. Assaults on eleven women nowhere near one an-other. Suspects with nothing in common. But their victims' being women. Assault and robbery of three more women. Three differ-ent times, same supermarket. Crippled for life, one my husband sent to ICU. Tenement building exploded, woman arsonist suspected, district-heating systems guilty. Woman exiting pharmacy pushed into traffic.

And AERS. Emergency PA system ordered voluntary electricity rationing. Everyone assumed themselves exempt. Snowstrain on the power plant and supply chains. They ordered the power plant to enforce rationing. From time to time just pull the plug, hotels, banks, neighborhoods thrown into the dark. Automatic Electricity Rationing Systems run full-time now, can't stop. Even when an algorithm's missing comma makes district-heating systems explode.

Rumor the city's bigwigs left the city. [. . .]

[CWL: Will & Testament cont.]

Sometime before Central Station filled with women, I was thinging on the platform. I was a closed door between a flooded restroom and the people waiting on the platform. A train arrived in a fascinating slowing, rising from underground to intersect at Central with overground routes. The graceful doors exhaled four teenagers, two girls, two boys, who elbowed their way to the street exit. They were laughing but also hard and overstrung. One boy looked over his shoulder as he ran. His subsequent near-collision with me enraged him. I'll never forget his youthful face becoming instantaneously hideous. One of the girls snatched the hand making for his pocket. And by that hand, with which he'd meant to do goodness knows, she dragged him away.

A Citizen-Watchman watches. His presence, uniformed and solid, discourages reckless behavior among passengers. This my colleagues and I have ever believed without needing to say so. Imagine my consternation when those four teenagers were suddenly all over the news. That day at Central Station, they'd been fleeing someplace they'd just robbed. They became newsworthy when they were charged with the CytyBox Murder.

Telling anyone about my experience was quite beyond my ability. I was sorely shaken, poring over the reportage on the trial. "Not guilty" meant the CytyBox Killers had done nothing wrong. Those kids van-dalized a defunct CytyBox outpost, murdered a complete stranger; the evidence determined that no one else could have done it. But "not guilty" meant that what they'd done was no wrongdoing. No moral education or behavioral adjustments were required. This made sense to everybody because the kids were kids and the stranger was a stranger.

When I was Little Lu, I was betimes a potted plant. I'd be a door or sideboard for a week or so. Not harming anyone, not making noise or mess. Lie still on the floor, be carpet. Stand still in the corner, arms aloft, silent: coatrack gets an evening off. That's thinging. Thinging was my delight. But to everyone around me it was wrong. Thinging was "antisocial behavior," was "shirking" and "not trying." Foster parents threatened to have me institutionalized if I failed to stop thinging. In contrast, the CytyBox Killers were absolved and free.

The possibility that I was to blame, that my thingly slowness was morally derelict after all, began to trouble me. I didn't know what they'd become when I did nothing to stop those people tear-ing through Central Station to get away with robbery. Even so, was I guilty by omission? Were all doors at Central Station guilty? If I'd arrested them that day on suspicion of suspiciousness, perhaps the CytyBox Victim would still be alive. She whose stepped-on face was ruined beyond recognition could've been a living thing of flesh instead of an irresolute pencil sketch.

I began, while sleeping, to have a dream over and over. In the dream, I am thinging against a wall in an unfamiliar room. I'm a wardrobe, either abandoned or undiscovered. A door like my own appears be-fore me, edged in light. I'm Big Lu again. I must open the other door which for that glowing moment was so like myself. Behind the door, moonlight or dawnlight slips into a dark room from a high corner. A small white box waits on the dust-and-gravel floor.

Things like this box could be the only flower buds of the future. It petals, petaling because of how it's made. It ravels itself in layers of itself. Its hidden secret is itself. It keeps its secret in itself for itself. It has nothing for you. It may choose to die rather than give you anything.

If I weren't dreaming but awake and dropped that little box on the street, it would be lost in its indifference from the snow. It is an existential paradox. As an impenetrable coil, it innately resists change. As plain paper, it cries out for change innately: white paper exists to be marked. The box exists in tension with its own constitution, exists in suspense towards itself like a bud. Its intrinsic tension is the power to meet and alter others.

I awaken from my dream thinking things I did not dream: three words: "white wicker totality." My mind is full of them. It is like this every time.

[Retrieval: "The Tragedy of *found secret*," *ART IN PUBLIC:* Messenger Delivery]

[. . .] The ZV Collection is where art and history live as one. A challenge of my job as curator is deciding what *art* and *history* mean.

Representations of potential or counterfeit events—stories, rumors, dreams—are also histories. *found secret*'s historiographic artistry is its use of found objects to stage, as in a tableau, a story that never happened. In an insight of pure genius, the creator of *found secret* realized any meeting of things, even in the privacy of a fallible imagination, is a moment of history. *found secret* was her quiet way of showing that history happens, history is made, when two incongruous objects come together.

The box, positioned as if at the moment of its discovery in the cabinet's secret compartment, symbolized things' entanglement in an indecipherable whole. The secret of *found secret*, an unassuming object made of crisscrossing papers as blank as fresh canvas, was like a gift wrapped in layers to keep the recipient guessing. It teased the viewer by hinting at its origins with uncompromising ambiguity. Was this box the loving work of hands or the mindless production of a factory? If the artist constructed it herself, she screened her involvement with the mythical café where, the story goes, she found the box. Then again, where some see a myth others see the truth in all its innocence.

The box's obvious fragility and the cabinet's battered condition represent the vulnerability of art and imagination, even their innermost secrets and private musings, to external influences. Social pressures and market forces, for example, which the artist felt to be her enemies, are conditions of contemporary life, and like the snow [. . .]

[AYJ: Email 3:
To puppymama37@mymailboxrightnow.free]

R, my loving sister,

Wondering if you're not replying because you think I won't receive it. See my previous email: Socket Medium, Socket Messengers. But to set your mind at ease. An email about life in the Queue at Central Station.

We have food. Street level: convenience store near restrooms. Candy, trail mix, jerky, dried fruit, protein bars, granola bars, cereal bars, cold coffee. A bar should take a day to eat. No less. Platform level: popcorn stands, two. Hot popcorn because they pop it right there. But can't risk it. If an upstairs queuer saw me sneak downstairs before the Queue took me downstairs, my rightful place would be forfeit. I'd be banished to the end.

I confess to nostalgia with milk. Sliver of uncooked apple. Cabbage leaf, sleek and wet. A spinach leaf. One stemmed wafer in memoriam of green. A grape of any color.

Up and down the Queue go the third-strangest of all beings. Knapsacks full of tea sachets, instant coffee, instant soup. Battery-powered kettles so it's nice and hot. Making more money than they made at jobs they don't have anymore because of shortages or snow. Third-strangest because they're strong enough to try to leave the city but not trying. Because they're making money. Feeding the despair binding queuers to the Queue.

Second-strangest of all beings import things to Central Station. And give them. One group gives to anyone who joins in praying to a deity. One group only gives to children, affirming the status quo. Strangest of the second-strangest wear sunset-pinkish purple and give only to women of the Refusal. Food, medicines, encouragement. Coming laden to be kind to us because they don't disagree that we should have to leave. Most of them are women too.

The strangest of all beings are husbands, children, siblings, frail parents. Crawling through the snow to wives, mothers, sisters swept up in the Refusal. To sons and husbands simply running away. My husband brings things he has no time for. Homemade dinners, books, overconfidence. Scared smiles glisten in his eyes, kisses. Then what? Goodbye all over again. Goodbye for good. Again. Because the train will come any minute, tomorrow when they come with month-old biscuits they might find a stranger in their loved one's place. Or nobody. The train might take everyone. The Queue may be no more, the station blank and silent as a ruin. R, it's torture. Again and again gluing my heart back together.

Overhead lights like upside-down flower buds in cages. Old fixtures, new bulbs. The kind of light that would invade all corners, hard-edge everything, flatten everything. Except the sconces' nostalgic dissonance. All daylight is snowlight. Snowlight: sifted light. Like a half-hearted reenactment of light. A boring memory of someone else's memory. Snowlight like a lid brought down over the city. The hardest light because it's easy to walk into.

Some people feel shriveled in the station. So used to snow on their faces. They go out for a change of ceiling. And get confused and scared. What snow does: Fill all places. Even when a place is full. Where you are, that's your place. They close in on you, they fall on you for your place. Snowflakes falling, queuers closing in. You move for a change of ceiling. They fill the place you left. It's frightening. Because you still are. Hurry back. Back in line, hurry scurry. You need a place. Because you exist.

My place is just inside the doors. My back against a wall that might be crooked. Sitting view: backs of benches, backs of heads, timetable. Posters: COZY, CLEAN, AND COOL. People laugh at these posters, spit at them. Claw the posters. Scrawl notes to the Socket Medium on the scraps. Standing view: revolving doors, six. Gray-green wall, graffiti stylized for unreadability. Distant restroom signs. Distant walls. Like a storeroom crammed with boxes stuffed with junk packed with unwanted memories, a dump. An expanse of bodies. Fidgeting, fretting, stoicing, stilling. Sprawling, pacing, rummaging, arguing, startling, the unchanging of the light, of their suitcases and clothes. Nighttime AERS snuffs everything. Except restrooms' signs, small and yellow like guttering candles. EXIT signs like fake emeralds. The Queue glutted with sleeplessness, bad dreams, queuers' own shrill laughter scares them. Us.

Rumor from City Hospital: The city in the snow is like the cat in the box. Long ago a scientist dreamed the cat in the box so scientists might learn something about themselves. Not wondering about the cat. How much she could bear or he. Of total colorless enclosure. Of the radiation they snowed into the box. They just wondered if it was their own daring to peek, their opening the box, that would decide whether the radiation had poisoned the cat. Unless they opened the box, the cat would be suspended. Alive and dead. Alive but dead. Dead while alive, a misdemeanor. What bigwigs aren't above: Poisoning their own city. Make us think we're meteorowarfare victims, scream revenge against innocent foreigners. War only fattens bigwigs. But that isn't what they've done. Lies they spread in hospitals aren't the lies they tell the public. They want doctors to think they're insiders. Still they had to use force to take my husband.

The snow is a ruin. A broken clock in a bigger ruin. The crumbling sky. The stars are missing. Talk of dream science and vast weaponry are the vanity that built this ruin in the first place. City of my exile, my living, my loves. The artist who inspired the Refusal named herself Counterfate. What she wrote: What society collapses at the sound of drifting snowflakes? Society was always what the snow has made of it, a ruin hiding underneath itself.

My children and grandchildren are at home. My husband at the hospital. My sister far away. Please let me know when you've received this email.

[CWL: Will & Testament cont.]

Because the CytyBox Killers were underage, their trial records were sealed. Only their arraignment for another, later crime required the court to loose its archive's fettered tongue.

A few months after their acquittal, the CytyBox Killers went rampaging with leaf blowers, bombarding the windows of a hotel with snow and little stones intended for potted plants. The attack coincided with the one-month anniversary of the death in childbirth of one of the Killers. They'd intended nightly bombings. But on the first night, the leaf blowers having gorged on stones and ice chips, the hotel had no sooner suffered starry microtraumas to its blue windows of vintage glass than did the bartender and two others charge into the night, tackle the unsuspecting "Snowbombers," and strip them of their leaf blowers. It was noted that the vandals were more listless than furious.

The hotel's owner had recently hatched a plan to restore her small establishment to nearer its former glory. From snow and competition she'd already suffered much. She and her guests were adamant that the Snowbombers be prosecuted to the full extent of the law, lest the hotel acquire an unsafe reputation just as she was trying to save it. The verdict this time was "guilty." The proceedings of both Snowbomber Trials and CytyBox Murder Trials entered the public online archive.

From records of the Snowbomber Trials, I learned:

(1) Their leaf blowers and ammunition were stolen from Garden SuperCenter, the very building where I no longer worked. That convergence of my history with the CytyBox Killers' lit a flare of recognition. By its bloodred light I understood the feeling with which I awoke from my strange dream: that throb of having recognized something I hadn't recognized. Seeing that the CytyBox-Killers-turned-

Snowbombers had robbed Garden SuperCenter, I understood that the throbbing energy wasn't just my own. It radiated, pulsing, from the box in my dream, drawing me into its orbit.

(2) Prosecutors were eager to connect the Snowbombings with the CytyBox Murders so the culprits could be made to take responsibility. Shown the official sketch of the CytyBox Victim (dead eyes, dark hair, strong jaw, odd front tooth), the hotel's owner thought she detected some resemblance to a local woman who used to patronize the hotel's bar but had never given her name.

(3) The bartender answered no to everything.

(4) The box for which the CytyBox Victim fought and died was "unavailable" for the Snowbomber Trials. When the Killers were acquitted of the CytyBox Murder, the box had been returned to them. It could not be found when they were rearrested. Guests and staff at the hotel claimed uncertainty, based on official photographs, as to whether or not they'd seen the box before.

From records of the CytyBox Murder Trials:

(1) The Victim recklessly pursued a small box made of white paper. The Killers murdered her with excessive ferocity to prevent her ever reaching it. The box in the official photos is so very like the box I dreamed it's almost as if that dream isn't mine but somehow found me. It was a shock to see in crime scene photos—a thing out of my own head. Serene, white, total, in the rubble of a broken cardboard palace: the likeness of the thing I'd never sought or wished to dream. Even before my waking eyes it wasn't exactly "there" but as if rumored, secondhand. For between it and my eyes were my computer, their computers, cameras. So even in official records, distance layering upon distance as if disguised the box in a veneer of unreality.

(2) The search for motives that would fit known criteria for making sense defeated everybody. Of what significance is a box that it's worth killing and dying for? A universal inability to convincingly address this question was invoked to support the defense lawyers' claims, upheld ultimately by the judge, that: (a) nobody was to blame, (b) the real culprits were snow and snowmadness, (c) a box

was insufficient to overturn the traditional assumption of a correlation between youth and innocence.

(3) A former CytyBox giftwrapper pointed the police to a blog about forged and stolen works of papercraft. The blog described a "pocket-size box, dizzyingly woven all in white, tapestry-tight, in defiance of every known template," which had been purloined from a local art gallery's chest of drawers. The artist who'd caused the chest of drawers to become valuable by putting the box in it denied that, by any stretch of the imagination, "her" box could have caused the CytyBox Murder. She said the white box at the crime scene was clearly a forgery of her work, calling it "the final straw."

(4) The CytyBox Killers fled the scene without the box; the Victim didn't clutch the box in her dead hand; the police didn't detain the box but returned it to the Killers—as if none of it mattered, neither the box nor its consequences.

(5) In her official portrait, the CytyBox Victim was so nondescript she could've been anyone. She wasn't anyone, though, except herself. She alone could've embarked on that doomed quest, searching a shuttered house of boxes for the box that didn't belong. Although I cannot believe she pointed from beyond the grave and cannot detect a divine hand in the decision, it's clear that I've been chosen to take her place: to make my own amendment to the records.

[Retrieval: "The Tragedy of *found secret*," cont.,
ART IN PUBLIC: Messenger Delivery]

[. . .] public statements history won't soon forget. On the steps of the ZVC, under the scrutiny of every camera in the city, the creator of *found secret* declared: "We're persecuted because we're vulnerable." Artists are more vulnerable than most in times of widespread economic hardship because in such times, as she put it, "society encourages art's value to fall to nil." She accused the highest authorities of fishing for connections between art and murder during the most ignominious trial in city history: "They want people to think it's dangerous or criminal to buy our work."

In one of her last interviews, she warned that artists could go the way of urban pigeons, reduced to begging on the steps of institutions, driven thence to extinction. But she refused to accept this as her destiny. Led by *COUNTERFATE*'s fearless mastermind, the ZVC sit-in erupted into the Women's March that launched the Refusal. "Our vulnerability is the same," she told the journalist with whom she spearheaded the March. "People think of art as a fun extra. Art's the free bobblehead society gets for phone-scanning proofs-of-purchase off a million cereal boxes. The status quo categorizes older women the same way. Fun but useless and in large numbers unhealthy." Whether the city can recover from the Refusal remains to be seen. It will be remembered as that young artist's greatest work.

That the life of the great *found secret* was curtailed by greed or malice is a tragedy. What motivated the thief we'll never know. They remain unidentified and, if not deceased, at large. But when the artist ramped up her work beyond the gallery, *found secret* found new life. Its story will live on longer than the piece itself, even without the vandalism, ever could. Its creator's greatest work was not even an artwork; for the Refusal was not done for its own sake, not even a little bit. Yet with the movement that began as the ZVC sit-in, an unheeded act of defiance by a handful of creatives, that young woman attained her long-desired goal. She accomplished an historic act.

As curator of the ZVC, I cannot help but wonder: What might she have accomplished if social obduracy hadn't cut her life tragically short? [. . .]

[AYJ: Email 4:
To puppymama37@mymailboxrightnow.free]

What I asked the Socket Medium: When you show me R's reply, will it be unedited and confidential? She said yes. So, R, don't be afraid. Just answer. I'm not carrying diseases. There are even tourists here.

Remarkable creatures. Exhausted themselves struggling to get into the city. Flew from snowfree haven to nearest working airport. Hitchhiked till highway too jammed to permit movement. Walked remaining miles (lots) in snow.

"Adventurers," they said. Coming to the city to risk coming to the city. Peek at "life in the snow bubble." Following online gossip, they went to a building they believed abandoned, went at night for thrills. But it wasn't abandoned. It was an AERS blackout. Tenants called the police. Tourists arrested, questioned, scolded, released. Found their hotel room given away. Homeless, they trudged to Central Station. Flopped down at Queue's end. Causing rumors of aliens. Queuers left their places, I left my suitcase, promised to return with news for my place-savers. News of worlds outside the city. Worlds without snow.

But the strangest thing. The tourists couldn't remember. Snowlight's monotony shocked their brains into amnesia. A week in the city and they couldn't find one word for their homeland. What the tourists said: We shouldn't be here, don't belong, never thought a civilized place would offer no way out, how have citizens not gone mad and disemboweled one another. But hope hasn't lost its daring, or the Queue wouldn't exist.

What I heard, eavesdropping, the eavesdroppee heard from someone waiting for the Socket Medium: Downstairs, overhangs above the platforms teem with sparrows, starlings, pigeons, ravens, crows, chickadees, finches. Black birds, brown birds, gray birds we forgot to see because we were used to seeing them. Dear drab colors of the city before everything went white. If it's true, the downstairs ceiling has a hundred thousand hearts. Two hundred thousand wings. Hundred hundred thousand feathers. A second ceiling of pure sound. Of chirp and chitter flutters like the tinkling ruckus of a restaurant from a distance elevated. Most people think birds vanished from the city.

Downstairs you watch the railway tracks tiptoe out. Watch snow swallow them. Watch for trains. Begin thinking you see trains, see the straight-pathed snow swirling itself into a train that will sweep you away from here. You're glad there's no breeze. Then the snow would come in where trains should come. You remember the last train. The last train slid closed quiet doors in your face. Leaving you on the platform because others got there first. And wouldn't make room for one more. You spend days hating everyone in front of you. Nights watching not sleeping. Every time you close your eyes the quiet doors slide closed.

Next time you'll be first. Even if a stampede. If the Queue collapses and you have to murder everyone. Under the overhangs must be crowded. And birds and bats. Rats. And fears and histories. Waste. And if downstairs the rules are not the same as upstairs.

When the birds run out of food. When the rats can't find anything except what's still alive. And the others. Worse than rats. Or birds or bats.

Rumor of a morning when AERS won't turn the lights back on. Rumor the Socket Medium went around the city buying battery packs. As if she knew even before. The Socket Medium won't confirm or deny anything about herself.

Disinfecting the floor where I sit with little wipes. Wishing I could spray and mop the whole station. Too afraid of losing my place. Quick, R, ask me a question. About our homeland.

[CWL: Will & Testament cont.]

The box on the blog, the box on trial, the box no longer in the gallery's chest of drawers and that might have never been at the Snowbombed hotel, the box that the CytyBox Killers stole not from CytyBox but somewhere else and that could've been the last thing the CytyBox Victim ever saw . . . The word I woke up thinking began to ring false. "Totality." "White wicker totality." The existence of the stories in the pictures in the records in the stories means there's always something more, meaning no totality is total, meaning—that false ring. For the box, all the stories began and ended in the middle.

But not for everybody. CytyBox closed. The shop the Killers had robbed when they were fleeing through Central Station was swallowed by the river. The pregnant mother among the Killers, the artist of the chest of drawers, and she whose heart gave out with the box within arm's reach are dead.

Of course, each thing has its own sides to every story. A thing's sides are the odd ones out (remainders) of an object's story. You look at objects, name and explain objects. You put objects to work. You reduce the object to what it is for you. The story of the object is: a "you" subjugates an object so the object is subject to the you. The you might be a box or a person. The object might be a secret or another person, it makes no difference. You're an object that uses objects.

But convergences between objects are partial. All encounters with objects are oblique. No you ever converges with all that is an object because an object is also a thing. A thing isn't for any you; a thing is for itself. A thing's real self is its secret self. Of course, a thing's appearance is also the thing, but when a thing appears it is an object. A thing never shows itself unpartially. The thing's side of the story remains secret and unsaid. There's always more to not be found. That's why, trying to trace the box to its genesis, I had to fail.

In a search for origins or meanings, the more you don't find, the more certain you become of things' strangeness. Thinging through the day shift, being a box for a few hours, I entertained the possibility that the records referred to a plural entity, a single box that was many. All these experiences of which I'd never known the like—my not colliding with the Killers, my adventures in public records, my transaction with the peddler whom I've not seen since—all seem to have been swayed, not by anything so grand as gravity or destiny, but by a smaller, meeker pull: the singular will that holds motley manifestations together as the actual appearance of an individual entity moving through space and time. Could this be "white wicker totality": the will of a thinging thing to be just one?

[CWL: Will & Testament cont.]

The self-denominated Peddler of Stolen Goods spread her wares on a black sheet on the floor at the end of an upstairs bench. Anyone coming or going from the bench at her end or from the benches in front and behind had to spare a glance for the Peddler and her stock or risk tripping over them. Our commanding officer said she was to be ignored unless she caused a scene. "Not licensed, but she has license," he said. I don't know what that means. The Peddler said, "I'm undercover-like" and winked, proffering the name "Max."

I'd encountered her on my patrols many a time but, following orders, taken no notice. On this occasion, stepping over suitcases, blankets, boots, paper cups, feet, sandwich wrappers, people on the floor, sometimes sleeping, sometimes weeping, I was wondering what had become of the little white box after the police returned it to the CytyBox Killers.

I really was. I'd swear to it. I was pondering the fate of the box when I saw it on the Peddler's black sheet.

This "Max" cultivated a miscellaneous and inconsistent appearance. It was as if she wanted everyone to think she was in disguise. I don't think I could identify her in a lineup unless she spoke. Even her voice could've been an affectation. Her sheet was a bazaar of boxes. They appeared to be jewelry boxes: dainty oblong boxes, precious little cubic boxes, music boxes, ornate boxes with tiny drawers, latches, and keys. And in a corner, almost overshadowed by its colorful conspecifics . . .

It was exactly as in my dream. Spiraling according to its impenetrable logic, its unblemished white crisscrosses over and around itself surely had no maker except the box itself. Self-contained, organic, alive. I was transfixed.

"Hello, birdie. Something you're wanting a peek at?"

It seemed impossible that I was there and not asleep. A thing out of the realm of dreams, out of the dreams of public archives, which could no more than dream events long receded into the past,

219

had no place in my waking, plodding day-to-day, in solid Central Station with queuers looking on in hundreds. As if reality had burst its seams.

"How it works, my pet, is we negotiate a price for whichever pretty box you choose. For one low price you get the box and its inner secrets both. Only no peeking before buying. No poking and shaking. Your eyes and heart alone shall lead you to your choice. And your brains if you've got any."

My gaze, my heart, my brains were full of one box alone. I thought (perhaps aloud!), "White wicker totality."

Max put her head on one side, followed my eyes with her beady ones. Took the box, *the* box, in her gloved hands.

She said, "You don't by any chance have sort of a thing for snails, do you, my flower?"

Gravity claimed my jaw as our eyes met. I'm afraid I was too slow to answer.

"I don't mean eating them," said Max.

I made an astonished, disorderly reference to malacology.

"And what's that, then?"

Zoology. Mollusks. Described with my usual efforts at deliberation and comprehensiveness. The Peddler became impatient.

"You pulling my leg, Officer?"

"No. I've got a textbook."

"And snails are mollusks, are they?"

"Yes."

"The Socket Medium's not gone and ratted on old Max?"

This question required thought.

I concluded: "I don't know what you mean."

Mark me, Courier, this was the truth. I'm hopeless at telling lies. Only *after* Max and I completed our transaction did I approach the Socket Medium for the first time.

"A snail," said Max, "is a symbol of hope. Because a shell is a symbol of elsewhere. Or of do-it-yourself roofing." She held the box up to the light as though it were a golden nugget. "Too bad really. The only snails left are man-made, aren't they. A real snail would be real hope. But never mind. We've got this, haven't we, ducky."

The box. And another of her winks. I took her seriously at the time. It was a conversation situation; that meant thinking had no time, only saying. Max said, "Let's say—" and named a price.

"May I ask . . . Where did you get it?"

"My darling dove, that'll cost you extra, won't it. Trades in stories too, Max does. Rumor says it's rumor that's Max's secret weapon. I've got stories that would make you rich if you knew how to use them. Wherefore and therefore my not using them myself comes at a price. Business, Officer, that's all. Nothing personal."

"That's fine. I'll take the story."

"Even the Socket Medium would pay handsome for it, I should think."

"I'll take the box as well, please." Money was exchanged.

"In good time, birdie, all in good time." And while she told the story, she held the box in her lap.

The first part of Max's story was too complicated for me to follow. It involved shops that no longer exist and some kind of illegal swap in which the box slipped through Max's fingers. What sparked her interest in it I didn't manage to understand. Lots of people were involved. Max mimicked all their voices, which made the story more confusing.

"Time passed, the shops were gone, but she found me anyway. What with my good name, I don't need premises to stay in business. The old girl told me straight as she'd no wish to pawn her box to anyone but me. I ask her why pawn it at all, and she starts shrieking, 'Because it's a commoditeeee! Because commoditieeees are red blood cells of commerce, engine of progress, dynamo of the civilized spirit!' After a good cackle, she calmed down and said she wasn't off her rocker, only starving. Lost her job, she had, and her brute of a super-visor wouldn't give her a reference, and there's nobody wanting to hire old women, and those bastards in government have stopped old people's pensions because it's snowing."

The pawner told Max she'd gone uninvited to a wake held in honor of a girl she'd briefly known who'd died in childbirth. The impoverished old woman knew the wealthy family was likely to send off their daughter with publicity and a buffet. She was making free with the refreshments when she overheard the girl's mother berating the deceased's young friends for trying to drop something in the coffin. The thing had ended up not in the coffin but in the possession of the dead girl's raging mother, who brandished it at her friends before rushing out of the room. Strong feelings drove the uninvited guest to follow her to the kitchen, where the hysterical mother mistook the old woman for one of the caterers. She threw the box at the old woman's feet and ordered her to get rid of it. The latter put it in her handbag when the mother turned her back. Later the family accused their daily housecleaner of stealing "a box-shaped keepsake." It made the news as one of many stories of Refusal.

Max laughed at everything Max said as if to distance it from the truth. She also charged me a month's wages: half my savings flying from my debit card to her phone. "Pay attention to the little things, my flower," she said. And I've not seen her since.

[AYJ: Email 5:
To puppymama37@mymailboxrightnow.free]

Fine, R. It's like this.

When are you wrong not to want to die? When can they convict you of survival? They say redundancy is our greatest fear, we of the Refusal. Unneeded by grown children. Unremembered by infant grandson who has my daughter for a mother. Irrelevant to husband requisitioned by the city. Unwanted by the city because I'm myself.

Like a box with nothing to give. A box no one can open. Maybe because it cannot open anymore. Aren't things most themselves when they're broken? The computer not responding isn't your equipment anymore, it's just itself. A city is a home, an institution, and a history, but a ruined city is.

I rarely saw my husband. Chronic snow flooded the ED with pneumonia, malnutrition, snowpsychosis, shortages rendering the treatable untreatable and his anguish. Every life's culmination in banishment.

Women of a certain age. Assaulted at bakeries, pharmacies, but not robbed. On buses and the underground humiliated, "Go hang yourself." Dismissed from work in terror, in shame for wanting to live, wishing away suffering. She, fifty-eight, lay down in the underground. She, sixty-two, slipped into the icy river. She ran down her gas tank through a hose into her window. Forty-four years old. "Redundant," they say in this city mine no longer mine. Her she-body no longer photocopies or seduces. Then they say she and she and she are "isolated incidents." What they mean by isolated: It's not a crime to throw away things that can't promise your persistence.

It happened to our journalist: Waiting room, Emergency Department, City Hospital. Young couple with child. What they overhear: Journalist, fifty-five, needs the same treatment they need for the same lung problem. Couple tries to bully her. Other patients join. "Go home, live or not, who needs you." Medication not made locally. And snow. Small mob including child pushing, slapping her. Knocked her to the floor. My husband stopped the scuffle. Took the journalist who'd become our journalist to an exam room, administered treatment. Administered treatment to couple with child. Refused to overlook unprovoked assault. Couple said she provoked them by existing: Why waste rations on her? Hospital forbade my husband to call the police. What they said: Disagreement. ED was crowded. And she won't have any more children. Her daughter and my daughter are the same age. Her daughter in danger because she doesn't want children. If I'd had my daughter at thirty-eight not twenty-five, she'd look like a teenager. She'd walk with me, my badge of worthiness. She carries my grandson everywhere for protection.

What our journalist wrote: Hate crime. Assaulted for wanting to breathe. In a hospital. City Hospital. What she wrote: Shortages are real, immortals not. My body demonstrates these facts. My body Refuses the myth that fecundity equals you going on forever. I Refuse that production must be in your own image and is only what life is.

Eighty-eight women joined the Refusal in one day. Police and politicians laughed. The March of Refusal was hundreds of women in the snow. Police watched from corners. Snow at their feet. They watched high windows strafe the marchers with empty prams, small refrigerators, garbage mountains. Rubbish bins and chairs and mirrors. A radiator flying from an office building. A mob of men and young women attacking with fists, stones, FEED OUR KIDS, blades, bricks, cars. They drove their cars into the March. Cars shot out of side streets to run down marchers on the boulevards. Cars nipping from the rear herded the women to the river. Cars forming a barrier across the esplanade. How many women died before a siren made a peep? What nobody's saying: Massacre.

I should've been with them. I was scrubbing a fund manager's toilets. My husband wanted to march. The hospital forbade it. Rumor at City Hospital: Calls from marchers to the emergency number, cries for help from the Refusal, were given low priority or ignored.

Counterfate led the March from the middle. Our journalist led from the front. Someone set a liquor bottle on fire. From a window. Counterfate, our artist, the young artist who inspired us. Looked up. The bomb landed on her upturned face. Women fell around her, called the emergency number and were told they'd send an ambulance. No ambulance came. Counterfate younger than my daughter. Our journalist watched her face fly off.

Rumor Counterfate was on a list. No recordings exist of calls pertaining to people on the list. Somebody deleted those recordings.

R, listen. You stayed. You chose the known over the unknown. But I'm a droplet in a diasporic wave. Those who fled so the guns couldn't take everything, every smidgen of security we'd clawed out of the ground. You put up with it. I couldn't. And you should've understood.

R, this city is different, but it's doing the same thing. There it was your ancestors, what they were. Here it's your age and gender. What our journalist wrote: Arbitrary criteria grounding pseudo-social decisions about who deserves to eat, work, live, and die. It's the same all over again. Again people pushing me to take their children. Just like then. It's appalling, people pressuring women of the Refusal to get their children out of the city. While they, the parents, stay and do not lose their jobs. What our journalist wrote and we of the Refusal swore: You won't punish us for not having any more children and then turn around and saddle us with your children. You rejected us because our future doesn't include your children.

Punishment for leaving you, R? I won't apologize. If I hadn't left you for this city, I wouldn't have met my husband.

[AYJ: Email 6:
To puppymama37@mymailboxrightnow.free]

PS: Sister. R, my sister. A woman ran weeping into the snow. Threw herself at the city through a door that kept on spinning. A young woman. Traveling maybe with her brother. They had a bench place near the escalators. What she screamed at him: There is no next train. When was the last time there was a train. Look it up.

She wanted to hear him say only a week ago. Two and three-quarters weeks ago. Only a month and a little while ago, a train arrived at Central Station in the city of snow and torment and took everyone away, so you see the probability. But his phone was dead. The girl who doesn't believe in trains dragged him to the sockets. What the socket hoarders shouted: Wait your turn or leave.

There must've been a previous train. Or the Queue would be even more uncontainable. We of the Refusal will be on the next train. If the train can't take everyone, the Queue must yield to us. The city's hatred demands it. R, I need a destination. I need you.

Madame, Madame, and Sir:

You may remember us from Room 4. We congratulate you on your new security measures. The blue walls boxing the hotel are stylishly formidable. The blue gate and window grilles are tastefully impenetrable. The camera-and-intercom system is state of the art. We congratulate you on effecting these improvements during difficult times. La Blue Boite is undoubtedly the best this city has to offer.

We'll always remember you, Madame La Boiteuse, describing your new partnership in the Boite's bar. We reiterate our congratulations to the other Madame, who served our drinks and cleaned our room. We congratulate you on becoming a partner after years of service. We congratulate you, Sir, loyal patron, on your retirement from television, investment in the Boite's improvements, and appointment as La Blue Boite's third profit-sharing partner. This partnership was born of pure friendship and dedication. It was obvious from how you handled the Snowbombing.

Madame La Boiteuse, you'll remember telling us the story. You and the gentleman were with us in the bar. The other Madame was elsewhere doing something for the Boite. You described the Snowbombers' unprovoked assault on the hotel. You said the other Madame ran outside screaming. She put herself between the Boite and the Snowbombers. She shielded the gentleman from shrapnel. She ran at the attackers. You and the gentleman ran behind her. The Snowbombers saw three people charging at them without coats or weapons. They were too surprised not to surrender.

You laughed at your own story, Madame La Boiteuse. You laughed even though it was a dangerous adventure. You said you thought we'd enjoy a thrilling story since we're "disaster tourists." You were right. You turned to the gentleman after concluding the story. You said, "She's almost ready to laugh about it, thanks to you." The gentleman will forgive us. We saw you blushing, Sir. We'd seen you press the hand of the other Madame. You were on that occasion wiping the table beside ours. She was dashing to the kitchen with our order. Your hand and hers met briefly on purpose.

Madame, Madame, and Sir, you and the Boite are the only lights in this doomed city. You inspire us to appeal to your authentic geniality.

You'll remember we were arrested. It wasn't our fault. We'd followed inaccurate information. Room 4 was reassigned by the time we returned. We accepted this. We settled our bill. We decided to return to our own country. We joined the Queue at Central Station. It's the only way out.

Madame, Madame, and Sir, the Queue is full of frightened people. Their impatience makes them dangerous. There's no system. There's only honor and dishonor. They function haphazardly. Vendors hover like flies. They prey on rationality. One vendor sells secrets in boxes. We heard complaints that this vendor refused to sell someone a certain box because of the Socket Medium. The Socket Medium said that box had to go to someone who likes snails. The box looks like a scrap of cement wrapped in copy paper. The absurdity of the matter is horrifying. We respect the Socket Medium. It's thanks to her we're turning our appeal into an email. She types every word. She edits nothing, questions nothing. She doesn't get offended. It's as if she doesn't process words like a human. Rumor says the Socket Medium sees the future. Rumor says she tells people what they want to hear. Rumors make queuers anxious and volatile. The tyranny of fear and illogic in the Queue terrifies us. We imagine ourselves barred from the train. They'd shut us out because we're foreigners or because we're men. They'd turn us away for no reason. We fear for our minds, trapped in this demented Queue.

We beg your permission to return to the Boite. We'll take a broom closet or storeroom. We'll pay your regular rates. We'll stay only until we've secured our passage home. We beseech your generosity. We appeal to your uncomplicated, fearless authenticity. We know we'd be safe at La Blue Boite.

Please reply to this address as soon as possible. The Socket Medium will give us your answer. Please remember your unlucky guests who admire you sincerely [. . .]

[CWL: Will & Testament cont.]

I know what you're thinking, Courier. You're thinking the box in my dreams, the box on Max's sheet, and the box at so many crime scenes couldn't be just one box. You think you're reading a perforated history of multiples, counterfeits, and clones. Granted, time and being could be discontinuous and plural; no evidence exists, besides rumors and feelings, that you're the same entity you were a minute ago. But everything will be simpler when you accept reality: The box is a living thing that chooses and causes things to happen. Its inner workings mayn't resemble ours, but once you've accepted that irreducible difference, you'll feel better. You'll realize, when the box takes you hither and yon, as it brought Max to set up shop in Central Station, causality needn't cling to its popular form with effects queuing meekly behind causes in an obvious order. It's just as reasonable for the box to invade my dreams as it is for the same box to get itself stolen from a chest of drawers I've never seen. Paradox is not eliminated, for being alive only makes a thing more vulnerable. As the box makes its way through the world, it's vulnerable to others that are doing the same thing. So small, light, and fragile is this box compared to others that it falls victim to the remotest coincidences: to accidents so probabilistically negligible, of relevance more distant than unheard-of planets, that to those of us relying on linear causality their impossibility seems absolute.

After I bought it, I no longer dreamed it because I no longer slept. I was as if wrapped up and knotted in dazzling and dashing fibers of white light. I wasn't distressed by this. Nor did I ever feel exhausted. I passed the time thinging with intensely thingly vigilance. I was a sofa cushion, a towel, a cabinet in my apartment. I was a chest of drawers. A portmanteau. A cardboard box unopened, just delivered. A new file box, empty. I approached it slowly, gradually. I became small. I wrapped myself in me, flattened all my features to white. I was very still. I waited to give my secret. I waited to receive. I thinged.

I understood nothing. The little white box itself was never far from me. I knew I was being called upon to be vigilant. I felt the humble pull, small but sharp, of a thinging will. But I couldn't understand what it wanted.

I'd never spoken to the Socket Medium. I'd seen her while patrolling and overheard much about her. Queuers begged me on their knees not to ask her for a license, and I agreed. Together the Socket Medium and her computer form a gathering point for stories like a shipping outpost, where things gather to go out again in all directions. She listens to suitcases, overhead lights, footsteps, floors, computers, snow, everything, every thing. Each thing, she told me recently, has a different form of life. Each thing experiences different kinds of being in different kinds of time. She tunes into each thing's emanations, allowing them to influence her feelings about futures. Through her, obscurities become clear: hidden things, the overlooked, things you'd thought imperceptible, including truths— truths including things' sides to stories.

Along with news and messages, the Socket Medium gives advice and comfort to queuers. Showing her the box (which isn't mine although I exchanged money for it) seemed the natural thing to do. Had she not been so busy with other people's messages, I believe the box would've overwhelmed and possessed her instantly. So sensitive is the Socket Medium to the ways and wiles of things, things' emanations being her gift of clairvoyance.

Of relevance to you, Courier, points from my discussion with the Socket Medium:

(1) Listen. By being itself, it will tell you what to do. But it won't tell you everything, especially about itself.

(2) Listening and thinging aren't the same. The Socket Medium said I mustn't try to be the box or try to make it me. We must stay as we are: apart, partial. That's the way to listen.

(3) The box could be or carry many things. Contingency makes it vulnerable at its core. Its form of life is flexible but fragile.

(4) It's both in danger and dangerous. See (1)–(3).

(5) It's made its way to Central Station. One thing you can do at Central Station you can't do anywhere else.

(6) I am Citizen-Watchman Lucrez of the Transit Authority Reserves. The box seeks my assistance in departing the city for purposes and destinations unknown.

[AYJ: Email 7:
To puppymama37@mymailboxrightnow.free]

Sister, I'll clean your house. Every day it'll feel new again. You think my profession degrading, but I love it. I love my husband. I didn't sell out. ~~You're a disgrace if you think I disgraced our family. And that's why you're not answering. No, please. From there.~~ For one email, R, I'll take care of everything. Every towel, every inch of wall and floor, every knob and curtain. For life if you want. It's getting too hard here. With nowhere to go.

My husband wishes life for me. He did this, he heard about it first: March of Refusal become Exodus of Refusal. From a nurse who was a patient because patients attacked. My husband refuses such a fate for me. I burned when he told me to go. As though he didn't wish for us to fight through this together. It isn't true. It isn't out of spite that I obey him. I won't believe he wants this. My diabetes medication will someday be denied me because I still am. He'll follow me. When the city releases him when the snow releases the city. Believe him. But I'll never forgive them.

What City Hospital did: Confiscate passports, licenses, papers of all physicians and nurses to stop them leaving. What my husband didn't say: City Hospital couldn't have made everyone surrender without threatening worse than termination.

Bigwigs think nobody knows they've fled. Like any bigwig would commit to austerities. What they say at City Hospital: They do it from afar. Instructions appear on computers. And people without knowing whom they just obey. Hostaging physicians while doing what about the shortages is a screen. They say citizens must have health care in this time of so on and so forth. They say they're taking care of them, of us. It's a screen screening that the city is already a ghost-city. They gave us up for dead long ago. For what? Developers? Buy our city cheap, speculate the snow will stop, raze the buildings if it stops! Dig for oil! Build casinos! A waste dump for other cities! Just like whatever cities where our city dumped its waste! Cities so broken you don't know they exist! And if the snow never stops, little is lost.

Please don't give me up, R. Your not answering feels like giving up. I'm losing track of days. Our journalist has a lawyer, a loan officer, and a professor. Corresponding through the Socket Medium with a railway company outside the city. What's to the company's advantage: Take us take our anguished many-more-than-eighty-eight on a soon train together override the Queue break the Queue tear out its dead womb we've pooled all our resources and they must take us because the city hates us as it hates the snow that will not die.

[AYJ: Email 8:
To puppymama37@mymailboxrightnow.free]

Ready to say get ready, ready or not here I come. Queue moved.

Sleeping at the escalator's summit up awake, let's go go on, move down go on go down down behind nudges me, I awake and see storming on the horizon, I nudge ahead, we all of us seize up our things. Down means a train, a train, we shuffle forward, don't care where we might be going, don't dare speak. We get as far as the first bench I mean the rearmost bench. What's happening, why stopping, people must be boarding slowly there are only so many doors, maybe the Queue began moving before the train finished stopping. Shouting behind what are you waiting for.

~~There. No train. No. Sorry. X it.~~

Hours we waited holding our suitcases trembling. And our journalist came. To each of us. She pressed our hands. She said there was no train. She said, and we trust her. People downstairs, people on the very platform. Just went out. Out on the tracks without a train into the distance. Some two dozen people and their things. And more people went to beg them to come back. They were walking into walls of snow. Queue closed over the empty places. Like snow buries footprints.

Now I have a bench. A back shaped like a scroll to put my head on crying. Leftovers visiting Queue, spurred by guilt or want of courage. Instant noodles, forever goodbyes again again. Bench queuers get more visitors than floor queuers. Easier to find your mother sitting on something like she's at the cinema. Hard to look for her in dark corners with muddy footprints and dropped crumbs.

Revising observations of the strangest of all beings. Visitors are only second-strangest. I made my husband subtract himself from the second-strangest. The man kept bringing me nice things he knew I shouldn't eat, fresh goodbyes he kept pretending weren't goodbyes, fresh tears, fresh rending. What I texted my husband: Train is here! Now boarding! Talk soon! May be a while can't charge phone. Love you always!

There was no train. There've been no trains. Just a little lie, but he trusted me. Left off visiting, it made sense. Shifts at the hospital are interminable. And he wants to save everyone. To survive, he needs his strength.

Floor queuers have better light. Bench queuers nearer to directly under the light, but theirs is a confused light unfriendly. My place on the floor was a half turn from the revolving doors. Now my back is to the doors all six. What I see from the bench: Great, vast, flat, never budges no-answer corpse of the timetable a more sucking dark does not exist. More bench queuers than ever I saw floor queuers trot back and forth to restrooms, take up smoking, pacing, cartwheeling, beg the Socket Medium to make them Socket Messengers, clean their shoes, I'm sick of people rubbing scrubbing at their shoes, bench queuers look long at their shoes, all around me weeping rocking breaking. Am I right that bench queuers are unsurpassably the strangest of all possible beings?

Rumor there's no trains anywhere. Rumor there's no cities to escape to. Rumor of a rumor from the sockets: Another city swallowed by an ocean, higher cities building battlements to keep out refugees. Rumor skitters quick because benchers are day and night shoulder to shoulder.

Benchers exhausted from being floorers. Benchers are strangers forced to prop each other with the force of inertia. So the bench can hold as many as our soft old bodies hold each other up. Fading but almost not our heads bob like bottles in the river. Sit up! Or you'll fall and lose your place! Used to sprawl or curl at night on the floor, lean my head on Suitcase. Like Suitcase was him. Now Suitcase stands upright between my knees. I drape over Suitcase like an excess sweater. I can't call him.

I won't ask you again, R. Won't beg anybody anymore, mustn't call him. Don't know where I'll go or if. But I'll do it alone. Like last time. When I left you. An exile is always withdrawn. An exile is no one's object.

[RRK: Email 23: To nbene@watanabesmith.law]

[. . .] and finally are you my lawyer or aren't you; for on the one hand, the hand which pays your retainer, it would seem that you are, but on the other hand, with which via the Socket Medium I've implored you do to something, anything, to expedite this situation, you've done precisely nothing whilst here I remain and remain in this travesty of a Queue where since the latest outrage people have gone tumbling over the threshold of insanity becoming in the best cases catatonic and in the worst cases disco dancing at the edge of psychosis, sending rumors flying: a train came but didn't stop, a train without a driver hurtled through the station, a train with driver came and stopped and fled the sight of this vast wailing filthy Queue, the crazies on the platform collectively hallucinated a trainlike shadow, the so-called authorities having banned incoming and outgoing trains until such time as all the women have given up, or if not our own authorities then every other governing body in the world has resolved never again to approach this hell of a city boxed up in snow, neither by train nor dogsled nor reindeer, determined instead to forget we ever existed until we've all died off so that archaeologists with camera-encumbered entourages can fight their way through the snow and discover a lost city complete with frozen corpses and wall-to-wall prophecies of COZY, CLEAN, AND COOL with which philologists will have terrific fun as they try on diagnoses for our downfall; and yet it appears not everybody's lawyers are doing nothing, for in the Socket Medium's queue-within-the-Queue are other people corresponding with their lawyers, but also there are those who address their correspondence to the transit authority, the police, the accountant general, various magistrates, news media outlets, railway companies, tabloids, psychiatric journals, software moguls, superstores, snowplow manufacturers, stunt performers, dictators in places which do not speak our language, the international court in charge of war crimes, and really one cannot scoff at people's crying out for help to universities and pop singers when one's own lawyer rakes in a retainer in exchange for doing precisely nothing, although you needn't think you are alone in shirking your responsibilities: this morning I saw a singularly large policeman walking up and down the Queue very slowly and in lieu of anything useful peering rudely at people and their suitcases and things, clothes, boots, hats, cats, canaries, there are rumors of a pangolin and of a large fish in a cool box, briefcases, makeup cases, laptop cases, the contrabass player's contrabass, the saddlebags which were ornately woven for a nonexistent camel and contain nothing but books, the potted plant in the instance of the lady with the potted plant, not touching anything, not patting down or whatever policemen do, but pausing in front of each and every queuer for an outrageously long time, making overwrought people tremendously uncomfortable to the extent that some burst into tears, "What do you want from me!," and begged the policeman to do something about the general situation, which apparently upset him for he appears to want people to take him for a gentle sort despite his being a giant municipal official who isn't right upstairs, and yet he managed to comfort the hysterics, which goes to show how wretched they've become: this huge idiot standing in front of them saying absolutely nothing before moving on to say absolutely nothing to the next person actually generated as if a phony sort of calm in these people who, so keenly do they yearn to believe official platitudes, made up platitudes to mutter to themselves, whereas despite his uniform I refuse to acknowledge him; his insistence on inspecting all of us as though we're criminals is unacceptable, his doing so without explanation is boorish, and the box he carries everywhere as though it were some mutant egg which he mustn't put down anywhere lest he miss its moment of hatching gives one the shivers as it forces one to look at it, quavering sensations of *déjà vu* or delusions of some vertiginous oscillation as if between a skittish then and a teetering now; my point being that something must be done not only about this fellow who, being underdeveloped in the brain department, has no business being a policeman, but especially about the trains, for it must be clear from the foregoing that this simply can't go on, people cannot hold on any longer, they could at any moment detonate or crumble [. . .]

[CWL: Will & Testament cont.]

And that's how I've come to bequeath a little box, via the Socket Medium, to someone I don't know. It's true the Refusal's journalist offered me a place on their train in exchange for my protection in a hypothetical altercation, and in such a situation I would honor that agreement. But I won't get on any train. My place can go to someone else.

There's no gallantry in this decision. There's no patriotism. I'm just one of those people who avoids change if they can. I want to be here when the city's snails awaken. Also it's one thing to be a bystander to the Queue. Becoming part of it, absorbed by it, would be quite another. As it is I am distinguished by my uniform and my departure at shift change, not by train but through a street exit, for my very own room in a corner of the city where I've lived all my life. Snowbound it may be, but it's still the same city where I recognize things. Learning a new one would be beyond my strength.

I'm less than eager to begin questioning potential Couriers. I don't like to judge, having been judged myself too often, too quickly, without grace. Of what to say to people I rarely have any idea. I suppose I'll look at how people treat their things. The Socket Medium warns me, quoting the Refusal's journalist, that it is wrong to expect any woman to bear the burden of one's own future simply because she's a woman.

But perhaps it's not I but the box to whom the choice will fall. That too has every chance of not going well. Max mentioned (and I'd forgotten, conversation being the stressful affair it is) some unspecified persons' ginger, fearful attitudes towards this box. Aversions of this nature led Max to wonder whether the little white box possessed magical powers. Set your mind at ease there, Courier. Max added: "It didn't do nothing to me or for me, neither made me a snowfree bubble nor rained pianos on choice individuals."

She expected a bit much. More apropos is what the box expects of us. That may be an open question, but in some respects it's simple. What the box requires of me is the same that it requires of you, Courier, and that it required of Max. It asks that we not harm it. The thing to keep in mind is that it's passing. To the box you're a passerby, as it is to you. That's why you are its Courier and not its owner. You are, as Max and I and others will have been, its medium. The CytyBox Victim vis-à-vis the box was in the same position, that of a passing passer-on, a passage. Only she didn't understand. Her extreme behavior leads me to suspect that she envisioned herself a possessor. But she couldn't realize that vision, no matter how she pursued it, because it was only a misunderstanding. A case of mistaken identity. It led her to go too far.

Don't take this, Courier, as any attempt to undermine your significance. To the contrary, my path shall cross yours but fleetingly, then our lives shall go on, and maybe we'll feel as if nothing notable has happened; but for the box a strange new life will begin, replete with novel experiences. It happens all the time in this mesh of miscellaneous realities. A human's nonevent is nearly always some other kind of thing's life-altering blow.

You'd doubtless like to know why you've been "chosen" to be a Courier. Given the reticence of the deciding party, I'm beginning to realize "choosing" will probably be a matter of stumbling into you by accident. With regret, I don't think I'll be able to provide the rationale you seek. I'll probably ask you some inane question to fill the awkward silence. I predict an arbitrary feeling revealing you to me as suddenly, alarmingly, and contingently as a dream of an unreal room revealed me to the box. I anticipate a feeling so unexpected that I'll wonder whether it's my feeling or something else's. Or an alteration in my understanding of my feelings (according to a conceptual schema that isn't mine but through which I can no longer help but think) as if at second hand. As if this little box has become a medium for me as I am for it. Between my feelings and my thoughts: a medium between myself and I.

The Socket Medium has agreed to convey this document to you by whatever convenient means. She is confident that you will seek her out. I wish you good health on your journey.

[AYJ: Email 1: To lucrez@tar.met]

Lu:

The way you stood. Not as watchman. Not as citizen. I didn't see your uniform. Just the box in your hand.

What I want in writing: I'll take the box. No more. What I said to you: My future is alone.

I have no family. They rejected me or stayed behind. I want that on record.

Also this: It was not I who stole a keepsake box from the CytyBox Killer's funeral.

And this: I accepted the box because of the box. Not for you.

How many stories it passed through to pass through ours. How hard it is for even a human to pass through this city. A paper box can't cry out for help. Wherever it falls, it has to trust whatever's there already. Lu, I read your knowing that.

What you didn't write: What is this? What's inside? What meaning? You didn't ask.

I understand. But if words came to you with it, it has wordable meaning. To you. It's important. All the words you could find for it you hunted down.

"White wicker totality." But what you didn't say, Big Lu: An all-white box is all surface. Its power is all repulsion. Is going-away power. Like a train. Unlike a train, the box has no visible opening. It can't take anything in, so everything's canceled. The timetable is empty. As the box is a container that no longer needs its content. And killed it. Killed the secret. Closed itself around the corpse of secret. A container that no longer has its tenants is a ruin. And a remainder and a ghost. A ruin is a premonition. You ask me to carry this.

I asked your story, which you wrote for me. Really me asking myself: Why I won't rip open this cheap-paper all-white box. You say it's alive. It's thing and it's convergences. And that is inexplicable, uncontainable life. Ruined maybe but alive. A ruin that's alive. Isn't a ruin. Is decomposing things' living coinciding. Things crossing in a nowhere that's still here.

What I could say in bitterness: A thing used to being used, put away, overused, dismissed, cries out in an explosion of pent-up ruined life, of life wasted because mistaken for nonlife. Like the fever that perspires too much snow.

What you'd write back: No, Courier, no thing is ever subjected. Only objects. And no object is fully subjugated. The object withdraws its secret self, the thing itself, from you. Each thing. Every you. A thing is an object that refuses. Is only itself.

Lu, you want this box, whatever it is, white-haired and barren, to stay itself. And to go on. Wherever. What you wrote: You're a medium. I'm a medium. I understand. Caring for things in passing. Bypassing what's not mine. Unpossessing everything. I'm used to it.

I think you know that too. But just in case. For the record.

You loomed like a tree. Stock-still and stared. Not like a wall or impossible cliff. I'm not afraid. I sat and stared as long as you stood and stared. Benchers all around, fear-deafened, intently unseeing. Four words you said to me. And no one else.

Your four words to me: What do you do?

What I said with pride, for the record: I clean houses. Apartments too.

I care for things that are not mine. And I take care of my things.

Lu, I thought all that was done. I thought I had no future.

What my husband gave me in my suitcase: Hard case for medications, for little first aid things, for a ring he gave me that doesn't fit me anymore. That's how the box will travel.

Misquoted and misinterpreted in this book are rumors instigated by: Theodor Adorno, Giorgio Agamben, Jane Bennett, John Berger, Lucio Cardoso, Fyodor Dostoevsky, John Robert Gregg, Graham Harman, Martin Heidegger, Alphonso Lingis, Clarice Lispector, Maaza Mengiste, Timothy Morton, Andrei Platonov, Marie Redonnet, Gerhard Richter, Erwin Schrödinger, W. G. Sebald, Antoine Volodine, and where applicable their English translators. An excerpt from *The Box* appears as "The Indoor Gardener" in *Arcturus*. Parts of the manuscript were written at the Three Rock Writers' Residency in Greece.

For giving this book life in one form or another, I owe endless gratitude to Akin Akinwumi, Gessy Alvarez, Rich Andrew, Amina Cain, Jen Cox-Shah, Yuka Igarashi, Heather Kettenis, Fiona McCrae, Ethan Nosowsky, Gregory Papadoyiannis, Three Rock Studio, Mark Wong, Marguerite and Roger Wong, Steve Woodward, and the production team at Graywolf Press. I am more grateful than I can say to Akin Akinwumi for taking a chance on this project, for inspiring discussions and support, and for leading me patiently from the middle of the ocean into the thick dark forests of the publishing business, wherein reside so many arcane myths and true legends.

Mandy-Suzanne Wong is a Bermudian writer of fiction and essays. Her works include the novel *Drafts of a Suicide Note*; the essay collection *Listen, we all bleed*; the chapbooks *Awabi* and *Artificial Wilderness*; and the exhibition catalog *Animals across Discipline, Time, and Space*. Her work appears in *Arcturus*, *Black Warrior Review*, *Cosmonauts Avenue*, *Entropy*, *Island Review*, *Necessary Fiction*, *Quail Bell*, *Stoneboat*, and the *Spectacle* and has won recognition in the Best of the Net, Aeon Award, and Eyelands Flash Fiction competitions.

The text of *The Box* is set in Perpetua MT Pro.
Book design by Rachel Holscher.
Composition by Bookmobile Design & Digital
Publisher Services, Minneapolis, Minnesota.
Manufactured by Sheridan Saline on acid-free,
100 percent postconsumer wastepaper.